DANGEROUS
DRINKS

KILLER
COCKTAILS

INSPIRED BY

✦ History's Most Nefarious ✦

CRIMINALS

Holly Frey & Maria Trimarchi

Co-Hosts of *Criminalia*

hachette
BOOKS

NEW YORK

Hachette Books
Hachette Book Group
1290 Avenue of the Americas
New York, NY 10104
HachetteBooks.com
Twitter.com/HachetteBooks
Instagram.com/HachetteBooks

First Edition: October 2024

Published by Hachette Books, an imprint of Hachette Book Group, Inc. The
Hachette Books name and logo is a trademark of the Hachette Book Group.

The Hachette Speakers Bureau provides a wide range of authors for speaking
events. To find out more, go to hachettespeakersbureau.com or email
HachetteSpeakers@hbgusa.com.

Books by Hachette Books may be purchased in bulk for business, educational, or
promotional use. For information, please contact your local bookseller or Hachette
Book Group Special Markets Department at: special.markets@hbgusa.com.

The publisher is not responsible for websites (or their content)
that are not owned by the publisher.

Print book interior design by Sheryl Kober.

Library of Congress Control Number: 2024939755

ISBNs: 9780306834110 (paper over board); 9780306834103 (ebook)

Printed in the United States of America

LSC-C

Printing 1, 2024

To the producer of the Criminalia *podcast, Casby Bias,*
and to the show's audience: You inspire us to tell great stories,
to celebrate the fun that is a good cocktail and mocktail.

♦

And to Brian: Thank you for being the most amazing supporter,
best friend, soulmate, playmate, and drink tester I could ever ask for. —H.

CONTENTS

INTRODUCTION

Cocktails and crime, together at last!

We're hardly the first folks to combine the two. Then again, making a beverage to accompany the historical crime stories we love seems like as natural a fit as gin and tonic. But it's not just that we love baddies and booze. Sure, that's a definite bonus, but the best part for us is that this exercise makes us really dig into these stories and think about history in a totally new way.

In some instances, the cocktail is a way to lighten the mood after a particularly grueling or grisly tale. In others, it's about celebrating someone who bypasses the law for the common good, or even someone who has transitioned from villainous to . . . *less* villainous? More than anything, it's about finding ways to give stories from the past a festive, exciting, and new spin—and have fun doing it. And it's not just about the alcohol, either, because we love a good drink whether it's a cocktail *or* a mocktail. Yep, that's right, we're all-inclusive when it comes to yummy bevvies, so every cocktail included in this book has a mocktail version to go right along with it.

All these drinks are meant to give you the confidence to try new things, test the waters, and choose your own adventure as you mix up your own refreshments. The most important thing to remember when it comes to mixing up a drink is that it's OK to play. Tweak your drinks to *your* tastes! Switch up the proportions if you want more or less spice, sweetness, or citrus zing, or—better yet—if you get so inspired, add in an additional ingredient to customize the concoction as your own.

And if your drink doesn't turn out quite the way you expected, well . . . it's really no big deal. You can always try again.

Thankfully, there's no such thing as cocktail jail. The worst thing that happens if you make a bad drink is that you'll mourn the ingredients and (hopefully minimal) time wasted as you toss it down the sink. After all, its family will not seek revenge. *Usually.*

If you're new to mixing spirits at home, don't worry too much about buying the "right" tools. It's totally OK to start with whatever you have on hand and just build up your arsenal if you find you want to up your game down the line. Don't have a shaker? Just sub in a blender bottle or another airtight, shakable vessel. No jigger? Anything that you know measures an ounce will probably do just fine. We've been known to use a mesh kitchen strainer to strain a drink in a pinch. A barspoon is great, yes, but a teaspoon will also work just about the same. You get the idea.

If you find you really like making drinks, and decide you'd like to expand what you're working with, here are some key tools to consider (but again, there is absolutely *no rush*):

Jigger—Listen, we love to measure with our hearts as much as the next person, but using something to measure out ingredients is really important if you want to start making drinks with consistent results. A jigger of alcohol is an actual unit of measure—1½ ounces—but jiggers come in a variety of shapes and sizes, so don't assume it's a 1½ ounce pour. Most of the time, you'll find jiggers that have an hourglass shape with a cup on each end, and one end is normally half that of the other. For example, a standard jigger with a 1½ ounce measure on one end will typically have a ¾ ounce measure on the other.

Shaker—The first thing to know about shakers is that there are several different kinds! Most beginners like what's called a cobbler shaker—that's the one that has a lid with a built-in strainer and a cap on top. (Most of the time, that cap is a 1 ounce measure, so you can use that if you don't want to buy a jigger!) The Boston shaker, on the other hand, is just two tins that fit together to create a seal. This one is *super* easy to clean, and it's often what you'll see used in bars and restaurants. The Parisian or French shaker is sort of like the other two shakers had a kid together. It has a lid, but there's no strainer. That last one is a good pick if you want something that looks sleek and has a top that seals nicely with the tin.

Strainer—Even if you have a cobbler shaker, it's a good idea to get a separate strainer so you can control the flow of your beverage into the serving glass. That means you can sometimes let a few ice chips through on drinks that work well with a little dilution, without over-diluting the whole drink. A Hawthorne strainer has a spring that lets you really control things because you can adjust its position to regulate flow. A julep strainer is like a large, wide spoon with holes in it that sits into the mouth of your shaker. The julep takes a little bit of practice for most folks, but once you get the hang of it, it offers a smooth, gentle pour, and it's very easy to clean.

Mixing glass—If there's no citrus juice, dairy, or egg in your drink, you probably don't need a shaker. On those occasions, a mixing glass is perfect; you just give your ingredients a stir before straining and voilà!

Barspoon—A standard barspoon holds the same volume of liquid as a teaspoon, but the longer length most of them have makes it easier to stir up drinks.

Muddler—A wooden spoon will do, but a muddler is a *lot* more efficient at crushing things like mint and other ingredients in your tin. If you're a big fan of mojitos, you're probably gonna want to add a muddler into your life.

As you travel through time with us, mixing tin in hand, you'll find a broad spectrum of flavors and styles of beverages within these pages—there's something for just about everybody in here. Some recipes are very simple and require just a couple of ingredients, and some may take a little advanced prep—we love a surprise hidden in ice or a custom syrup flavor—but none of them have a high difficulty rating. Most of the flavored syrups in the recipes are readily available for purchase, and we've included recipes for those that aren't. The most important thing here is that we want you to be able to make the drink with ease so you can enjoy it, right alongside the story!

So come on in, take a seat, and get ready for some wild tales about poisoners, pirates, body snatchers, art thieves, and a whole bunch of other truly bizarre stories and characters. ♦

CHEERS!

PART 1

What's Your Poison?

When one thinks of poison, it's only natural that images of Victorian-era detectives and deviants come to mind. After all, my dear Watson, there's something inherently mesmerizing and mysterious about murder by poison. When it comes to weapons, poison is a great equalizer: the poisoner doesn't need to be stronger, savvier, or even smarter than the intended victim to wield the power of a fatal potion—they just need to know how and when to administer the lethal dose. Whether nestled within the pages of a fictitious detective serial or listed as the official "cause of death" by real-world homicide investigators, scholars generally agree that murder-by-poison reached its heyday around the Victorian age. Though poisoners at this time had a number of toxic tonics to choose from, arsenic was by far the favored form, mainly because it was virtually colorless, odorless, and tasteless when mixed into food or drink. What's more, it was readily available to literally anyone, as it could be found in just about everything, from rat bait to wallpaper to cosmetics.

As popular as poison was during the Victorian era, it's suspected that the first intentional homicide by poisoning took place much, *much* earlier than that—as far back as 70,000 BCE. What could've motivated that person to commit murder? Was it to settle a score? Maybe a hungry power play? Or perhaps, even an accident? Without much left in terms of context or evidence, experts can only speculate on the circumstance. Since then, however, there have been numerous accounts of poisonings across almost every culture around the globe—from ancient Sumerians, Egyptians, Greeks, and Chinese to Indians and Persians. And though poisoners come in all shapes, sizes, and genders, we're focusing first on women who used poison to achieve their own goals, whether motivated by ambition, vengeance, mercy, or circumstance. ♦

HIERONYMA SPARA AND
HER SECRET SOCIETY OF POISONERS

Outside of her work with poisons, Hieronyma Spara, who went by the professional name "La Spara," is basically a total mystery. There are a number of problems with that, but here's the biggest one: over time, the story of her life has gotten mixed up with that of another famous poisoner, her contemporary, Giulia Tofana. And, really, it's easy to see why there's been so much confusion. In seventeenth-century Rome, poison and politics were ridiculously intertwined, but interestingly, neither La Spara nor Giulia got into the poison business with the intent of becoming wealthy or powerful. Instead, both were known for primarily supplying poisons to women who wanted to get out of their marriages. There was, however, a subtle difference: while Giulia tended to assist women who wanted to get out of abusive situations, La Spara was more focused on helping her clients get a financial leg up on their spouses.

La Spara was known around the city as a sorceress or a witch, and though she was a practicing astrologer and fortune teller, she considered those more like side gigs. In reality, most of her time and attention went to a very different role, as the head and hostess of an all-female secret society—one that was a *lot* deadlier than a knitting circle. The purpose of this secret society? Well, it wasn't some sort of benign book club or a place where ladies could gossip about the latest fashions. The true objective was much more sinister: this club catered to women—primarily young women, many who came from some of the most elite families in Rome—who wanted to learn how to effectively use poison to become wealthy widows.

Keep in mind: around this time in Italian history, it wasn't like women could just get a divorce. So, regardless of whether it was through natural means, the teachings of a secret society, or a well-timed "accident," if you wanted to get out of a marriage, you needed your spouse to die. In her personally handcrafted toxic concoctions, La Spara primarily used arsenic, in a liquid poison she herself made. Conveniently for her clients, a fatal dose of arsenic is just about the equivalent in size to a pea. In other words, La Spara wasn't handing out poison by the gallon; she was simply supplying these dames with deadly drops.

She ran her secret society for years, until, well . . . there's always someone who can't keep their mouth shut, isn't there? Eventually, someone disclosed in a Catholic confessional that they had poisoned their husband using La Spara's fatal formula. Despite the rules of the confessional (i.e., that it's supposed to stay between the penitent and their God), the local priest grew alarmed and notified papal authorities. Following some cursory investigation, authorities discovered that there seemed to be a lot of young, wealthy widows living in Rome, whose young, and presumably healthy, husbands had suddenly died. Exactly how they ascertained that, your guess is as good as ours. Door to door with a clipboard? Chatting it up with civilians at the local watering hole? Nevertheless, they were definitely skeptical.

Eager to catch the group in the act, authorities set up a trap in which a young woman infiltrated the group. After the spy feigned distress over the infidelities of her wealthy, ill-tempered husband, La Spara—not suspicious in the *slightest*—invited her in. The plant stayed for the evening's events and left with a few drops of a colorless, tasteless poison. When the liquid was later analyzed by authorities, they confirmed that it was, indeed, a slow-acting poison. La Spara and a dozen of her associates and pupils were immediately implicated in running a poison ring.

Though interrogated on the infamous rack, La Spara never confessed to committing any crimes. However, one of her accomplices, a woman named La Gratiosa, did confess under torture—and that's all that was needed under the law. All of the accused were found guilty and hanged. In addition, many who had personally attended La Spara's "lessons" were publicly whipped through the streets of the city, while others—typically those belonging to the highest class—were punished with fines and banished from Rome.

Despite the ruthless methods used by the papal authorities to punish these poisoners, they'd underestimated others in town with a penchant for poison. ♦

POISON SOCIETY PUNCH

What sort of refreshments might a woman serve for a gaggle of ladies who are coming over to learn how to poison their unsuspecting husbands? In thinking about a punch that would have appealed to a wide range of palates and would be refreshing but not too much of a heavy drink, we came up with the idea for a drink we're calling Poison Society Punch. It's a simple libation that you can either whip up for a single serving or scale up for a punch bowl, simply by multiplying the three easy-to-find ingredients.

INGREDIENTS:

- 4 ounces cranberry juice
- 1 ounce Amaretto
- 4 ounces champagne or sparkling wine

METHOD:

Combine the cranberry juice and Amaretto in a shaking tin with ice.

Shake, then pour into prechilled flutes.

Top with the champagne or sparkling wine.

◆ MAKE IT A MOCKTAIL ◆

In lieu of Amaretto, use orgeat (which is made with almonds) or make your own almond simple syrup (see below) and substitute ginger ale for the champagne/sparkling wine.

ALMOND SIMPLE SYRUP:

Bring 1 cup of water and 1 cup of sugar to a simmer for about 5 minutes, then remove from heat. Add ½ teaspoon of pure almond extract, then allow to cool and store in a clean receptacle.

BELLE GUNNESS, THE "COMELY WIDOW" WHO WANTS YOU TO STAY . . . FOREVER

PERSONAL. Seeking: Comely widow who owns a large farm in one of the finest districts in La Porte County, Indiana, desires to make the acquaintance of a gentleman equally well provided, with view of joining fortunes. No replies by letter considered unless sender is willing to follow answer with personal visit. Triflers need not apply.

That "comely widow" was Belle Gunness, a woman who killed an estimated forty victims—maybe more—across both Chicago, Illinois, and La Porte, Indiana, between 1884 and 1908. And then, POOF! Just like Keyser Söze in *The Usual Suspects*, she simply vanished.

Born Brynhild Paulsdatter Størseth, Belle immigrated from Norway to America—Chicago, to be precise—in 1881 and, like many of her fellow immigrants during this era, quickly "Americanized" her name. Three years later, she married a man named Mads Sørensen, but their marriage was riddled with a series of misfortunes right from the start. First, they opened a candy shop, but it burned down. Then, two of their young daughters died, out of the blue. Initially, no one was suspicious about these events; these were presumed to be nothing more than unlucky coincidences. But the bad luck just kept on coming. Soon after the deaths of their daughters, their home mysteriously burned down. When Belle asked her husband to take out a bigger life insurance policy on himself, he did. And then, on the one and only day that his two life insurance policies—the newer, bigger one and the older, smaller one—overlapped, Mads conveniently died, allegedly of heart failure. Pretty convenient timing on that for Belle.

With her three foster children in tow, she moved to a forty-acre farm in nearby La Porte, Indiana—about seventy miles outside of Chicago. There, she remarried a widower who had two young daughters of his own. But, as often seemed to happen whenever Belle was around, bad luck—if by "bad luck," you mean "death"—quickly followed. One of her stepdaughters died in her care, and then, after just eight months of marriage, her husband died under peculiar circumstances. Just how peculiar? Well, he was struck over the back of the head when a sausage grinder fell off a high shelf in the kitchen. A grisly ending for Husband #2, to be sure, but not so much for Belle, who was building quite a nest egg for herself with all these insurance payouts.

A widow twice over, Belle turned to the personals, ostensibly in search of love. (Spoiler: it wasn't for love.) Fortunately for her, she caught the interest of many men through the matrimonial ads she placed in local Norwegian-language papers, which she followed up with sexually suggestive correspondence once a potential suitor was hooked. But lest you think Belle had romantic intentions in mind, remember: for her, it was all about money. One of her farmhands later told the *New York Tribune* that whenever these men came to visit her on the farm, Belle concealed their identities; if the neighbors ever inquired, she would introduce these gentlemen simply as her cousins. As it turned out, Belle had a *lot* of cousins from Kansas, South Dakota, Wisconsin, and the greater Chicago area. In an effort to win her affections, these doomed souls signed over deeds, handed over bank account numbers, and promised to pay for everything, including her mortgage. Belle didn't marry any of them, nor were any of them ever seen again after leaving her company. Even so, the cavalier courters kept on courting, and accounts from her mail carrier suggested that Belle received as many as eight letters per day. While we don't know how much mail the average household received in a day at that time, not including circulars or advertisements, it was enough for the postal service to take note.

Eventually, however, the families of these missing men started to wonder what had happened to their loved ones. When the brother of one of Belle's "cousins" arrived to talk to Belle personally in April 1908, her farmhouse suddenly went up in flames. Buried deep within the ashes of the basement, police were horrified to recover the bodies of three children and one headless woman. The children, officials believed, were Belle's foster children, but there was no way that the headless woman could be Belle. The adult victim was five feet tall and weighed roughly seventy-five pounds, while Belle stood six feet tall and weighed two hundred pounds. Plus, in an interesting turn of events over the course of the investigation, it was discovered that the headless woman had been poisoned with strychnine before the fire even got started.

The sheriff, suspicious, rounded up a dozen men and headed over to Belle's farm to see what they could, literally, dig up. In addition to finding the remains of more unidentified children, they recovered about a dozen additional adult bodies, along with miscellaneous body parts. There were numerous teeth and bones—and watches, too—adding up to possibly forty people. Though no body matched her measurements, the coroner declared Belle dead after her dentures were found among the debris. Curiously, they were intact, with no fire damage at all.

When questioned about the nefarious activities that had supposedly transpired on the property, her former handyman spilled some secrets: Belle's MO was that she would poison her suitors' after-dinner coffee with strychnine, then hit them over the head with her meat cleaver to finish the job. Afterward, she butchered their bodies in the basement, and distributed body parts among the hogs. The handyman also didn't believe Belle was actually dead; instead, he suggested that she had most likely fled with her money and taken up a new identity.

For years, there were reports of Belle sightings all around the country, including a particularly eyebrow-raising claim that she changed her name to "Esther Carlson." This same "Esther" was later arrested in Los Angeles for poisoning her boss in an attempt to steal his money, which—come on—*does* sound a bit like our Belle. What's more, people who'd both known Belle in real life and seen photos of "Esther" claimed that they were the same person. In the years since, scientists have tried to link "Esther" and Belle through DNA; however, so far, things have been unsuccessful, as the samples have significantly degraded over time.

Sadly, "Hell's Belle" has, it seems, taken her spine-chilling secrets with her to her grave—wherever that grave might be. ♦

ESTHER CARLSON

Since Belle changed her identity throughout her life, going from a coquettish flirt to an unabashed arsonist to a stone-cold killer, the best cocktail to represent her is something that changes flavor as you're drinking. This one is relatively simple, but be warned: it does take a little more prep time.

INGREDIENTS:

- Cranberry juice
- Jalapeño juice (from a jar of pickled jalapeños)
- 2 ounces vodka
- 5 ounces ginger ale

METHOD:

Fill an ice cube tray halfway up with cranberry juice and freeze.

Once it's set, add 3–5 drops of jalapeño juice to each ice cube (an eye dropper is your friend here) and pop the tray back in the freezer.

After the jalapeño drops are frozen, top up the tray with cranberry juice and freeze.

Combine the vodka and ginger ale in a glass and stir. Add in a couple of cranberry jalapeño ice cubes. As you drink, the flavor will get fruitier and will finish with a little bite. Just like Belle.

♦ MAKE IT A MOCKTAIL ♦

Substitute sparkling water or low-sugar apple juice for the vodka and make as above.

SALLY BASSETT AND
HER WHITE TOAD POWDER

Sarah "Sally" Bassett was an enslaved woman who was executed for allegedly attempting to poison her granddaughter's enslavers. Her story is divisive among Bermudians. To some, she's an innocent victim. To others, she's a convicted criminal. And still others see her as a representation of the fight against the injustices of slavery. Whatever you believe, one thing is for certain: her life gives us a fascinating look into the complex dynamics of race, gender, and medical knowledge in Bermuda during the eighteenth century.

The island's very first inhabitants were British sailors seeking shelter after the wreck of their ship, the *Sea Venture*, in 1609. Although these first settlers were white, the island's population quickly became racially and culturally diverse, mainly due to the flourishing slave trade of the era, as well as a sizable influx of immigrants from Portugal and the West Indies. However, even though the population itself became a melting pot, to be Black at this time in a British colony was to be enslaved—and that was true for Sally Bassett.

As far as we can tell, Sally's captivity began when she was enslaved by a blacksmith named Francis Dickinson. When he died in 1727, give or take a year, his children inherited his property, which included his Southampton estate— and Sally. Some retellings of Sally's story suggest that at some unknown point after his death, her servitude may have been transferred to a new enslaver named Thomas Forster, who was the grandson of the former governor of Bermuda and an overall man of means. While we can't pin down if Sally herself was or wasn't enslaved by him, we *do* know that one of Sally's grandchildren, her granddaughter Beck, most certainly was.

Many who were enslaved on the island worked in maritime capacities. But there was still domestic work to be done, as well as work in the fields. Because it wasn't uncommon for enslaved women like Sally, who had roots in West Africa or the West Indies, to have some medical knowledge, they were tasked with providing care not only to the enslaved community, but also to the white inhabitants of the island. Even so, the practice was steeped in the racial tension that has existed on the island as far back as 1623, when slave revolts and uprisings became commonplace. As fear rose in the white community, some enslavers began to accuse those they enslaved of poisoning them, whether or not it was true. Unfortunately, back then, there really wasn't a good way to discern if a person who fell ill was the victim of poison or a naturally occurring disease, as many poisons caused similar and common symptoms such as vomiting, headaches, or dizziness. On top of that, many alleged poisoners were cooks or assumed other domestic duties in white households, and it wouldn't have been hard to sprinkle a little extra seasoning into the soup—if you know what we mean.

According to Bermudian lore, and for reasons we can't begin to know, before Christmas in 1729, Sally made a deadly powder for her granddaughter to use against Thomas Forster and his wife, Sarah. Some speculate that something specific must have happened to Beck, but again, all we have is speculation. Whatever the motivation, the Forster family fell seriously ill, as did another enslaved woman who had discovered the leftover poison in a bag in the kitchen. When Beck appeared to be the only one in the household unaffected, she was accused of poisoning the family—and she eventually confessed that her grandmother had slipped her the powder.

Consequently, Sally was accused of being an "agent of the devil." Beck testified against her grandmother, which may sound surprising but was likely a way of bargaining for her own life (a move that might have been done with Sally's encouragement, no less). According to trial records, Sally's white poison powder contained ratsbane (a.k.a. arsenic), manchineel root (which comes from the most dangerous tree in the world), and a toxin that was known as "white toad." All of these ingredients are known to cause complaints ranging from burning eyes, irritated mucus membranes, and less-than-ideal gastrointestinal symptoms, all the way to—in higher doses—a dangerously slow and irregular heartbeat, seizures, and hallucinations. Ingest enough of any of these three toxins and you *will* die. Mixed together into a powder, they'd look as innocent as a bag of sugar.

"White toad"—which literally comes from the skin of toads—was not a substance that would have been found in Bermuda back then, mainly because the toads it was extracted from were not indigenous to the island. However, these toads *were* known to be used in ceremonies in areas of West Africa, and their use carried over into *obeah*, or vodou, traditions carried out in what is now called the West Indies. While it's possible Sally had a stash of her own, the toxin doesn't actually have a very long shelf life at room temperature—only days or weeks at most. To import such an ingredient, Sally would have had to have asked for a favor from a mariner, who could have picked it up for her on their routes to and from West Africa.

Beck wasn't the only one to testify against Sally on attempted murder charges. Sarah Forster also did—as did *nine* additional unnamed white Bermudians. Sadly, Sally's jury, made up of twelve white men, rather predictably concluded that she was: "Guilty, and we value her at one pound, four shillings and six pence." Sally was also found guilty of encouraging other enslaved people to poison their enslavers, even though there was no hard evidence to prove that she did.

When she stood to hear her sentence, Sally declared that she never deserved it, but nonetheless, she was burned alive.

And out of her ashes, according to local legend, grew a small purple flower known as the Bermudiana, which is now Bermuda's national flower. ♦

THE WHITE TOAD

Sally was found guilty of attempting to murder her granddaughter's enslavers, and she was sentenced to a particularly gruesome death that was intended to scare other enslaved people of Bermuda into submission. While the natural choice for a drink that relates to a story set on Bermuda would be rum, let's sidestep the triangle trade that linked rum to enslavement, and instead honor Sally with a refreshing ginger drink, perfect for hot summer days.

INGREDIENTS:

- ¾ ounce ginger liqueur
- 1 ounce vanilla vodka
- 5 ounces ginger beer
- Fresh ginger, for garnish

METHOD:

Combine ginger liqueur and vanilla vodka in a cocktail shaker and shake with ice.

Strain over ice.

Top with ginger beer, and garnish with a thin slice of fresh ginger.

♦ MAKE IT A MOCKTAIL ♦

Substitute 1 ounce of vanilla ginger syrup (see below) for the vodka and liqueur. Combine with 5 ounces of ginger beer in a glass, then add ice and enjoy.

VANILLA GINGER SYRUP:

Bring 1 cup of water and 1 cup of sugar to a simmer; once the sugar is dissolved, add several slices of fresh ginger and ¼ teaspoon of vanilla extract.

Simmer all together for about 5 minutes, then remove from heat.

Allow to cool, then strain into a clean receptacle.

WHY YOU SHOULDN'T DRINK MARTHA GRINDER'S HERBAL TEA

Martha Grinder was known as a self-sacrificing woman who spent many nights caring for those who were ill and keeping bedside vigils for sick neighbors. She cooked meals for families and was revered far and wide for her beef broth and herbal tea remedies. In the years following the American Civil War, Martha was widely regarded to be one of the kindest and most open-hearted women in the Pittsburgh area.

No one would've ever guessed that she was also one of the most prolific serial killers in US history.

You see, as it turned out, Martha's famous tea included a special ingredient: arsenic. She was what we now consider to be an "angel of death," someone who fatally poisoned people and then cared for them until they met their death. In fact, the number of people who died under mysterious circumstances while in her care is unknown still today.

She might've continued her nefarious activities in perpetuity if it wasn't for the suspicions of a neighbor, who fell ill along with his wife, after the two drank tea with Martha. The severity of their symptoms even led to a visit to the hospital. After hearing they'd met up with Martha earlier that day, doctors grew suspicious of what they may have been served. Postmortem testing of another person, one who'd died in Martha's care, was ordered. The results were consistent across the board: arsenic poisoning. When she was arrested soon after, the press dubbed Martha the "Pittsburgh Poisoner" and the "American Borgia." She was eventually taken to trial for the poisoning of another neighbor, Mrs. Caruthers, as well as a domestic worker named Jane R. Buchanan. Several witnesses testified that they had fallen ill after visiting with Martha, whose indiscriminate victims included men, women, and children, and none of which had a clear motive.

Martha confessed to the murders of Mrs. Caruthers and Jane Buchanan and was convicted in October 1865, though she denied guilt in all of the other cases in which she was suspected. Found guilty of murder in the first degree, Martha was executed for her crimes. According to the *New York Times*'s coverage of her trial, the evidence was "entirely circumstantial, but so complete was every link in the chain of testimony, that when the last witness left the stand, a universal murmur of guilty was heard from every part of the room." One reporter remarked, alarmingly, that "the record of the trial [read] like an account of an epidemic." ♦

THE CONVERSATIONALIST

This drink gets its name from a description of Martha that appeared in the *New York Times* on September 3, 1865, in which she was characterized as having "remarkable conversational abilities." Compared to whom or based on what criteria, we just don't know. Because she committed her crimes in Pittsburgh, we're going to fuss around with a drink that is native to the area called a Fussfungle. The Fussfungle is itself a play on an Old Fashioned, which uses burnt brown-sugar molasses. For our version, we'll include a spirit that always seems to loosen the tongue—tequila.

INGREDIENTS:

- 1 ounce reposado tequila
- 1 ounce rye whiskey
- 1 ounce brown sugar simple syrup (see Method)
- Angostura bitters, 2–3 dashes, or to taste
- Orange twist, for garnish

METHOD:

Combine all ingredients in a shaking tin with ice, shake, and strain over fresh ice into a rocks glass. Garnish with an orange twist.

Brown sugar simple syrup: Bring 1 cup of water and 1 cup of brown sugar to a simmer. Once the sugar is dissolved, simmer on low another 5 minutes, then remove from heat and allow to cool.

♦ MAKE IT A MOCKTAIL ♦

Combine these ingredients in a shaking tin, shake with ice, then strain over fresh ice and add your garnish:

- 1 ounce aloe vera juice
- 1 ounce cold blonde coffee
- 1 ounce brown sugar simple syrup
- Angostura bitters, 2–3 dashes, or to taste, or pinch of white pepper

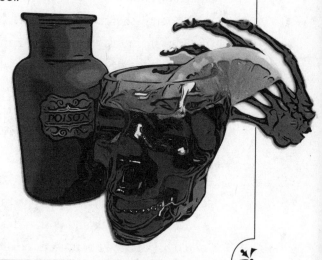

THE LEGEND OF LOCUSTA, THE IMPERIAL POISON MAKER OF ANCIENT ROME

The scene of this particular poisoning tale takes us right to the doorstep of a woman named Locusta, who lived in ancient Rome during the Imperial period. Though her name has remained in the Roman historical record for centuries, we don't have much information about who she really was—other than the fact that she was a woman who could be hired to whip up poisons on demand. Think of her more like a botanist or chemist who just happened to specialize in toxins. She probably would have been right at home compounding drugs in an apothecary, had she chosen to go that route; she was a bonafide expert at her craft. But she wasn't exactly easy to get a hold of; if you really wanted to find her, you needed to look deep within the shadows of the city.

Back in the heyday of Ancient Rome, poisoning, particularly politically motivated poisoning, was so ubiquitous that it was often just assumed that those in the Imperial Court never died of natural causes. So, as you can imagine, her talents were in demand.

Locusta was as discreet as she was adept. Because she was adamant that she didn't want to know her clients' business regarding their plans for the compounds she concocted, when authorities eventually came knocking, she couldn't share any such details. All she wanted to know from her clients was, did they want the death to play out as something sudden, or were they imagining more of an agonizingly long and painful affair? Either way, she could provide them with a silent killer—for a price.

Locusta's poisons were mostly plant-based, and she probably relied on toxins like belladonna, deadly nightshade, mandrake, hemlock, and wolfsbane, which was known as the "Queen of Poisons." Rumors claimed that whenever Locusta formulated new poisons, she tested them, at the emperor's request, on convicted criminals and enslaved persons—though, if she *really* wanted to, she could have tested her poisons on *anyone*. She was just that good.

Whether or not she actually administered any of her own poisons, she didn't come through her work completely unscathed. She was arrested and thrown in jail a few times. Twice she was bailed out when high-ranking, ambitious, and impatient Roman politicians intervened—after all, you can't have your assassin in jail when there are still political rivals out there just waiting to be poisoned. Another time, she was freed by Emperor Nero, a fervent supporter of her work.

Locusta and Nero had a mutually beneficial relationship. She was instrumental in his rise to power, and he used Locusta's concoctions against members of his own family—as well as his colleagues and counterparts in the Imperial Court, of course, as one did. Though we have no idea exactly how many people were poisoned with her products, we do know that Nero alone proved himself to be quite the busy bee. To thank her for her assistance, he even rewarded Locusta with a not-so-subtle official title: Imperial Poisoner.

When Nero's reign ended, though, so did Locusta's. She was executed, shortly after Nero's suicide. ◆

THE BOTANIST'S LATTE

Because Locusta was a knowledgeable botanist, she could have easily worked as an apothecary instead of a poison maker. Had she gone down a more pharmaceutical path, we'd like to think she might have made soothing concoctions like this one to help her clients relax and unwind.

INGREDIENTS:

- · 2 cups almond milk (or milk of your choice)
- · ¼ cup culinary rosebuds
- · 1 Earl Grey tea bag
- · Sweetener of choice, to taste
- · 1 ounce brandy (or more, to taste)

METHOD:

Combine the almond milk, rosebuds, and tea in a saucepan and heat on medium until the milk is steamy and *just* starting to bubble around the edges. Turn off the heat, give it a quick stir, and leave it to sit for several minutes.

Strain into a mug and sweeten to taste.

Add in 1 ounce of brandy (or more).

♦ MAKE IT A MOCKTAIL ♦

Make a brandy substitute by simmering 1 cup of white grape juice with a dash (2–3 drops) of vanilla extract for 5–10 minutes. Once cooled, funnel into a sealable bottle and it's ready to use.

HOW JUDY BUENOANO GOT
ALL THAT MONEY (AHEM: POISON)

❖

This "Black Widow" poisoned multiple partners, poisoned *and* drowned her paralyzed son, and even attempted to murder a fiancé by blowing him up with a car bomb . . . after slowly poisoning him for an unknown period of time with poison-laced vitamins (yikes). We may not know exactly what motivated Judy Buenoano's attacks for sure, but it's worth mentioning that she made *quite* a bit of money in insurance policy payouts.

Strange and unexplained deaths followed Judy for years before anyone caught on. Shortly after returning from a tour of duty in Vietnam in 1971, Judy's first husband, James Goodyear, died in Orlando, Florida, but the reason for his death was unknown. Since there was no immediate cause for suspicion, it wasn't initially cause for investigation. A year later, in 1972, Judy's new boyfriend, Bobby Joe Morris, *also* died after showing similarly mysterious symptoms, including severe gastrointestinal issues and hallucinations.

A few years after that, Judy's son, Michael, visited his mother while he was on leave from the army; shortly thereafter, he fell ill. Doctors said that he was suffering from arsenic poisoning, and yet, somehow, it was casually blamed on possible exposure during his time in the military. Though the poison ended up incapacitating his upper and lower limbs and he became partially paralyzed, the toxin did not kill him. Sadly, though, his bad luck continued when he later drowned during an outing with his mother; the pair were in a canoe, which capsized. Judy, of course, made it safely to shore.

And Judy's murderous streak didn't end there. In 1982, she got engaged to a businessman named John Gentry. She convinced her fiancé to take vitamins—laced with arsenic, as it turned out. Sick with gastrointestinal symptoms requiring hospital care, John never once considered that Judy might be poisoning him. *But. Then.* On his way to a liquor store one day, John's car exploded. Yes, *exploded.* A search of Judy's home revealed some interesting evidence against her:

namely, wire and tape matching those found on the bomb in her fiancé's trunk. Until the car bomb incident, investigators hadn't thought to take a serious look into Judy's extracurricular activities. When digging deeper into her past, the sheriff's office was surprised to discover that in both of the policies taken out in her son's name, his signature appeared to be forged. And that was only the tip of the iceberg. After exhuming and testing the bodies of James Goodyear, Bobby Morris, and Michael Buenoano, investigators determined that each had been a victim of arsenic poisoning.

Though Judy was later suspected to be responsible for several other homicides, she was already on death row in Florida when they came to light— and so, she was never made to answer for them. Judy's last meal consisted of broccoli, asparagus, strawberries, and hot tea. When asked on her day of execution if she had any last words, she simply said, "No, sir." ◆

THE FAKE SPANIARD

Because Judy used the name Buenoano, an incorrect Spanish translation of the name "Goodyear," we'll take inspiration for her drink from Spanish cocktail culture. The Valenciano is a delicious, dessert-y drink that combines Valencia orange juice, vanilla ice cream, and orange liqueur. Our version has a little added kick because nothing about Judy's life was really all that sweet.

INGREDIENTS:

- 5 ounces orange juice
- 1 ounce orange liqueur
- 1 ounce vodka
- ¼ ounce sriracha (other hot sauce also works)
- 1 small scoop vanilla ice cream

METHOD:

Combine the orange juice, orange liqueur, vodka, and sriracha in a mixing tin and shake with ice. Strain over fresh ice into a tall glass and top with ice cream.

♦ MAKE IT A MOCKTAIL ♦

Make as above with 6 ounces of orange juice, 1 small scoop of vanilla ice cream, 1 ounce of orange syrup, and ¼ ounce of sriracha.

THE SECRET INGREDIENT
IN NANNIE DOSS'S COFFEE

I was searching for the perfect mate," Nannie Doss explained to authorities, after she was arrested. "The real romance in life."

A hopeless romantic who married five times, Nancy Hazle, known to history as Nannie Doss—as well as by several nicknames including the Giggling Granny, the Lonely Hearts Killer, the Black Widow, and Lady Blue Beard—was responsible for murdering as many as twelve people between the 1920s and 1954, when she was finally arrested in Oklahoma. Officials in several states speculate that she was responsible for the murders of her husbands, a mother-in-law, a grandson, a granddaughter, her mother, her sister, and two of her own daughters—all of whom she killed by lacing their food with arsenic. There are also some spotty theories that she may have stabbed and smothered some victims, though we still don't know for sure. However, we do know that it was when she poisoned her fifth and final husband, Samuel Doss, that she was finally apprehended.

Though Samuel's doctor suspected foul play might be behind his severe gastrointestinal symptoms when his patient initially complained, he had no evidence to back it up. Nannie probably would've gotten away with it, too—had she not made a big mistake. She'd laced a prune cake with poison, which sent Samuel to the hospital but didn't kill him. A few days after he returned home, however, he died after drinking coffee she'd spiked with poison—a *lot* of poison. Hoping to get proof, the doctor convinced Nannie, who was poised to receive two life insurance payouts after Samuel's death, to let him perform an autopsy. For reasons we can't fathom, she consented to it, and, of course, he found his proof: Samuel's body contained large amounts of arsenic. Like, all-caps *LARGE*. The hospital promptly alerted police, and after Nannie was arrested, she confessed to killing four husbands. When those bodies were exhumed and tested, each tested positive for arsenic, also in huge amounts.

Nannie always blamed the killings on a head injury that she had sustained at age seven, which she claimed had given her chronic headaches. She chose to forgo her right to a trial and instead pleaded guilty to murder. Despite likely being to blame for a number of fatal poisonings, she was convicted solely for the murder of Samuel Doss, in Oklahoma, and sentenced to life in prison. Her life ended a decade into her sentence at the Oklahoma State Penitentiary, when she died from leukemia at age fifty-nine. ♦

HOPELESS ROMANTIC

Because Nanny Doss was a self-confessed romantic, it seems only right that her drink—a whiskey sour, with a fruity syrup note—matches the sweet exterior that she showed to the rest of the world.

INGREDIENTS:

- ½ ounce strawberry syrup
- 1 ounce lemon juice
- 1½ ounces bourbon
- 1 egg white
- Lemon coin (a circular cut of lemon rind) and a fresh strawberry, for garnish

METHOD:

Combine all components in a shaking tin. Shake dry (without ice) first to get the egg white nice and frothy, then add ice for your final shake. Strain over fresh ice into an old-fashioned glass and garnish with a lemon coin and a strawberry.

♦ **MAKE IT A MOCKTAIL** ♦

Make as above but substitute black tea for the bourbon.

OH, WHAT DAISY DE MELKER COULD DO WITH A PINCH OF STRYCHNINE

W idely considered to be South Africa's first female serial killer, a label surely *no one* really wants, Daisy Louisa Hancorn-Smith (a.k.a. Daisy de Melker) married men with the intention of killing them for her own financial gain.

Yep, you guessed it: she was in it for the insurance payout. From March 1909 to February 1932, Daisy married three times and killed two of those husbands. She also killed her twenty-year-old son, Rhodes.

Daisy's primary weapon of choice was a white, slightly bitter, powder called strychnine (once prescribed in much smaller doses as a medication)—though Rhodes's official cause of death was attributed to cerebral malaria. Because he'd become ill at work after drinking coffee from a flask his mother had prepared for him, cerebral malaria was highly unlikely. Poison was, though, but let's not get ahead of ourselves. The motive for his murder was never clear, but there's speculation that it was related to an alleged inheritance—which matches up with his mother's typical motive for killing: money.

For two decades, no one raised a flag about the number of suspicious deaths around Daisy. It wasn't until the younger brother of Daisy's second husband grew concerned and notified authorities after Rhodes died in a very similar way to her husbands. Bodies were exhumed, and experts examined what was left behind in their graves. The bodies of Daisy's two former husbands were both saturated with strychnine. However, her son, it was discovered, had actually been a victim of arsenic poisoning. Bad luck for them, but also bad luck for Daisy.

In April 1932, she was arrested. Her trial began six months later in Johannesburg and lasted one month. Though she was charged with the three murders, Daisy was convicted and executed only for the murder of her son; due to lack of evidence, she was acquitted for the murders of her husbands. ♦

TAINTED FLASK

Daisy's story is a deeply sad one because of Rhodes; it's basically unfathomable to imagine a mother murdering her own child. What's more, Rhodes's true cause of death may never have been revealed had it not been for the arsenic-tainted coffee flask. As such, this drink is really more for Rhodes than Daisy, and it combines a coffee note with a drink that comes from a plant native to South Africa, where their story unfolded: rooibos.

INGREDIENTS:

- 1 ounce rooibos tea
- 1 ounce coffee liqueur
- 1 ounce vodka
- ¼ ounce anisette

METHOD:

Shake all ingredients vigorously in a shaker with ice, then strain into a pre-chilled cocktail glass.

♦ MAKE IT A MOCKTAIL ♦

Eliminate the coffee liqueur and the vodka, and use 1½ ounces of rooibos tea and 1½ ounces of coffee, plus ½ ounce of anisette or licorice syrup.

MAYBE LUCREZIA BORGIA WASN'T THE DEPRAVED AND MURDEROUS WOMAN HISTORY SUGGESTS

On the day Lucrezia Borgia was born in April 1480, her father, Rodrigo Borgia—who later became Pope Alexander VI—summoned astrologers to their home just outside of Rome to reveal the future of his newborn daughter. While we know that they foretold a remarkable future for her, the details of that particular prediction are lost to history. However, we do know that she grew up in a very prominent family of military leaders, dukes, two Popes, a saint—and a whole lot of murder and scandal.

Over the past several centuries, Lucrezia has maintained an infamous reputation as a political schemer and poisoner—most of us, when we hear her name, immediately think of all the terrible things she supposedly did during her lifetime. This is somewhat to be expected; after all, the legacy of the Borgias is not one of generosity, inspiration, or saintliness. Their reputation, dating back to the 1300s, centers more around their greed, bribery, sex scandals, violent political corruption, megalomania, and power-hungry control. Quite a list of achievements and attributes in that family tree. As such, Lucrezia has long been characterized in literature, film, and other forms of art as a woman who embodied the nefarious traits of her family: vicious, extravagant, and also guilty of nepotism, incest, and murder.

However, scholars no longer believe there is irrefutable proof that the real Lucrezia lived like her notorious family members. Sure, *maybe* she did. But it's also possible she was villainized unfairly because of the power she wielded. Historians today note that she was frequently left in charge of the papal court during her father's absences—which was a *big* deal for a woman back then. Before you go and think Lucrezia held all the cards, keep in mind that she still played the role of a political pawn in her father's game. She was married three times, and not once for love. Her marriages were strategic, as all three aligned the Borgias with other influential families and helped her father build up the family's collective political power.

Like many other important and ambitious families at the time, Lucrezia's father and brother likely both *did* use poison to their political advantage; there were even rumors that they'd poisoned a cardinal or two. Their poisons, allegedly, could be added to anything, including food and drinks, clothes, gloves, pages of books, and even flowers; in fact, the phrase "tasting the cup of the Borgias" came to be used as a euphemism for death by poison. Lucrezia is often linked to this poisonous pedigree, and there were rumors that she wore a poisoned-filled ring and sprinkled a little of it into wine glasses during dinner parties. As murderous details come, it's impressive—but it's also likely not true. If there was a ring, and that's a BIG IF, it's believed it was her brother who actually wore it for nefarious purposes. So much for a femme fatale.

We might never know whether or not Lucrezia's infamous reputation as a poisoner is deserved—but we're going to hold steady at *maybe?* After all, she *was* a Borgia. ♦

THRICE WED

Since Lucrezia's personal history has been mired in myriad accusations of scheming and wrongdoing over the years, it's only fitting to focus on something that we actually know is *true* about her for this cocktail. Her many weddings conjure up thoughts of light and refreshing celebration drinks, and so each marriage is represented by a different fruit in this particular concoction. It's delicious—and full of antioxidants!

INGREDIENTS:

- ¼ cup diced watermelon
- ¼ cup diced plum
- ¼ cup diced apricots
- About 5 drops Elemekule Tiki Bitters
- Prosecco

METHOD:

Puree fruit in a blender until smooth.

Fill one-half of a champagne flute or coupe with fruit puree. Add bitters.

Pour in a little prosecco, then mix gently with a cocktail spoon.

Once the fruit and prosecco are incorporated, top up the glass with prosecco and enjoy!

◆ **MAKE IT A MOCKTAIL** ◆

Make as above using sparkling grape juice or ginger ale instead of prosecco.

PART 2

The Chasers (but Not Really)

As we've learned from countless thrillers and true crime documentaries over the years, there's often a *really fine line* between love (or even friendly admiration) and obsession. When two people are in love, you don't think twice about the fact that they can't get their lover out of their mind, or that they want to spend as much time with the object of their affection as possible. But when only *one* person feels that way, and the other doesn't return the same feelings, things can get dicey (and even dangerous) quite quickly.

And once you cross over into stalking territory, well—there's really no return. Today, around half of all stalkers are the former partners of their victims, but the demographics of the stalkers themselves are broad and diverse; basically, *anyone* from any race, religion, class, or walk of life can find themselves compelled to engage in stalking. And just as anyone can be a stalker, anyone can find themselves on the receiving end of this kind of incessant and often terrifying unwanted attention. As you'll see across the next several stories, though the circumstances surrounding these incidents vary greatly, one thing remains the same: unrequited love rarely comes with a happily ever after. ♦

THE NIGHT RUTH ANN STEINHAGEN
SHOT EDDIE WAITKUS

While Eddie Waitkus lay on the floor with a gaping chest wound, Ruth Ann Steinhagen laid down her .22 caliber rifle and called the hotel desk. "I just shot a man," she calmly stated.

Earlier on the night of June 14, 1949, Ruth had tipped a bellhop at the Edgewater Beach Hotel in Chicago to deliver a handwritten note to another guest, a man named Eddie Waitkus. Eddie, a former Chicago Cub, was the first baseman for the Philadelphia Phillies, who were in town to play against his old team. Ruth, a nineteen-year-old typist for an insurance company, had become infatuated with Eddie while he played with the Cubs, largely because he'd been one of their most popular players. She went to every Cubs game, always hoping to catch his attention. But as time went on without any recognition from the object of her misguided affection, Ruth's crush took a dangerous turn into full-blown obsession.

In her note, she referred to herself by the name "Ruth Anne Burns" and invited Eddie to come up to her room—which he did, around 11:30 p.m. Ruth's plan was to stab him, she later told authorities, but her plans changed when he walked by her too fast and then sat down before she could grab the weapon.

"I have a surprise for you," she said, as she reached into the closet for her gun and shot him point-blank. According to *Life* magazine, as he was bleeding out on the floor, Eddie allegedly cried out to Ruth, "Baby, what did you do that for?"

Ruth had a history of falling in love with unattainable people, especially celebrities. Before her obsession with Eddie Waitkus, she confessed to the police that she had had crushes on both actor Alan Ladd and Cubs infielder Peanuts Lowrey—but she'd admired them both from afar. Her crush on Eddie felt different, and so was the extent of her infatuation. During Eddie's three seasons with the Cubs, she'd collected numerous photographs of him, and, according to her family's recollections after the incident, she spoke of him incessantly. This crush, it seems, went way too far.

Fortunately, Eddie survived the attack, but he didn't return to the field until the next season. Meanwhile, Ruth was arrested and charged with assault with intent to commit murder. During her trial, which began about two weeks later, she was found not guilty by reason of insanity. After undergoing roughly three years of psychiatric treatment at the Kankakee State Hospital, she was released, and she intentionally disappeared into near obscurity. ♦

CAN WE JUST FORGET THIS?

Perhaps one of the most fascinating things about Ruth is that after the incident and her stay in a mental health facility, she managed to live out a very quiet life. She never married, but for nearly her entire life she did live close to the hotel site where she'd almost killed Eddie Waitkus. If she ever had a job, as a typist or otherwise, there's no record of it. It's as though she wanted to forget the whole thing, and hoped everyone else would forget it, too. So for the cocktail version of this drink, we're including a spirit known for its ability to affect the hippocampus, the part of the brain that helps both your short-term and long-term memory.

We also couldn't resist the temptation to make this a drink with an apple note, since apples—like baseball—are often associated with Americana.

The sad coda to this story is that Eddie Waitkus developed alcoholism in the years following the incident. Out of respect for that, we're putting the mocktail first here.

INGREDIENTS:

- ¾ ounce lemon juice
- ¾ ounce demerara syrup
- 1½ ounces agave juice
- 3 ounces low-sugar apple juice

METHOD:

Shake with ice, then strain over fresh ice.

MAKE IT ALCOHOLIC:

- ¾ ounce lemon juice
- ¾ ounce demerara syrup
- 1½ ounces reposado tequila
- 3 ounces low-sugar apple juice

Shake with ice, then strain over fresh ice.

THE CHARACTER ASSASSINATION OF EDGAR ALLAN POE BY RUFUS GRISWOLD

Rufus Griswold was the kind of person who made enemies everywhere he went and was generally considered to be kind of a nightmare by many who knew him socially and professionally. He was a successful journalist, literary critic, anthologist, and editor who was said to have an expression of smug defiance and a "glib tongue." However, what he's probably best known for is assassination—that is, the character assassination of his peer and arch-nemesis, Edgar Allan Poe. Rufus's fixation on Edgar following the poet's death just about consumed his life.

The two men first met in March 1841, when they were both around thirty years old, give or take a year or two. Edgar, a budding poet, was editor of *Graham's Magazine*, and Rufus was working on his first anthology, *The Poets and Poetry of America*, a work that included Poe's writing. By all accounts, it was the anthology that allowed for a small but amicable introduction to each other. They talked for hours about the possibilities for Rufus's book, and Rufus paid Edgar to write a review. He did write one, but Rufus never could've anticipated what Edgar had in store.

In his review, Edgar criticized a considerable number of the poets Rufus had selected, including Longfellow, whom Edgar accused of plagiarizing Alfred, Lord Tennyson. Edgar had a reputation as a harsh critic, and given their brief interaction, Rufus had been expecting a rave review. Rufus believed his acquaintance thought too highly of himself, and the whole affair sparked a rivalry that became possibly one of the longest-standing smear campaigns in literary history.

Things got even weirder after Edgar died in 1849. The circumstances surrounding his untimely death remain one of the great literary mysteries, and speculation has long fueled the idea that he lived a life of debauchery. Amid this ambiguity, Rufus saw opportunity and went on—*and on*—to defame Edgar after he died. His assault on Edgar's character began when he penned his rival's obituary, which was so libelous that he wrote it under the pseudonym "Ludwig." He essentially called Edgar morally bankrupt and a drunken womanizer—things we now know were all vengeful lies. And that obituary was just the beginning.

Rufus devoted the rest of his life to spreading as many lies about Edgar as possible and became the wellspring of pretty much all misinformation about him, some of which is still mistakenly circulating today. As part of his toxic campaign, he also decided to write Edgar's "memoirs." You may be asking yourself, "What in the WHAT?" We did. And here's how that went down. We're going to preface this by saying it can't be completely ruled out that Edgar *may* have named Rufus to be his literary executor, and if that's the case, it was probably during a time when the two were . . . more civil.

However. Many historians believe the whole thing was actually pretty shady, and that Rufus convinced Edgar's mother-in-law to sign away the rights to the writer's work. With all of his rival's literary papers in hand, Rufus was able to pick and choose facts from his life and twist them to fit the character he was creating. Ultimately Rufus ended up inventing a mad-genius version of Edgar, one of a poor, wandering madman with addiction problems who talked to himself on the streets.

Despite Rufus's best efforts, Edgar still went on to become a literary legend, though still a mischaracterized one. That's not to say the real Edgar Allan Poe didn't have a sense of humor about himself or his work. The real Edgar was so recognizable after his poem *The Raven* was published that children followed him in the streets of Baltimore, flapping their arms and making "cawing" noises at him, hoping to get a response—and he didn't disappoint; he'd spin around and exclaim, "Nevermore!" and the kids would run away, laughing and shrieking. Sounds like a *terrible* madman, for sure. ♦

BITTER RIVAL

Rufus Griswold's obsession with Edgar Allan Poe was rooted in envy and hurt feelings. Over time, he became as bitter as burnt coffee about Edgar's criticisms and ultimately tarnished the famed writer's reputation by writing an unflattering—and largely false—account of Edgar upon his death. To mirror the bitterness of Rufus's heart, and to find some solace, here's a drink that includes cold coffee, but the addition of lemon juice and simple syrup gives it a bright and sweet flavor.

INGREDIENTS:

- 4 ounces cold coffee
- 2 ounces rum
- 2 dashes Angostura bitters
- 1 ounce simple syrup
- ¾ ounce lemon juice

METHOD:

Combine in a shaker with ice, then strain over fresh ice.

♦ MAKE IT A MOCKTAIL ♦

Use 5 ounces of cold coffee, and instead of rum,
add a scant ¼ teaspoon of nonalcoholic rum extract.

THE SOCIALITE WHO LOVED
CHARLES DICKENS WAY, WAY TOO MUCH

Charles Dickens was the man behind classic novels including *Oliver Twist*, *David Copperfield*, and *A Tale of Two Cities*. Popular and charismatic, Charles was a hot ticket on the literary tour circuit in his heyday and is still often described as the ideal master of ceremonies: dynamic, quick, observant, and filled with a palpable zest for life. Basically, Charles was a born entertainer. His seventy-six-date book tour across the United States in 1867 was like the Victorian version of the 1960s British invasion, a hugely influential cultural phenomenon. Forget Beatlemania; this was known as *Dickensmania*, and his fans, giving him a warm and often frightful welcome, literally tried to tear the shirt off his back—and the fur off his coat—to get themselves a souvenir.

This type of celebrity status and fan obsession may seem commonplace today, but in the mid-1800s, it most certainly was not. As such, Charles was among the first modern mass media celebrities, and if ever there was a great way to describe a Victorian rock star, this description of him could be it: "Dickens, who had a gleefully gaudy fashion sense that attracted attention and some revulsion, was a particularly striking celebrity to encounter."

Touring put him in the position to meet all sorts of people, and he was on the road when he met John and Jane Bigelow at the Parker House Hotel in Boston. And it's upon this meeting, over an evening of games and conversation, when this story takes a turn from celebrity infatuation to celebrity stalking.

Jane "Jenny" Tunis Poultney was a socialite from Baltimore who married an attorney and writer named John Bigelow. John was an influential diplomat who openly credited his wife for his success—but Jenny was not exactly popular among her peers. Or his peers, for that matter. There are a bunch of tales of her inappropriate behavior, including one anecdote involving her slapping the Prince of Wales on the back. That was *unheard* of at the time—and, frankly, probably wouldn't go over well today, either. Jenny was well known in political circles because of her husband's work but also because of that whole slap on the back thing. Girl just couldn't live it down. She was also, and more importantly, known for her generosity and patronage of emerging writers, including Charles Dickens, to whom she quite literally opened her New York home.

However innocent this admiration may have started, it didn't take long before Annie Fields, the wife of Dickens's publisher, nicknamed her the Bigelow Terror. Jenny's fondness for Charles quickly escalated into possessive behavior, but things *really* began to sour when she started regarding Charles as her personal property after hosting him. She threatened any woman who vaguely expressed interest in him, whether they were flirtatious or not. One time, Jenny even verbally and physically attacked an elderly widow who had tried to call on Charles after a reading in New York City. Fortunately for him, fans had already become so persistent that the author had been forced to hire security guards to stand outside his door 24/7 while on tour. After that attack, security guards were ordered to specifically keep Jenny away from his hotel room at all times. Now banished from Charles's social circle, she was left to wait around in hotel lobbies for hours on end, hoping to catch a glimpse of her beloved author in the lobby or a hallway, all while Charles did his best to avoid her at all costs for the remainder of the tour.

It was the best of times; it was . . . the worst of times? ♦

SLOPPY BISHOP

Dickens was reportedly fond of a popular warm punch called Smoking Bishop, which is made in large batches and features oranges roasted with cloves, lemons, red wine, and ruby port, among other ingredients. Our own Sloppy Bishop is inspired by the punch Dickens loved, but instead, it's a cold cocktail that you can dole out in single servings much more quickly.

INGREDIENTS:

- 3 ounces ruby port
- 2 ounces cranberry juice
- 1 ounce triple sec
- 1 ounce gin
- ½ ounce black cherry puree
- Optional: Dash of bitters (a bitters with cinnamon is great)

METHOD:

Combine in a shaker with ice, then shake and strain over fresh ice.

♦ MAKE IT A MOCKTAIL ♦

- 3 ounces Concord grape juice
- 2 ounces cranberry juice
- 1 ounce orange juice
- 1 ounce flat tonic
- ½ ounce black cherry puree
- Dash of bitters (see Note)

Combine in a shaker with ice, then shake and strain over fresh ice.

Note: *If the small amount of alcohol in bitters excludes them from usability for you, you can skip them. Another option is to add a couple drops of saline to season your drink and bring out the flavors of the other ingredients. To make cocktail saline, combine one part salt to four parts water and stir or shake until thoroughly dissolved.*

ADÈLE HUGO'S ROMANTIC OBSESSION WITH LT. PINSON

By all accounts, Adèle Hugo was a sullen child who spent a good part of her day at the piano. She was the youngest child of the French poet, novelist, and dramatist Victor Hugo, and his wife, Adèle Foucher. You'll probably recognize her father's name from his famous novels, including *The Hunchback of Notre-Dame* and *Les Misérables*. Born in Paris in 1830, much of Adèle's childhood centered around music, art, and the intellectual and literary conversations of her father's famous friends, so it was no surprise that she grew into an intelligent and ambitious young woman. Adèle was particularly revered for her beauty, and she sat for portraits by several well-known Parisian artists. However, though Adèle's life may have started out rather charmed, it quickly took a tragic turn into mental illness and romantic obsession—which incinerated the young woman's prospects down to ash.

While Adèle was in her early twenties, the Hugo family lived among the Channel Islands, an archipelago in the English Channel. That's where Adèle first met Albert "Bertie" Pinson, a lieutenant in the British Army. A lot of what we know about Adèle comes from biographies written about her famous father, but she, herself, was a prolific writer and journaled pretty much everything, from her thoughts about horse racing to love affairs, including her relationship with Albert. Because of this, we know now that their affair began as a summer romance, of which she wrote, "I was absorbed in my book and I didn't see him. But he saw me, and from that day . . . he loved me."

It's true that Albert became close to the Hugo family, though there's a good chance that he was likely more attracted to the allure of their wealth than that of their daughter. When Albert proposed to Adèle, she refused him, but as Albert moved across Europe with his regiment in the years that followed, Adèle would often visit him, depending on where he was stationed.

In an unexpected turn of events, however, Adèle slowly started losing contact with reality and experienced symptoms like delusions and hallucinations, symptoms that were mostly overlooked by her family and Albert. And, unfortunately for all involved, Adèle's obsession did not dim with his absence. In fact, it worsened. Though she had previously turned down his proposal, she not only began insisting that they were to be married, she also began referring to herself as Mrs. Pinson. She continued to travel to be closer to him, and Adèle's family, believing that there must be some sort of arrangement between the pair, shipped her clothing and other odds and ends. By this time, though, Albert had lost any interest in Adèle whatsoever and started to ignore all of her romantic advances. Undaunted, she began disguising herself while pursuing him. She peered through his windows and rented rooms near him and, at night, paced in her room while talking to herself. Though not officially diagnosed with any specific type of illness, people who met her recognized that she was clearly unwell—so unwell that she didn't even realize that Albert had married another woman.

Today, experts believe it was probably undiagnosed mental illness that fueled Adèle's fire of irrational and obsessive behaviors. It is always a tricky proposition to diagnose someone who is not around to be assessed by a mental health professional, but modern biographers and historians believe untreated schizophrenia could have been to blame for her worsening delusions and paranoia. As it became increasingly clear that she wasn't doing well, Adèle's mother was the first to express concern over her daughter's mental state and wrote to her husband, "She is forced in upon herself. She thinks a great deal, and her ideas—often erroneous, since nothing flows in from the outside to modify them—become like burning lava." Eventually, Adèle's parents moved their daughter into a psychiatric hospital, where she lived for forty-four years, until her death at age eighty-five. She was never arrested or prosecuted for stalking Albert and leaves behind only a sad story of a confused young woman. ◆

VICTOR'S PARTY TRICK

While researching Adèle's story, we learned a fun anecdote about her father that inspired our cocktail-loving hearts. Victor loved hosting large dinner parties, at which he would often, as a party trick, shove an entire orange in his mouth. Immediately afterward he'd add lumps of sugar in his cheeks and chew, then swallow it all down with two glasses of kirsch. Quite a party trick, indeed. Our tip of the hat to Victor's spectacle is much more sippable—and tastes a little like a creamsicle!

INGREDIENTS:

- · 1 ounce vanilla syrup
- · 2 ounces triple sec
- · 2 ounces vanilla or whipped cream vodka
- · 3 ounces hard seltzer

METHOD:

Combine in a shaker with ice, then strain over fresh ice into a Collins glass.

Top with hard seltzer.

♦ MAKE IT A MOCKTAIL ♦

- · 1 ounce vanilla syrup
- · 2 ounces orange syrup
- · 1 ounce water
- · 4 ounces orange seltzer

Combine in a shaker with ice, then strain over fresh ice into a Collins glass.

Top with orange seltzer, or, if you love a sweet, sweet drink, you could also use orange soda.

HEARTTHROB (AND HEARTBREAKER)
FRANZ LISZT AND HIS
NINETEENTH-CENTURY GROUPIES

Imagine your excitement: Franz Liszt is the hottest artist on the scene, and you have a ticket to see his show in Vienna. But once you find your seat, you notice that there are three pianos on stage. Who will be the guest artists, you might wonder? Surprisingly, no one—they were all for Franz. He gained notoriety for using multiple pianos in his performances, playing one after the other as each broke under his dynamic and passionate technique. A very physical musician, his long hair would grow slick with sweat during his shows, and he'd whip it around as he played—kind of like an early headbanger. And there was also one other aspect of his performance style that set him apart from his contemporaries. Unlike any other pianist in his day, or even those before him, Franz placed his piano, or pianos, in such a way on stage so that the audience could see his face as he played for them. And that was *scandalous*.

Women swooned and screamed and, allegedly, threw their nineteenth-century undergarments at him during his performances. Which, given their intricacies, were probably difficult to remove at a show, but we'll go with it. Like more modern artists on the celebrity level of, say, Mick Jagger or David Bowie, there are also stories of women not just throwing their clothing onto the stage but also stealing things from Franz, or surreptitiously clipping off locks of his hair. In other words, whatever they could get their hands on, they took. And this ever-growing delirium that surrounded him became known as Lisztomania.

Far from just a composer or musician, Franz Liszt was a talented, charismatic showman with a larger-than-life personality, and his performances showcased a combination of skill and flamboyance. During what's known as the Romantic period of music, he composed many pieces you'd recognize today, including the *Hungarian Rhapsodies* and the *Faust Symphony*—in total, this prolific artist wrote more than seven hundred (!) compositions. Many of us today don't think about classical musicians like rock stars, but in his time, Franz was *super* famous. And he was also *super* good looking. Put those two things together, and here come the groupies.

Enter: Olga Janina.

Olga was a cigar-smoking feminist—although if we're being period correct, she was a proto-feminist, as the feminism we'd recognize today was still forming up through the late nineteenth century. Undeterred by others' opinions, Olga stood out from other women because she was outspoken and wore menswear at a time when women didn't do such things. But she also stood out because of her reputation for being rowdy, notoriously unstable, and aggressive. She carried a revolver in her handbag, and there's even an anecdote about her beating a newspaper editor with a cane when she didn't like his review of her own piano performance.

Franz and Olga met in 1869, when he was fifty-eight and she was nineteen. Olga was not just one of his students, she was also one of the many women who swooned over him—though in Olga's case, "swooned" turned into threatening his and her lives in revenge after he broke off their affair. While Franz, who was known to be a playboy, quickly moved on from their short-lived fling, Olga remained madly infatuated—and madly jealous. She followed and threatened the women she considered to be her rivals. She also wrote Franz letters, even though he rebuffed her advances. In a final act of desperation, she decided to abandon her husband and children to follow Franz full time. It's too bad she didn't live to see what her lover inspired a century later: the 1975 movie *Lisztomania*, with Roger Daltrey, the handsome singer of the rock band the Who, playing Franz Liszt. You just can't make that up. ♦

SMASHED PIANO

For this drink, let's mix up something that conjures the white of piano keys and also gives a hint of the joy that Lisztomaniacs must have felt watching their idol play piano with abandon. What better than elderflower liqueur, which seems to make any drink it's added to more delicious? (True story: it's nicknamed bartender's ketchup because it's such an easy way to improve a drink.)

INGREDIENTS:

- 1 ounce white rum
- 1 ounce elderflower liqueur
- 1 ounce milk of your choice (oat, almond, dairy, etc.)

METHOD:

Shake with ice and strain into a chilled glass.

♦ MAKE IT A MOCKTAIL ♦

- 1 ounce white grape juice
- 1 drop almond extract
- 1 ounce elderflower syrup
- 1 ounce milk of your choice

Shake with ice and strain into a chilled glass.

THE TALE OF GEORGE HARRISON'S STALKERS (YES, PLURAL)

We remember George Harrison as the Beatles guitarist who wrote and sang classics like "Here Comes the Sun" and "While My Guitar Gently Weeps." Former Beatles producer Sir George Martin once described him as a "very peaceful person who hates violence of any kind"—which made it that much harder for the musician to stomach the fact that he had at least two experiences with obsessed fans, both of whom actually got into his home, one of whom almost murdered him.

Let's begin with a woman named Cristin Keleher. Cristin once approached the caretaker and manager of George's Maui estate, a man named Don Carroll, to tell him that she hoped to run into the quiet Beatle one day. Unfortunately, one day in December 1999, she took that opportunity into her own hands and broke into that same Maui home. The sixty-one-acre grounds were thick with trees and bushes intended to discourage paparazzi and fans like Cristin from getting in. But Cristin, amazingly, reached the mansion, and when she arrived, she entered through an open sliding glass door. Once inside, she made herself right at home—and she even made herself lunch. She cooked a frozen pizza, drank root beer from the family's refrigerator, did some of her personal laundry, and called her mother, long distance, back in New Jersey. ("Hey, Mom, you'll never guess where I'm calling you from!") Cristin was discovered about an hour later by in-house security, who proceeded to call the police. She had become obsessed to the point of delusion, believing that George would be happy to meet her but admitted to authorities that there was actually no particular motive or reason for her visit to the Harrison home. She just "thought [she] had a psychic connection with George."

Believe it or not, Cristin's break-in wasn't even the scariest incident that George and his family faced where stalkers were concerned. In fact, *just one week* after Cristin's arrest, George encountered yet another intruder, a man named Michael Abram, this time in the middle of the night, at Friar Park, his estate in Henley-on-Thames, Oxfordshire.

There had been burglary attempts at Friar Park over the years, and a reported arson attempt as well. After all that, plus a number of written death threats going back for decades, George's security team had installed some pretty serious equipment, from lights and cameras to electronically controlled gates. The grounds were protected by a high brick wall that was topped with barbed wire. *And yet.* Despite all the security measures in place, Michael Abram somehow scaled that wall, broke a window, and entered the home. He stabbed George several times in the torso with a seven-inch knife, puncturing his right lung. He also tried to choke George's wife, Olivia. Despite their injuries, the pair were luckily able to overpower the intruder and hold him off until authorities arrived.

When family, friends, and neighbors were initially questioned about Michael after the incident, they gave the ever-so-common and ever-so-clichéd answer that he was quiet and "mild mannered." But family later admitted that he'd recently developed an obsession with the Beatles. Michael later told authorities that he believed he had been sent by God to murder George, and that he believed all the Beatles were witches. George, specifically, he noted, was trying to possess him. Though he did not attend the trial because he was still recovering from his injuries, George wrote in a statement to the court, "There were times during the violent struggle I truly believed I was dying." He continued that the "whole magnitude of [the Beatles'] fame made me nervous."

Although George was clearly shocked by the incident, he did maintain his sense of humor. Mark Gritten, chief executive of the Royal Berkshire hospital, said that upon being admitted, George told him, "the man wasn't a burglar but … he certainly wasn't auditioning for the Traveling Wilburys." Ba-dum-ching. ♦

PEPPERY SERGEANT

There are approximately a kazillion recipes for drinks called Sergeant Pepper. So, let's do something a little unexpected in honor of the legendary George Harrison. This is a simple drink, but trust us—like George, it packs a lot of flavor.

INGREDIENTS:

- 1 tablespoon jalapeño jam
- 2 ounces whiskey of choice
- Club soda, to taste (1–2 ounces)

METHOD:

Add the jam to the whiskey and let sit for a few minutes, then stir to combine. Add ice cubes after the sugar of the jam is dissolved, and top with club soda.

♦ MAKE IT A MOCKTAIL ♦

- 2 ounces chai tea
- Dash of salt
- 1 tablespoon jalapeño jam
- Soda, to taste

Mix as above. In the mocktail, the salt helps amplify the flavor of the jam—something the whiskey tends to do on its own, but that tea has a hard time replicating.

PART 3

The Imposters

Imposters pretend to be someone else—either a real or a fictional person—for the purpose of public deception. Of course, that's just a basic definition, and you'll find a lot of different motives behind these impersonations, but when we were looking into famous deceivers of the past, two kinds of imposters really seemed to stand out. The first kind were those who were in it for power, status, and/or money, like those who claimed to be royalty or built up a career out of fleecing unsuspecting victims. The second kind were imposters who never really intended to hurt anyone; at the end of the day, they were really all about having fun and not taking life too seriously. Strangely enough, most of the time they got away with it, too—that is, *most* of the time.

Like other kinds of criminals, imposters come from all backgrounds and in all shapes, sizes, and genders, but there is one thing that ties them all together: at some point, they realize that in order to achieve their goals, they must sacrifice a bit (or all) of their true identity first.

Because the tales that come next are all about imposters, we're switching things up here, too. We'll be featuring the mocktails in this section and then adding in the alcoholic versions of each drink as the secondary recipe. Bottoms up! ♦

THE MYSTERIOUS
PRINCESS CARABOO FROM JAVASU

With a single counterfeit coin in her pocket and assumed to be homeless, the locals of Almondsbury in south Gloucestershire couldn't decide if the woman calling herself "Princess Caraboo" should be tried for vagrancy. When she first appeared in their town in the spring of 1817, she was found speaking an unknown language and didn't seem to know a word of English. Residents were bewildered both by her language and her manner of dress; for example, the black turban she wore was totally foreign to the villagers.

Word quickly spread about the alleged princess, and despite their earlier suspicions, locals began treating her as if she was a visiting head of state. It wasn't until a Portuguese sailor—or pirate, depending on who tells you the story—arrived in town about a week after her that her narrative started to unfold. Well, her fake narrative, anyway. The sailor claimed that he understood her dialect and gestures. He said that she was from a royal family, and she had been born in China, though she had a different name for the country: Congee. "Princess Caraboo" had apparently been kidnapped by pirates and was forced to jump overboard to escape them, before swimming across the English Channel to safety. Her true home, he explained, was on the far, far away island of Javasu. He basically stayed long enough to tell her fake story and then continued on his journey. It's a strange coincidence that the mysterious sailor showed up when he did, and you, like us, might be wondering, were they in cahoots? History doesn't have a good answer for that—or, any answer.

Fictitious or not, the princess's yarn enthralled the townspeople, who were head over heels for their new eccentric guest. And she put on quite a show for them. She informally entertained curious locals but formally entertained experts, too, such as linguists, craniologists, and physiognomists. Whether a vagrant or dignitary, the princess's strange and scandalous behavior did *not* disappoint. She wore flowers in her hair and swam naked in the lake. She knew how to use a bow and arrow, and she gave fencing demonstrations. Before eating or sleeping, she prayed to a god she called Allah-Tallah.

But the princess had secrets, starting with the fact that she wasn't actually a royal, nor was her name Caraboo. Mary Willcocks—though you'll also find her referred to as Mary Baker and Mary Burgess, likely from her marriages—was a native English speaker who had grown up in a poor family in England and adopted the royal disguise and fake language hoping it would make her seem more interesting. She listened to what everyone was saying while they thought she couldn't understand them—and the knowledge she gleaned from that played a big part in how long she was able to effectively pull off her hoax. She always seemed credible to the villagers, but they never suspected that she was reading them—their body language, their tone of voice, their word choices—in order to manipulate them.

Alas, the ruse only lasted about three months before she was ultimately undone by the press. When a local newspaper published a story about her arrival with an accompanying engraving, a woman who ran a lodging house nearby recognized her as a lodger named Mary Baker who'd stayed there about six months prior to the whole "Princess Caraboo" affair. After this revelation broke, only months later during the summer of 1817, the residents of Almondsbury were done with her—they wanted her to move on and out of their village. They pooled their money to purchase Mary's boat fare, sending her off to the United States. She may have been booted out of England, but because the story of the infamous "Princess Caraboo" was already well known in America, Mary was greeted there as royalty—*even though Americans already knew she was a fake*. There, she held performances in her royal character and achieved some success, likely due to the sheer curiosity of the general public. Several years later, she returned to England, where she continued to give performances as "Princess Caraboo," in London as well as in Bath and Bristol. The cost of a ticket to see her final appearance? A shilling. Was it worth it? Who are we to judge! ♦

TENDER NERVES

In some accounts of Mary's life, even the ones where she was already outed as a fraud, she was often noted as being delicate and nervous. So, let's cook up something that might soothe her (and anyone else), but also something that feels just a little bit outside the normal—just as many people thought something was off with the whole "Princess Caraboo" story, even though they usually liked the woman at the heart of it all.

If you can't find a spicy mango syrup for the recipe below, you can make one by simmering 1 cup of water, 1 cup of sugar, about a half cup of chopped mango, and 1 teaspoon cayenne pepper until the cayenne is incorporated. Then, let it cool and strain it into a clean container. You can also sub out another syrup if you prefer, with bite or without. And you could make this one warm if you prefer a very cozy version.

As an added bonus, if you keep the strained fruit, you've essentially got yourself a spicy mango compote that's delicious on toast. You could also use this as an ingredient in our next drink!

INGREDIENTS:

- 6 ounces tea, brewed and cooled
- 2 ounces milk of choice (nondairy is fine)
- ½ ounce spicy mango syrup (see headnote above)

METHOD:

Combine in a shaker with ice and give it a good hard shake, then strain over ice.

MAKE IT ALCOHOLIC:

Add 1 ounce of vanilla vodka.

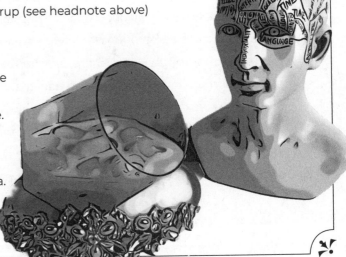

SOME SAY KORLA PANDIT WAS THE FIRST LIBERACE (BUT LIBERACE WASN'T A FAKER)

Assuming the identity of "Korla Pandit" wasn't the first time that John Roland Redd had passed as someone other than a Black man. But it was this identity that made him successful.

Born in Missouri in 1921, John was an American musician and composer who moved to Hollywood in the 1940s seeking a career in music—and fame, too, if it was in the cards. There, he reinvented himself as, well, *many* other aliases. The problematic thing about John wasn't his music—he was very talented—or even that he gave himself new names; rather, it was the way that he assumed the racial identities of each persona he took on.

John was a Black man when racism and racial prejudice was incredibly rampant across America, meaning it was hard for him to find steady work. However, he was eventually able to book jobs when he posed as a Latin performer in Los Angeles night clubs, under the alias "Juan Rolando." At the time, Mexican music was really popular, and passing as Mexican meant he was allowed to join the whites-only Musicians Union, which meant he could book more gigs.

John changed his identity yet again after he married Beryl DeBeeson, who was employed in Disney's special effects department. Together, they created the persona of "Korla Pandit," a French-Indian musician from New Delhi, India—and with that, John's star was born. As "Korla," he was always smartly dressed, in a suit and tie or silk brocade Nehru jacket. He wore a turban adorned with a single jewel. Beryl also did his eye makeup.

According to "Korla's" made-up legend, he was a child prodigy (which John actually was), born to a Brahmin priest and a French opera singer (which John wasn't). He claimed that he'd been classically trained in the United States. As "Korla Pandit," John played a Hammond B3 organ, which was an unpopular instrument at the time; however, he transformed it into something magical, fusing musical compositions from the East and West into a new kind of musical genre that became known as "Exotica." John, as "Korla," also starred in his own nine-hundred-episode show on Los Angeles local television called *Korla Pandit's Adventures in Music*; he bought a house in the Hollywood Hills; and he socialized with celebrities of the day—big names, like Bob Hope and Errol Flynn.

Following the success of Korla, John—and Beryl, too—took his true identity and life story to the grave. But three years after his death, journalist R. J. Smith discovered that the backstory of the person calling himself "Korla Pandit" was a lie and discovered that he was actually the American-born son of a Black minister. R. J. Smith's article, titled "The Many Faces of Korla Pandit," was published in *Los Angeles Magazine* in 2001 and spilled all of John's secrets. ◆

THE RUSE

John's utter commitment to the "Korla Pandit" persona would be admirable...were it not so fraught with cultural appropriation. The idea of assuming an entirely new identity is something most people likely ponder at least playfully at some point in their lives. But in John's case, this also meant that he was perpetuating a completely false idea of Indian identity for the viewing public, based on a pastiche of things John thought would work to sell his performative personality.

To make a drink that mirrors this story, let's borrow a few of India's most popular flavors—mango, Darjeeling tea, and orange juice—and combine them into a yummy drink with a creamy texture, thanks to the puree.

INGREDIENTS:

- 2 ounces Darjeeling tea
- 2 ounces orange juice
- 1½ ounces pureed mango
- ½–¾ ounce simple syrup, to taste (optional)

METHOD:

Combine all elements in a shaking tin with ice. Shake vigorously, then strain over fresh ice.

MAKE IT ALCOHOLIC:

Use a Darjeeling-infused vodka in lieu of tea. Steep a Darjeeling tea bag in 4 ounces of vodka for 30 minutes, then strain and use 2 ounces for the drink— you'll have enough infused vodka to make two.

IF FRED DEMARA COULDN'T BE A SOMEBODY, HE'D BE SOMEBODY ELSE

Ferdinand Waldo Demara, Jr.—a.k.a. Fred Demara—had a knack for spinning tall tales and running a good con. Whether he was talking about the time he allegedly gave Steve McQueen his last rites or "adopting" new careers at the drop of a hat, Fred knew that storytelling was the key ingredient to a successful con, which made him one of the most effective imposters of his day.

The very first con that Fred ran was when he was a kid, convincing a local chocolatier to give out chocolates to his entire class at school—when he had no money or intention of paying for the treats. But the first time he faked another identity was as a young adult. In 1941, during World War II, Fred enlisted in the US Army but deserted after serving only a year. Afterward, however, he reenlisted in the navy—this time under the name Anthony Ignolia, a *real person* who had been one of his army buddies—so that he could train as a corpsman. When he realized this job meant he'd be on the front line, though, he immediately tried to back out of it, forging credentials that would allow him to enroll in officer training, instead. Unfortunately for him, his forgery was discovered, and with that, Fred went on the run.

Fred was always on the prowl for a new opportunity and a new life to vanish into. He didn't have any real credentials, but that didn't stop him from teaching psychology at a college in Pennsylvania. He then posed as a professor at a school in Washington State; in fact, while in Washington, Fred was so popular with locals that he was asked to stay on as the sheriff of Pullman. Afterward, he moved on to La Mennais College in Maine, founded by the Brothers of Christian Instruction, who welcomed their new teacher, "Brother John Payne." Though he wasn't a sailor nor a Canadian citizen, he next took to the Royal Canadian Navy—as a surgeon named "Dr. Joseph Cyr." When he was commissioned as a surgeon-lieutenant, Fred actually did perform real surgeries, from dental work to amputations—and it's a miracle that none of his patients died. When the Canadian Navy discovered there was an actual Dr. Joseph Cyr whose medical records Fred had stolen, authorities ultimately declined to take any action, presumably hoping to keep the whole embarrassing thing as quiet as possible. *Especially* those surgeries. As such, Fred was honorably discharged.

As his next adopted persona, he used the name "Robert Linton French." Robert was a real person, and a real doctor. And through what we'd now call social engineering, Fred was able to talk his way into getting copies of Robert's credentials, including his birth certificate—though, unlike today, he had to do it all by mail. As "Robert French," he studied, briefly, at DePaul University in Chicago. Next up on his resume, Fred went on to work as a counselor at the Union Rescue Mission in downtown Los Angeles. The monastic life was something Fred returned to on and off throughout his life, but he left every time he was close to taking vows. He had his first ministerial assignment as pastor of the Cherry Grove Baptist Church in Oregon, but around this time, he couldn't escape rumors of his previous life of fraud. Some members of the church enjoyed his presence, though others worried they too were part of a con. Eventually, Fred resigned.

Fred was intelligent and had a remarkable memory, but he didn't have any kind of education or training in any of the careers he tried. Unlike other imposters, he didn't con for the money—his main goal was to attain prestige and status. There were rumors at one point that he became Frank Sinatra's bodyguard, which was not at all true, but can you imagine the huge ego boost he got from knowing people thought that? Fred soon became so well known that he was even name-checked in mainstream publications, including *Time* magazine, which called him an "audacious, unschooled but amazingly intelligent pretender who always wanted to be a Somebody, and succeeded in being a whole raft of Somebody Elses."

Over the years, Fred maintained that his goal was status and fame—and just one more cheat, one more thrill. And whenever he was asked to describe his motives, Fred replied simply, "Rascality, pure rascality." ♦

PURE RASCALITY

This is a mocktail with a lot of character—just like Fred. It initially started as a base with the intention of adding additional components, but everything that we tested detracted from the flavor instead of enhancing it. And you can just make it right in the glass with no other vessels involved!

The cocktail version is a good on-ramp for people who may struggle with the bold nature of brown spirits. This combination of flavors makes bourbon less prominent as a flavor, so you may find yourself taking the time to pick out the flavors and notes that the spirit imparts to the drink.

INGREDIENTS:

- 4 ounces pink lemonade
- 4 ounces ginger beer

METHOD:

Combine in a glass with ice and enjoy!

MAKE IT ALCOHOLIC:

Add 1–1½ ounces of bourbon and stir gently with a bar spoon.

NO PROFESSIONAL SPORT WAS SAFE
FROM IMPOSTER BARRY BREMEN

In 1979, a stranger in a Kansas City Kings uniform, now the Sacramento Kings, joined the basketball team for a warm-up. Before anyone could stop him, this same stranger made his way onto the court again at half-time, with the name "Johnson" splashed across the back of his jersey. "There were thirteen Johnsons in the NBA," the man later stated, "so it was almost like I fit right in." Like everyone else in the stadium, the pros were quickly taken in by this guy's infectious charm, charisma, and genuine love of life—which probably explains why, even though he wasn't supposed to be there, they started feeding him the ball.

No one loved a gag quite like Barry Bremen. Barry earned a living as a marketer and salesman—he represented toy and novelty manufacturers and sold novelty goods (think gag gifts like Pet Rocks). He also loved sports and was an enthusiastic but amateur athlete. But more than anything, Barry was known for his high-spirited and fun-loving pranks, in particular, sports pranks.

It was sports journalist Dick Schaap who first put the spotlight on Barry as "Sportsman of the Week" on NBC's *TODAY Show* after he crashed that 1979 NBA All-Star game. Next, Barry appeared on *The Tonight Show Starring Johnny Carson*—by invitation, not by prank—which also led to a legit appearance on *Late Night with David Letterman*. Before long, Barry became a staple of pop culture, and even became the answer to a *Jeopardy!* question.

No professional sports were safe from Barry's antics. During batting practice at a Major League Baseball All-Star Game in Houston, Barry—wearing a #13 New York Mets uniform with no name—caught the attention of Los Angeles Dodgers manager, Tommy Lasorda, who, with a whole lot of expletives, booted him off the field. In 1980, Barry stood in as an umpire for the World Series game between the Philadelphia Phillies and Kansas City Royals but was, again, escorted off the field. In 1982, Barry tried to crash the Super Bowl while impersonating the famous San Diego Chicken, a sports mascot played by Ted Giannoulas, but was stopped before he got onto the field. Barry's dream prank, though, was to appear as a Dallas Cowboys cheerleader. He finally made his move at a Dallas Cowboys–Washington Redskins game. In hot pants, boots, breast enhancers, and a blonde wig, Barry danced with the squad during the last two minutes of a game. He also got out a single cheer—"Go Dallas!"—before security nabbed him.

Though most of his pranks were sports-related—and in no way did we cover all the sports or games he crashed—one big prank was not. In 1985, Barry brazenly accepted actor Betty Thomas's Emmy award. Throughout the 1980s, she was nominated seven times for her role of Sergeant Lucy Bates on *Hill Street Blues*, and this was the night she won at last. When Betty's name was announced, Barry, in a rented tuxedo with a pink tie and cummerbund, strode to the stage from his third-row aisle seat at the Pasadena Civic Auditorium and, to the surprise of everyone in the auditorium, accepted her award for "Outstanding Supporting Actress in a Drama Series," explaining in a short speech that Betty was unavailable. But here's the kicker: Betty *was* in the audience. He later said there was no specific reason he chose her, stating, "I never met Betty Thomas, and I've never seen *Hill Street Blues*." He added, "I should have accepted for Jane Curtin." Jane Curtin, named "Best Actress in a Comedy Series" that year, had been a no-show. Barry had reached a level of celebrity where, on his way out, he signed autographs for some of the police officers.

When prompted to give advice to people curious about trying a prank of their own, Barry joked, "Don't do it. It's against the law. Stay away . . . This is my act." Asked about what was next, he admitted, "I have no idea. Maybe Johnny Carson will ask me to be on his show, and they'll say, 'Here's Johnny,' and I'll come out." Imagine that. ♦

JOIE DE VIVRE

A fun, bright, crisp beverage is the perfect way to celebrate the way Barry lived his life—always embracing possibility and hoping to make people laugh along the way. While he was described by his widow as having a no-guts-no-glory approach to life, we like to think of this libation as something you might grab in your more relaxed moments.

INGREDIENTS:

- 6–10 mint leaves
- Juice of ½ lime
- 3–4 blueberries
- 4 ounces passion fruit juice
- Splash of club soda
- Mint sprig, for garnish

METHOD:

In the base of your cocktail shaker, gently muddle the mint leaves in the lime juice, then add the blueberries and make one more muddling pass.

Add the passion fruit juice, then shake in a cocktail shaker, strain over ice, and top with club soda.

Garnish with a sprig of mint.

MAKE IT ALCOHOLIC:

Add 1–1½ ounces of white rum to get essentially a blueberry passion fruit mojito.

THE COLD WAR SPY WHO WAS
FORSAKEN BY THE UNITED STATES

L t. Col. Michael Goleniewski was a senior officer in the People's Republic of Poland's Ministry of Public Security (*whewf*, what a mouthful), the deputy head of military counterintelligence, and later, the head of the technical and scientific section of Polish intelligence. He was also a spy. Except, he wasn't just a spy for Poland—he also happened to be a spy for the KGB (a.k.a. the Soviet Union). Playing one side against the other, as you can imagine, Michael rose up the ranks very quickly, in no doubt thanks to the fact that he had the goods on a *lot* of people.

Except, hold up: Michael was actually a *triple* threat. In 1959, he began working undercover with the US Central Intelligence Agency, sharing both Polish and Russian secrets with both American and British intelligence. Under his CIA code name SNIPER, he smuggled over detailed reports about Soviet spy activity while simultaneously holding a senior position in the Polish security service *and* conducting daily meetings with senior Soviet intelligence officers.

Over the years, Michael's complicated undercover work proved incredibly helpful for the US government. In addition to exposing George Blake, the KGB's man inside Britain's MI6, Michael also exposed the Portland spy ring, which was a group of Soviet spies who shared British Admiralty secrets with the KGB. Perhaps most importantly, he also uncovered the names of some of the most successful and damaging Soviet spies.

So when he defected at the US embassy in West Berlin in 1961, the US Congress, on the recommendation of the CIA, quickly passed a special bill, enabling Michael to apply immediately for American citizenship and then waived the requirements for him to do so. After all, their spy had earned it.

But. Then. Once in the United States, Michael became unhappy about his new situation, claiming that since he'd arrived, he was mistreated, ignored, and persecuted by the American government. He accused CIA and US state department agents of betrayal and claimed they were trying to discredit him—which, depending on who you talk to, they were. (Let the record reflect: *they were.*) In 1964, the CIA started pulling back on promises they'd made to Michael, after another spy-turned-defector sneakily and successfully convinced the CIA's counterintelligence office that *he* was the only one who could be trusted. He worked hard to discredit Michael, and the United States trusted his misinformation, when the reality of the situation was that they had no reason to doubt Michael.

As this went on, Michael became increasingly paranoid and mentally unwell in the years that followed his defection. He began to claim he was really Tsarevich Alexei Nikolaevich, the youngest member of the Romanov Russian royal family, whom we now know was killed with his family by Bolsheviks in 1918. In his rendition of historical events, however, Michael said that Yakov Yurovsky, one of the assassins, had actually helped the family to escape. In the end, he was abandoned by the same Western intelligence community who'd promised him the American dream in return for his work. And he lived the remainder of his life in Queens, New York, still claiming he was Tsarevich Alexei. ♦

TRIPLE AGENT

Because Goleniewski had ties to Poland, Russia, and the United States, let's whip up a mocktail that combines the various beverage traditions of all three countries. There is a shot that's popular in Poland called a Mad Dog, which is made with vodka, raspberry syrup, and Tabasco sauce. This conveniently covers both the Polish and Russian elements of the drink because raspberries are a common crop in Russia. The American element we're throwing in here comes from a summertime classic: iced tea.

INGREDIENTS:

- 1 ounce raspberry syrup
- 5 ounces cold black tea
- 3 drops Tabasco sauce

METHOD:

Combine in a shaking tin with ice, shake, then strain over fresh ice.

MAKE IT ALCOHOLIC:

Use 1½ ounces of rye whiskey in lieu of tea and top with club soda or ginger ale after you've shaken and poured over fresh ice.

THIS JUST IN: ELIZABETH "BETTY" BIGLEY WAS NOT REALLY THE DAUGHTER OF ANDREW CARNEGIE

You may know Elizabeth "Betty" Bigley by one of her many aliases: Lydia Devere, Lydia Scott, Cassie Hoover, Elizabeth Cunard, Emily Heathcliff, Marie LaRose, or perhaps her most famous fake name, Cassie Chadwick.

Betty pulled off lots of scams over the years, but her biggest success was convincing high society in the early 1900s that her real name was Cassie Chadwick. As "Cassie," Betty claimed to be the illegitimate daughter of industrialist Andrew Carnegie, one of the world's richest men. It started out like this: during a visit to New York City right around the turn of the twentieth century, "Cassie" asked James Dillon, a lawyer and business associate of her husband, to take her to her "father's" house, which was located at 2 East 91st Street and Fifth Avenue, in the Upper East Side of Manhattan. To the associate's surprise, they wound up right in front of Andrew Carnegie's mansion, where Betty shamelessly knocked on the door and was allowed inside. The reality of the visit had nothing to do with seeing Carnegie; it was really all about appearances.

"Cassie's" cover story was to ask after the credentials of a domestic worker named Hilda Schmidt, whom she claimed she was hoping to hire for her own home. In truth, there was no Hilda Schmidt; that was just a name and excuse to get in the door. Between asking after a fictitious person whom, of course, no one had heard of, and general chit-chat with the domestic staff, Betty was able to stretch her time inside the mansion up to about thirty minutes. When she returned to the carriage, Betty "accidentally" dropped a promissory note for $2 million with Carnegie's signature—*coincidentally* right in front of her acquaintance. She then demurely shared that she was Andrew Carnegie's secret child and that her father kept her flush with money to support her lifestyle, though she was also set to inherit $400 million when her father died.

Of course, all of this was to be kept a secret. Ever the observant con artist, she had actually selected this particular person—James Dillon—because she thought he wouldn't be able to keep that secret. And her instinct was right. Suddenly, it seemed *everyone* thought that Andrew Carnegie was her father.

"Cassie Chadwick" and Andrew Carnegie, however, were far from related; in fact, Betty and Andrew had never even met. Not *once*! Andrew Carnegie and his wife, Louise Whitfield, had only one child, a daughter named Margaret, who was born in 1897 and lived with her parents in New York. Keep in mind: she was still a baby when all of this was happening.

What motivated Betty to perpetuate this façade? Money. Because of her now-alleged association with Carnegie and the Carnegie fortune, Betty—as "Cassie Chadwick"—was able to withdraw large sums of money from banks, as well as borrow money from wealthy friends. Word about Betty's alleged pedigree spread quickly, and banks lined up to offer her loans. They also let Betty's loans compound annually, which meant any interest Betty earned on the principal of her loan immediately began earning interest on itself. In other words, Betty was smartly and effectively making money *from* her money. Financial experts refer to it as interest-on-interest. And if there were any problems, the banks assumed Carnegie would vouch for any debts. Ultimately, she amassed debts totaling between $2 to $20 million—to this day, no one seems to agree on just how much debt she accumulated, just that it was a staggering sum.

Betty's eventual downfall came at the hands of a man named Herbert Newton, a banker in Massachusetts who had loaned nearly $200,000 to "Cassie" and then requested repayment. That's when Herbert learned that this was a woman with a huge number of loans, and that she was scamming him. Naturally, he filed suit against her to recover what he'd lost. He also contacted his associate, Andrew Carnegie, to ask about the repayment of his daughter "Cassie Chadwick's" loan. Carnegie was surprised—his daughter was still quite young, and her name wasn't Cassie. It was at this moment that the two men discovered the depth of Betty's scam.

Betty was promptly arrested and stood trial in Cleveland, and the proceedings attracted a great amount of national attention. In response to questions about Andrew Carnegie's relationship to her, the family issued a press release, simply stating, "Mr. Carnegie does not know Mrs. Chadwick of Cleveland." At the trial, Betty denied all charges, and also denied that she'd claimed any kind of relationship with Andrew Carnegie. But, in perhaps a surprise move, Carnegie personally attended the trial, and upon examination of the promissory notes in question, he stated to the court, "If anybody had seen this paper and then really believed that I had drawn it up and signed it, I could hardly have been flattered," and went about highlighting several errors in spelling and punctuation. He continued, "Why, I have not signed a note in the last thirty years." He added that if anyone had ever bothered to ask him about "Cassie" or any of the loans, the whole scandal could have been avoided.

Betty was found guilty of conspiracy to defraud a national bank and sentenced to ten years in prison, but what we really want to know is this: What was the look on her face when Andrew Carnegie unexpectedly walked into that courtroom?!?! ♦

THE CALLING CARD

Since the key prop in this ruse was a calling card, what could be better than to name a drink after it? We want to make a drink that, like Betty/Cassie, might not appeal to everyone but will probably be *really* enjoyed by folks who love these flavors. Coincidentally, around the time that "Cassie" was launching her ruse, absinthe—far from everyone's favorite liquor—suddenly became more readily available and popular across North America, making it a fitting source of flavor inspiration for this beverage.

INGREDIENTS:

- 2 large sprigs of dill
- ¾ ounce anise syrup
- 5 ounces coconut water

METHOD:

Muddle the dill in a cocktail shaker,
   then add anise syrup and coconut water.

Shake vigorously and strain over ice.

MAKE IT ALCOHOLIC:

Just drink absinthe!

Or: Add ¾ ounce of Anisette
   instead of anise syrup
   and ¾ ounce of vodka.

ANNA EKELÖF WASN'T THE CROWN PRINCE OF SWEDEN...EVEN THOUGH SHE SAID SHE WAS!

Imagine, if you will, eighteenth-century Sweden, during what was then known as "The Age of Freedom." Still primarily under monarchical leadership, the country was set up as a dual-party system—the Nightcaps (or just "Caps") and the Hats. A little backstory: Until 1738, the pro-monarchist Nightcaps were the party in power, and they tread lightly so as to not provoke conflict with Russia, which was in the air. But between 1738 and 1765, the Hats came into power, and they focused on making alliances as well as drafting up treaties with France. The Hats took a hard line on foreign policy, seeing impending and unavoidable war with Russia—a war that took place between 1741 and 1743. In 1757, Sweden entered into war with Prussia, which continued until 1762. And though the Hats tried to elevate Sweden's economic status, war costs led to inflation, which ended in financial collapse; their reign eventually came to an end in 1765, amid rising political confusion.

And that was the tumultuous Sweden that Anna Ekelöf grew up in.

Anna Eleonora Ekelöf was a serial imposter who took on several false identities, including but not limited to: a *mamsell* (an honorific title used for unmarried women in Anna's time and place), a noblewoman, and Count Carl Ekeblad. Perhaps the most impressive of all, she even pretended to be the Crown Prince of Sweden—that is, until she was arrested at age twenty, in 1765.

Much about Anna's early life is unknown, until she began trying on new identities and generally living the high life of a con artist and imposter. What would have been particularly scandalous about her crimes back then was not exactly hidden from the public eye, either: Anna preferred to dress in male attire, and the characters she chose to impersonate were, except her first few tries, male. In addition to trying out what life would be like as a count, she even managed to get away with impersonating royalty—her backstory on that one was that she'd been forced into exile after plotting uprisings against the Swedish throne. Alas, that last con marked her final curtain call, and she was arrested while trying to cross the border into Norway.

Don't worry too much about her, though; ever the chameleon, she escaped custody and fell back into historical obscurity. ♦

CROWN PRINCE

When considering a story like Anna's, it's hard not to be at least a *little* impressed—after all, she convinced some people that she was *the* royal heir! This Swedish story gives us a great opportunity to play with aquavit (also spelled akavit), a popular spirit in Scandinavia frequently made with caraway seeds. But since we're starting with a mocktail, we're going to brew up some caraway tea first. Additionally, we're going to give a nod to a popular Swedish soda called *julmust*, which has a flavor that's often compared to root beer.

INGREDIENTS:

- 2 tablespoons caraway seeds (or a caraway tea bag)
- 2 ounces root beer
- 2 ounces club soda

METHOD:

Combine 8 ounces of hot water with caraway seeds or tea bag and steep for 15 minutes. Strain into a clean container and allow to cool.

Once the tea is cool, combine 2 ounces of the tea with the root beer and the club soda and pour over ice.

MAKE IT ALCOHOLIC:

Use aquavit instead of caraway tea and combine in equal parts as above.

PERKIN WARBECK WASN'T A DUKE;
HE WAS JUST A LIAR

Let's now travel together over to England, in the time between the late Middle Ages and the very early beginning of the Renaissance. Richard, Duke of Gloucester (whom you may know better as Richard III, but we'll get to that title in a moment), and his older brother, Edward IV, who was the then-King of England, were both hungry for power. Importantly, Richard was hungry to be *king*—a position currently occupied by his brother.

On April 9, 1483, King Edward IV's death came suddenly and quite unexpectedly. But here's the kicker: when he died, it wasn't his brother, Richard, Duke of Gloucester, who assumed the crown. The king had several children, including sons: Edward, Prince of Wales, and Richard, Duke of York. Upon his father's death, young Edward, about twelve or thirteen years old, the heir apparent, was now first in line for the throne. Edward was declared king, and his little brother Richard, Duke of York, was named the new heir presumptive.

Young King Edward V was immediately moved into the Tower of London, which was, traditionally, where a monarch lived prior to their coronation. Back then, the infamous Tower functioned as a palace-plus-fortress-plus-prison. Palace AND prison? Yes. Can you smell the foreshadowing? Smells like . . . *regicide*.

About a month after the move, Edward's brother joined him at the Tower. However, just before the big event was to take place, the young king's uncle and guardian, Richard, Duke of Gloucester, delayed the coronation—but never set a new date. And *then*, in a strategic power play, Uncle Richard seized the throne from his nephew and crowned *himself* King Richard III. Edward IV's sons were never seen again—and with the kind of reputation Richard, Duke of Gloucester, had (i.e., not a good one), nobody dared to ask whatever happened to the young royals.

Many historians today assume that at this point in the story, the boys were executed by order of their uncle Richard, though no one is quite sure when. It's an unsettling story, to be sure, but we're not finished quite yet.

Upon King Richard III's death in 1485, a man named Perkin Warbeck seized an opportunity for himself. Since there was no firm evidence about the fate of either of Edward IV's heirs, Perkin assumed the identity of Edward IV's son Richard, Duke of York, and wasted no time claiming his right to the throne, explaining that he'd been spared from death in the Tower because of his young age. To explain his absence, he claimed that he'd been smuggled into Europe by Yorkist sympathizers, where he'd spent the past few years living in secret.

As far-fetched as it might seem today, important people of the time were taken in by Perkin's ruse. The king of France, for example, recognized Perkin as the rightful king of England, as did Maximilian I, Holy Roman Emperor. One of the most influential supporters of fake Richard, though, was Margaret of York, Duchess of Burgundy—who was actually the aunt of the *real* Duke of York. With her support, Perkin solidified his new identity, and many aristocrats promised to aid him in his efforts to recover both the throne and his inheritance. Meanwhile, the current king, Henry VII, was not messing around with this Duke of York situation and did his part to ensure that he wouldn't be unseated—by an imposter or even, perhaps, the real Duke (anything seemed possible). Through his personal spy network, he quietly identified the people who were not loyal to him and removed them from the picture (which is a nice way of saying he had them executed).

Perkin made a number of plays for the throne, but he never quite pulled it off. Various scenarios played out as he'd round up supporters but then lose them due to his general lack of leadership ability. After several failed attempts, Perkin sought sanctuary at an abbey in Hampshire before surrendering to Henry VII's men and confessing his true identity. He was later executed on November 23, 1499, but surprisingly enough, it was not as punishment for impersonating a Yorkist royal—it was for participating in a plot to overthrow Henry VII. ◆

THE ROSY PRETENDER

During the era in which Perkin made his claim for the throne, cider was incredibly popular, so we'll use that as a base for this drink. And since Perkin was called the "White Rose" at times (a nod to his claimed lineage, the House of York), there will also be a rose note, though it somewhat recedes to the background following the tart cherry note.

INGREDIENTS:

· 5 ounces low-sugar apple juice
· 1 ounce tart cherry concentrate
· 1 ounce rose syrup

METHOD:

Combine in a shaker and shake vigorously to integrate all the components. Strain over fresh ice and enjoy.

MAKE IT ALCOHOLIC:

Keep it neutral and add 1–1½ ounces of vodka.

STEPHEN WEINBERG HAD SO MANY ALIASES, WE COULDN'T EVEN COUNT THEM ALL

Born in Brooklyn, New York, right around the end of the nineteenth century, Stephen Jacob Weinberg once explained his fondness for impersonation to a judge like this: "One man's life is a boring thing. I lived many lives; I'm never bored." Be it talent or luck, he played all these different parts perfectly—right down to small details. For instance, as an army officer, he never made the mistake of mingling with troops. As an aviator, the street crowds of New York cheered him on for feats he'd never performed—especially notable considering he'd never even flown a plane.

But things didn't start out this way. Initially, Stephen wanted to become a doctor. However, when his parents couldn't afford his schooling, he pursued a less virtuous path. And, as far as we can tell, he may have never used his given name again.

Stephen's "career" began with a series of dead-end jobs, and it was during this time that he began to imagine and live other lives. In those other lives, he never impersonated a real person, but instead concocted many different aliases for himself: Ethan Allen Weinberg, Royal St. Cyr, Sterling C. Wyman, Rodney S. Wyman, S. Clifford Weinberg, C. Sterling Weinberg, Allen Stanley Weyman, and Stanley Clifford Weyman. Once he reached middle age, he began to use his favorite alias, Stanley Clifford Weyman, as his permanent name. These aliases weren't necessarily intended to hide who he really was, but rather functioned like a "suit" that he'd choose to wear for a time. And speaking of that, Stephen was a snappy, or at least interesting, dresser, with a fully stocked wardrobe at hand. He had the right clothes and the right uniforms for all of the characters he created. And no matter what alias he was using, he always had an air of distinction about him, a mix of dapper and eccentric.

Using all those names, Stephen pretended to be many things, including a lawyer, an aviator, and a sanitation expert. He pretended to be a psychiatrist, twice, and a physician several times. Once, he was even appointed to be the personal physician to silent screen star Pola Negri. More surprisingly, even after she found out his ruse, she *still* wanted him as her doctor. He impersonated several officers in the US Navy, ranging in rank from lieutenant to admiral, and also impersonated US Army officers, a state department naval liaison officer, many consuls-general, and a United Nations expert on Balkan and Asian affairs. The *Montreal Gazette* reported that one time, as he inspected a battleship, the USS *Wyoming*, he donned "a stunning light-blue uniform dripping with gold braid and wearing an admiral's hat," and he was given a twenty-one-gun salute in the New York Harbor. As the alleged State Department Naval Liaison Officer Rodney Sterling Wyman, he was also notably photographed meeting President Warren G. Harding and his wife, Florence, on the White House lawn.

Though mostly nothing came of his antics, Stephen did serve prison time on thirteen different occasions. Six of those occasions were for parole violation, though, usually because he missed a visit with his parole officer, not because of a new crime.

In the late 1940s, Stephen, for reasons unknown, veered back to the right side of the law. He passed the Georgia Bar, got a real job as a correspondent, attached to a legitimate news agency, and hosted a radio broadcast series featuring interviews with diplomats. But it was at his job at the Dunwoodie Motel in New York that managed to be the riskiest of all. There, he worked as the night manager, up until one night, when he was shot twice in the abdomen and once in the back of the head during a holdup. In an attempt to stop the perpetrators, he ended up dying from his injuries. Remarked the detective in charge of the case, "[Stephen] did a lot of things in the course of his life, but what he did [at the Dunwoodie] was brave." ♦

MANY LIVES

Because Stephen Weinberg wanted the thrill of living many lives, it only makes sense to craft a mocktail that has its own chameleon quality, depending on what syrup you choose to include. It's a little bit of an imposter of the popular Lemon Drop cocktail, but hey, you can choose your own adventure!

INGREDIENTS

- 6–10 basil leaves
- 3 ounces lemon juice
- 1 ounce simple or vanilla syrup
- ¾ ounce any other syrup
- Club soda, to taste (1–2 ounces)

METHOD:

Muddle the leaves in a cocktail shaker, then add the lemon juice and syrups and give it a good shake.

Strain it over ice or, if you're going for a mock Lemon Drop, into a chilled martini glass with a sugar rim.

Top with club soda.

MAKE IT ALCOHOLIC:

If you want to make your own version of its alcoholic progenitor, simply add these before the shaking step:

- 1 ounce vodka
- ½ ounce triple sec

PART 4

The Groggery

From *Treasure Island* and *Peter Pan* to *The Pirates of Penzance*, *The Princess Bride*, and *Pirates of the Caribbean*, pirates have long enjoyed a rather romantic (and often comedic) rendering in the public imagination, thanks to Hollywood. When you hear the word "pirate," what kind of images immediately come to mind for you? If you're anything like us, you're probably thinking: swashbuckling adventures, liquor-induced romps through port cities, eye patches and peg legs, and, of course, wooden chests overflowing with treasure like gold coins and gems.

As it is with many Hollywood reimaginings, the reality of life as a pirate—particularly a pirate several centuries (or more!) ago—was not quite as exciting as you'd think. Though gold and gems were definitely a score back then (and still would be today, honestly), for many pirates, the more reliable "treasure" they looted was the food, water, clothing, alcohol, and weapons that they'd stolen from the ships they raided. And sometimes, the treasure was more intangible, like the satisfaction of revenge or the thrilling high of freedom from polite society.

In this next section, we're exploring the tall (and occasionally terrifying) tales of pirates who plundered the world several times over, and over quite a span of time, too. It may be true that dead men tell no tales. But lucky for you . . . *we do.* ♦

CAPTAIN CHARLES JOHNSON, THE PIRATE WHO WASN'T

Little is known about Captain Charles Johnson except one thing: if he ever did exist, that was probably *not* his real name.

There's no record of a "Captain Charles Johnson" in the Royal Navy dating back to the eighteenth century or earlier, nor is there any evidence that a self-titled pirate captain of that name plundered the seas. However, in 1724, a certain "Captain Charles" wrote a book called *A General History of the Robberies and Murders of the most notorious Pyrates*, which contained biographies of both historical and fictional pirates—including names many of us recognize, like the very real Edward "Blackbeard" Teach, Anne Bonny, and Jack "Calico Jack" Rackham. It read like a pirate encyclopedia, or maybe a yearbook. Most importantly, whoever wrote it clearly had great knowledge of the sea and the pirates who roamed across it, and it remained an influential book on piracy for a long time.

It was mostly thanks to this book that the Western world developed their own presumptions regarding what pirates looked like and how they talked and behaved. Think of the stereotypical things like eye patches and wooden legs. Whoever he really was, "Charles" knew the language—and the pirates. Some pirates, such as Henry Every (who was actually a real pirate), were romanticized, helping their story of seafaring crimes take a more permanent hold in popular culture. Thanks to this record, Henry gained recognition as one of a few, if not the only or perhaps the first, major pirate captain to escape with his loot without being killed in battle or apprehended. In other words, he got to cash in his pirate 401(k) when most pirates didn't have a chance to retire.

Many have tried to guess the identity of this mysterious "Captain Charles" in the years since that book was first published. It was once suggested that perhaps the actual person behind the book was author Daniel Defoe—the same guy who wrote the famous eighteenth-century novel *Robinson Crusoe*, which was inspired by the story of Alexander Selkirk, a Scottish seaman. Defoe often wrote under pseudonyms, and among his *three hundred* works, he sometimes wrote about piracy. While an interesting theory, not everyone is convinced that Defoe was the true author. Some believe the name behind the pen was actually Nathaniel Mist, an eighteenth-century publisher and former sailor familiar with the West Indies. Alas, me hearties, he, too, is unconfirmed, and the real identity remains elusive, seemingly lost to Davy Jones's locker. ♦

CRYSTAL CLEAR

Because Johnson's identity remains cloudy, let's flip things upside down and make a cocktail that is crystal clear. There are lots of clear drinks! Any clear spirit plus soda will land you there, but we want something with a little more flavor than that.

Since Johnson's histories of pirates are a little fantastical and bring up stereotypical visions of tropical adventures, we find ourselves drawn to the flavors of a piña colada but still want to craft a clear, lighter version.

INGREDIENTS:

- 1 ounce white rum
- ¾ ounce clear coconut syrup
- 8 ounces pineapple hard seltzer

METHOD:

Combine rum and syrup in a shaking tin with ice,
   then shake and strain over fresh ice into a large glass.

Top with seltzer.

♦ MAKE IT A MOCKTAIL ♦

Use 1 ounce of clear coconut syrup and
   8 ounces of pineapple sparkling water.

WHY TEUTA, QUEEN OF THE ILLYRIANS, WAS CALLED "UNTAMABLE"

She's been called "Teuta the Untamable." She's been called the "Fierce Queen." She's often considered the pirate queen of antiquity, but that may actually be a little bit misleading; Teuta was not actually a pirate, herself—at least, not on the regular. While she might not be known for personally pillaging and looting captured ships, she *is* known for commanding an army of pirates across the Adriatic and Mediterranean Seas from 231 BCE to 228 BCE—and for defying the Roman Republic in the process.

Teuta was the second wife of Agron, King of the Illyrians, and stepmother to his son, Pinnes. Agron was the first king to unify the tribes and regions between the Adriatic coast, from land that's now considered modern-day Slovenia, all the way to part of the Balkan peninsula in modern Albania. The Illyrians were a loosely tied nation made up of tribes and states of people that shared similar language and customs, who happened to live in the same region. Under his rule, Agron centralized control of Illyrian vessels. Previously, these sailors had been independent—let's call them entrepreneurs (ahem, they *were* pirates), violently taking all they could hoard for themselves. Argon made their acts—which he may or may not have called acts of piracy but much of the rest of the world sure did—part of his state policy. When he died suddenly in 231 BCE, it was decided that Agron's son and only heir, Pinnes, was too young to rule, and so, Teuta stepped in to act as queen regent over the kingdom in the meantime. What we know of her rule comes primarily from accounts of pro-piracy laws she enacted.

Queen Teuta outwardly supported and encouraged legalized piracy. To the Illyrians back then, it was considered a respectable way to make a living. Those engaging in acts of piracy were given licenses issued by the government, making it legal for private citizens to, basically, become legal pirates—today, we'd consider those kinds of seafarers "privateers."

Teuta's assembly of pirates became infamous for looting merchant ships—that is, when they weren't busy fighting among themselves, which was a common problem for crews at sea, or raiding Roman and Greek ships and coastal settlements. However, when their piracy in the Adriatic finally caught the attention of the Roman Republic, the Romans feared that Queen Teuta's rising power could become problematic. In response, Rome sent two envoys to meet with her, whom she promptly had killed. Even though the Roman Republic had the largest presence in the Mediterranean Sea at the time, Teuta refused to submit to them time and time again. But then, the tables *turned*. Perhaps seeing that their odds were not good against Rome, or maybe out of fear, Teuta's advisor-slash-military general turned traitor and switched sides, acting as Rome's counsel in their war against Teuta. It was only a matter of weeks before Rome effectively destroyed Teuta's kingdom, and the queen was forced to surrender.

There are a few versions of the story that detail the end of Teuta's reign, and though so much time has passed that we can't point to which is true, there is one thing that seems to hold steady across all of them: she was forbidden from ever again setting sail with more than two ships beyond southern Illyria. This was obviously to ensure that she didn't officially engage in piracy and/or with pirates in the future. There are many rumors about what happened to her after her last battle with Rome, but when it comes to this ancient queen, there are still a lot of unknowns. Whatever her role in the act of piracy itself, we do know that she intimidated the crap out of the Roman Republic, a feat in itself. And that's *so* pirate. ♦

TEUTA'S CURSE

For this drink, we want to pick a spirit associated with the Mediterranean—and though Albanian beverages are often fruity and delicious, let's go with another spirit common in the Mediterranean: ouzo. To top it off, we can throw in some citrus, which is common in the area. Don't let the name fool you; this divine drink is less of a curse and more of a gift from above.

INGREDIENTS:

- 1 ounce ouzo
- 1 ounce vodka (citrus vodka is great)
- 5 ounces lemonade

METHOD:

Shake together with ice and strain over fresh ice.

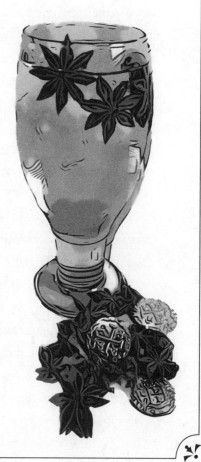

♦ MAKE IT A MOCKTAIL ♦

- 3 drops anise extract
- 7 ounces lemonade

Add the anise extract to a glass with ice, and pour the lemonade over.

ARTEMISIA I OF KARIYA TOLD XERXES WHAT TO DO (AND SHE WAS RIGHT)

Artemisia I was the queen of the ancient city of Halicarnassus and is best known today for two things: the prosperous era of her reign and the role she played in the naval Battle of Salamis in 480 BCE.

She rose to power in the ancient district of Kariya in southwestern Anatolia (which is considered modern-day Turkey) when she began acting as queen regent for her young son, Pisindelis, after the death of her king-husband.

Though much about her remains unknown or unverified (which, to be fair, *can happen* after one and a half millennia), we do know that she was an ally of King Xerxes I of Persia. It's also believed that Artemisia led a fleet of five ships, and that she was the only woman among Xerxes's military commanders; in fact, she often advised him on tactical matters, and she was pretty much— OK, *always*—right. She was especially famous for her tactical skill and daring, and there's a particularly juicy anecdote about the time she escaped enemy pursuit by ordering her crew to ram a friendly Persian warship (sorry, friends!). It worked, causing the attacking Athenians to pull back, believing that she was actually on their side.

Though not a pirate in the modern sense, she certainly had the maritime gravitas we often associate with pirate captains, and it's *that* story of her life that history continues to tell.

Herodotus of Halicarnassus, who was her contemporary and historian of the Greco-Persian Wars, notably wrote about her in his book, *The Histories*. Though he does confirm some basic important facts (like that she was real, she was a queen, and she did engage in naval battles for the Persians at Salamis), other claims aren't necessarily quite as convincing. Like, was she *really* the admiral of a Persian navy with upward of six hundred warships? *Six hundred!?!?* Quick, does anyone know if Herodotus was known for hyperbole? ♦

FIT FOR A QUEEN

Artemisia's life story is one of extraordinary strength, adventure, prowess, and a little heartache. As such, she deserves a drink that feels regal and powerful, but also beautiful and enjoyable—like any drink worthy of a fleet-commanding warrior queen should be.

INGREDIENTS:

- ½ ounce cinnamon liqueur
- 1½ ounces bourbon
- 1 ounce passion fruit liqueur
- ¾ ounce lemon juice
- 2 ounces agave juice

METHOD:

Glaze a rocks glass with cinnamon liqueur and add ice.

Combine bourbon, passion fruit liqueur, lemon juice, and agave juice in a cocktail shaker with ice, shake, and strain into the glazed, chilled glass.

◆ MAKE IT A MOCKTAIL ◆

Instead of passion fruit liqueur, puree passion fruit and use 1 tablespoon of it.

Sub in black tea for the bourbon, and cinnamon syrup for the cinnamon liqueur glaze. (To make the syrup, simmer 1 cup of sugar with 1 cup of water and a few cinnamon sticks; let it cool and strain out the sticks.)

RACHEL WALL:
NEW ENGLAND'S "LADY" PIRATE

O ften referred to as New England's only female pirate, Rachel Wall, who was *probably* born under the name Rachel Schmidt, earned a fear-inducing nickname for herself due to her antics during the mid-eighteenth century: The Dread Pirate Rachel. She may or may not have been the first American-born woman to become a pirate, but she most certainly was the last woman to be hanged in Massachusetts—though not ultimately for piracy.

We're a bit lucky when it comes to Rachel Wall's life history, or at least *parts* of her history. And that's because, before the end of her life, she wrote a piece called "Life, Last Words and Dying CONFESSION, OF RACHEL WALL." It's important to stress that this was a confession that was penned shortly before her execution; it was not a journal, and historians acknowledge there are embellishments and inaccuracies in these kinds of documents.

Rachel left home in Pennsylvania at the age of sixteen and soon met a fisherman named George Wall, a meeting that would change the course of her life. The pair married and settled in Boston, but not long after, George left Rachel for the sea. Rachel admitted that she had no idea where he was when she was questioned about her husband's whereabouts, but historians now believe that George may have found work as a privateer during the American Revolution. Regardless of his initial behavior during their newlywed years, George did, eventually, return to his wife, and when he did, she joined him and they began a new life together in piracy.

Rachel and George were a husband-and-wife pirate team, the proto–Bonnie and Clyde of the seas. Their legend claims that they stole a ship named the *Essex*, and, together, plundered as many as twelve ships, killed twenty-four sailors, and allegedly amassed thousands of dollars. They primarily worked after storms had hit, when ships might be shipwrecked or otherwise susceptible to boarding, and they notably made use of their unique situation (a.k.a. having a woman on board) to lure in their victims. One of their favorite moves was for Rachel to stand on the deck or mast of their ship and pretend to be a lady in distress, screaming for help until nearby sailors came to her rescue. And that's when George and the crew would swing into action, plundering and murdering and causing general mayhem.

Alas, before long, tragedy struck, and George and most of the crew drowned at sea during a particularly treacherous storm. Rachel survived but gave up piracy and returned to Boston, where she found employment in domestic work. One night while she was walking home from work, she passed seventeen-year-old Margaret Bender on the road. Whether she did the crime or not, Margaret accused Rachel of violently stealing a bonnet, as well as shoes and buckles, from her—and possibly a few shillings, too. There's an odd and highly unlikely salacious detail that sometimes appears in this story, too: Margaret allegedly claimed that Rachel tried to rip her tongue out during the attack.

Eventually, Rachel was arrested and jailed. To her credit, she never denied that she was a criminal, and that she'd been previously arrested for petty theft and for larceny. While technically no longer a pirate, she did also loot a few important people on land. But in the end, her arrest wasn't for piracy or petty crime. It was for highway robbery, which, in Massachusetts at the time, meant that she could be executed if found guilty.

Rachel pleaded innocent before the Supreme Judicial Court in Massachusetts but was found guilty. She was executed by hanging at the Great Elm on Boston Common on October 8, 1789, when she was only twenty-nine years old. Rachel was the last woman hanged in Massachusetts, and despite her pleas to be hanged as a pirate, she was hanged for highway robbery—no more, no less. ♦

THE HANGED WOMAN

Because Rachel lived in New England at a time when ciders were very popular, and because she died in October, we're infusing this drink with some classic autumnal flavor. The bubbles make it a good candidate for celebration toasts, and unlike Rachel's life, this one is easy, both to make and to sip.

The mocktail version is a great candidate for fall parties with kids or nondrinkers, as it still feels fancy and celebratory.

INGREDIENTS:

- Splash of pumpkin syrup
- 3 ounces hard cider
- 3 ounces champagne

METHOD:

Pour the pumpkin syrup into a chilled coupe or champagne flute, then add the hard cider and champagne.

♦ MAKE IT A MOCKTAIL ♦

Sub in nonalcoholic cider and ginger ale.

LAGERTHA, VIKING SHIELD-MAIDEN AND PROBABLE PIRATE

Oftentimes, history gets in the way of separating fact from fiction—mostly because the sourcing is so ambiguous. For example, much of what we know about the Viking era comes either from mythology or stories that were told for hundreds of years *after* these events supposedly took place. Sometimes, those who battled with the Vikings did live to tell about it and were able to record their experiences, although those stories were surely told with a one-sided angle that did not favor the Vikings, as one might imagine. All that being said, let's talk about Lagertha, a Viking shield-maiden who might have also plundered the high seas.

From approximately the ninth to the eleventh century BCE, Vikings were known to attack and pillage up and down coastlines, and especially during exploratory voyages. But their culture wasn't all about menacing and plundering; they were also traders and settlers. While we frequently talk about them today collectively, calling them Vikings or Norsemen, it's important to remember that they weren't actually organized under one big hierarchical umbrella; they were a bunch of chieftain-led tribes, not a unified group. The women in Viking communities were smart, hard-working, and resourceful. Most were wives and mothers, and they were responsible for managing the family's home and tending to the family farm while the men were at sea. Surprisingly, Vikings were also pretty progressive in terms of rights for women back then. For example, it was their right to request a divorce and to reclaim their dowries if their marriage ended. They could also inherit property. Even though they had (comparatively) more rights than women in other cultures, there were still some Viking women that just didn't fit the mold and marched to the beat of their own drum. Some were entrepreneurs, some were master craftswomen, and some, like Lagertha, are now thought to have fought in combat or perhaps sailed the high seas looking to raid and plunder.

Whether referred to as Valkyries, she-warriors, warriors, pirates, or shield-maidens, stories about strong women like Lagertha aren't uncommon in Norse lore. We know about Lagertha by name because Danish theologian, chronicler, and historian Saxo Grammaticus included her in his Danish historical record, *Gesta Danorum* (or *Deeds of the Danes*), though her real name, in Old Norse, would have probably been something more like Hlaðgerðr. Saxo Grammaticus wrote about how Lagertha fought with the Vikings in their battle against the Swedes during the invasion of Norway. In his narrative of events, she was a shield-maiden who led an army that would end up being the downfall of the King of Sweden. Shield-maidens were Viking women who carried a sword and, yes, a shield, and who were known for their brutality and abilities in battle on land as well as at sea; essentially, they were warriors and pirates, just like their male peers. Or at least some historians think they were.

And remember, Lagertha isn't the only example of a Viking warrior woman. Saxo Grammaticus's records and mythology mention as many as three hundred shield-maidens who fought alongside Viking men, including Freydís, Brynhildr, Hervor, and Veborg. Unfortunately, because there are so few records of Lagertha's life that are even remotely close to verifiable, her life story is controversial and there are a lot of skeptics. Some believe that Saxo Grammaticus's description of her might have been of his own creation, combining the actions of more than one female warrior he learned about into a single character. Other historians argue against his record of events, suggesting that there's no way any Viking woman ever raided, and that any descriptions of them doing so are totally fictional. Very open-minded. So, what we end up with is the history of a people—and a woman—that relies not on their own historical and factual record, but on ancient Scandinavian legends, folklore, sagas, and sometimes what other people said about them, which could be good or bad. And the truth is buried deep underneath all of that, perhaps never to see the light of day again. ♦

THE HORNED HELMET

Lagertha's story conjures up the comedic and not-historically accurate image of a horned helmet à la Bugs Bunny in an old *Merrie Melodies* cartoon. And that's because it's tied to a false ideology, which parallels the concept of stereotypical male/female dichotomy that's often assumed has always been part of every historical culture. But discoveries of Viking artifacts have shown us that the possibility that such a narrow view of things may not really apply, so we want to make a cocktail that combines components that are stereotypically thought of (incorrectly) as feminine—like flowers—and masculine—like brown spirits—so that we can concoct something that brings out the best of both.

INGREDIENTS:

- ¾ ounce lemon juice
- ¾ ounce violet syrup
- 1½ ounces whiskey of your choice
- Club soda, to taste (1–2 ounces)

METHOD:

Combine the first three ingredients in a shaking tin, shake with ice, strain over ice into a rocks glass, and top with club soda.

♦ MAKE IT A MOCKTAIL ♦

- 1½ ounces long-steeped black tea, plus a dash of bitters (optional)
- ¾ ounce lemon juice
- ¾ ounce violet syrup
- Club soda, to taste (1–2 ounces)

Combine and shake as above and top with club soda.

CAPTAIN HENRY EVERY: THE PIRATE WHO GOT AWAY WITH IT

Henry Every was in his late thirties when he became one of the most successful pirates in history—a feat he accomplished over the span of just two years. That's quite something when you're pirating during the Golden Age of Piracy, competing for the "honor" against thousands of now-infamous pirates like Captain Kidd, Calico Jack, Black Bart, and Blackbeard. And yet, according to his legend, Henry's reputation-making heist was one of the most profitable acts of piracy ever, putting all those other names to shame.

His story on the seas begins in the 1670s, when he joined the Royal Navy as a midshipman on a sixty-four-gun ship named the HMS *Rupert*. But Henry didn't stay on the straight and narrow for long. After spending time in the navy, he worked as a privateer—basically, he was paid by the government to practice acts of piracy against ships from enemy countries. He built an impressive career for himself, and then, when he took command of the royal warship, the forty-six-gun *Charles II*, he announced his intention to turn pirate full-time, declaring, "I am captain of this ship now. I am bound to Madagascar, with the design of making my own fortune, and that of all the brave fellows joined with me."

As Captain Henry Every, he renamed the *Charles II* as the *Fancy*, and she, with her new captain and crew, sailed for the African coasts, where trade routes were full of English, Spanish, and French ships just *waiting* to be preyed upon. Henry operated in both the Atlantic Ocean and the Indian Ocean, following what was known as the "Pirate Round," which was a sailing route popular among English pirates. It was largely the same route that was used by East India Company ships, a company incorporated by royal charter and formed, essentially, for the exploitation of trade with East and Southeast Asia and India.

After months of plundering trade routes, Henry and his crew amassed a fleet of five ships, giving him enough power to attack even the most well-armored vessels. So, when he learned that there was *real* treasure to be taken, he was ready to go. The target was a Mughal empire armada sailing from the Red Sea on a voyage home to Surat, India. The convoy would primarily be carrying Muslim pilgrims on their way to the holy city of Mecca, but that's not what interested him. The fleet would also include several treasure-filled merchant vessels owned by the Emperor Aurangzeb Alamgir. And *that's* what Henry wanted. Their flagship *Ganj-i-Sawai* was equipped with several dozen cannons and upward of four hundred riflemen, which was more firepower than Henry's entire pirate fleet possessed, but, ambitious and undeterred, Henry attacked anyway. Henry's crew was brutal and murderous, and in the end, they were victorious, which quickly turned Captain Every into the world's most prosperous—and most wanted—pirate.

Following the devastating loss, the East India Company feared for the safety of their own trade agreements and placed a bounty on Henry's head. They called him and his crew "notorious rogues" and offered a reward to anyone who took part in their capture. But despite the promise of fortune, Henry was never brought to account for his crimes. Much of his crew retired after that haul, but Henry? Well, he just vanished. And in doing so, he became one of the very few pirate captains—some will tell you the *only*—to escape with his loot before being killed in battle or arrested and hanged.

During the time of Captain Henry Every, not many pirates died rich, or even in their own beds. Tales we hear about the end of Henry's life run the gamut, so let's indulge in them for a minute. It was said that Henry married an Indian princess. (He didn't.) There was also talk of Henry founding a new monarchy . . . though no one knew where. (He didn't.) Some believe he changed his name to Benjamin Bridgeman, after using it for an alias for many years, and quietly lived out the rest of his life in an undisclosed location. (He . . . didn't? This one is intriguing, but hard to prove definitively one way or another.) And there were also accounts that suggested that Henry had squandered his fortune and died on the streets of London. (As far as we know, he didn't.) In the end, all we have left are tall tales, and Every's story is more than worth its weight in gold. ◆

THE VANISHING PIRATE

Just like Henry, this cocktail vanishes very quickly. And if you drink enough—which is easy to do (but *don't!*)—your stories will get very hazy. It's a delicious sip—perfect for relaxing while you're whiling away your days under the radar.

INGREDIENTS:

- 1 ounce elderflower liqueur
- 1 ounce strawberry vodka
- 6 ounces ginger beer

METHOD:

Pour the liqueur, then the vodka, then the ginger beer into a glass and stir, then add ice and stir once more.

♦ MAKE IT A MOCKTAIL ♦

- 1 ounce elderflower syrup
- 4 strawberries, cut in half
- 6 ounces ginger beer

Muddle the syrup and strawberries together, then top with ginger beer and add ice.

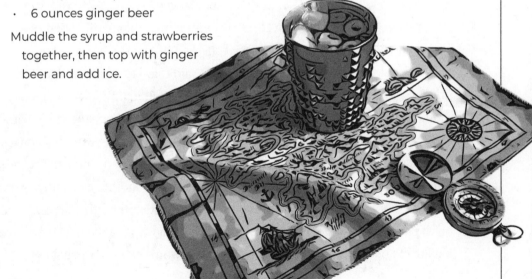

CHARLOTTE DE BERRY, THE MUTINOUS, ROMANTIC (AND POSSIBLY FICTIONAL) PIRATE

The earliest known reference to Charlotte de Berry can be found in London-based publisher Edward Lloyd's popular penny dreadful series, in a story called *History of the Pirates*, which was published in 1836. Notably, that story came out *two hundred years after* her alleged birth date. Here's why that's important: Lloyd was very influential in shaping the modern popular press, but he played *real* fast and loose with authorship and ownership—and fact and fiction. Basically, he wrote the story that would sell, not necessarily the story that was true. And it was through his paper that readers were often introduced to popular stories of the time, told in *his* words—serializations that often needed to be taken with a grain of salt.

According to the sources we do have, Charlotte was born in 1636 in England, and, as a teenager, fell madly in love and married a sailor—against her parents' wishes—and eventually found herself wrapped up in a life of piracy. At first, she disguised herself as a man to accompany her husband, since it was considered bad luck to have a woman onboard a ship. Then, an officer discovered her true identity—i.e., that she was a *she*—but since he'd developed feelings for her, he kept quiet about her presence. Instead, he assigned her husband to dangerous work that put his life at risk, hoping it would result in his, *oops*, accidental death. After surviving task after task thrown at him, Charlotte's husband was then accused of mutiny—and executed. Now, her husband's wicked shipmate assumed Charlotte would finally be his. But when they next landed in port, Charlotte took her revenge and murdered the officer. She then fled the ship and began working on the docks, where . . . stay with us, things take a turn . . . she was (allegedly) kidnapped by and (allegedly) forcibly married to the captain of a merchant ship passing through. We're not saying that marriage didn't happen, but this is when her story begins to . . . well, get a little shaky.

During the journey to the African coast with her new husband and his crew, Charlotte incited mutiny, according to Lloyd's version of events. She killed her kidnapper/husband and subsequently captained the ship herself. She married again, this time for love, but when the ship and its crew became marooned on a small island, her bad luck returned. It's said that the crew, starving, turned to cannibalism, and that Charlotte's new husband drew the short straw. Other storytellers insist that the marooned crew was being rescued by a Dutch merchant ship, from which Charlotte then jumped to her death. We may never know exactly what happened, but there's no doubt she was a bonafide badass. ◆

VENGEFUL WIDOW

If Charlotte's story is true, she was one exceptionally fierce woman. What struck us the most about her story was her drive to punish the men who wronged her; while we don't condone violence generally, both of the men that she murdered had definitely done shady enough things to earn her ire.

Thinking about what might best represent such a woman, we lean toward something with a touch of peppery spice—but still unexpected. Thus, the Vengeful Widow, which looks at first very much like a classic Collins but has a unique surprise taste.

INGREDIENTS:

- ½ teaspoon white pepper
- 4 ounces gin (you'll have enough for two cocktails)
- 1 ounce grapefruit juice
- 1 ounce simple syrup
- Club soda, to taste (1–2 ounces)

METHOD:

Add the white pepper to the gin and soak overnight in an airtight container, shaking occasionally.

Fine strain 2 ounces of gin into a shaking tin with the grapefruit juice and simple syrup.

Shake with ice, then strain into a tall glass over fresh ice.

Top with club soda.

♦ MAKE IT A MOCKTAIL ♦

Make as above, but sub out the gin for flat tonic water.

ANNE DIEU-LE-VEUT, THE PIRATE OF "GOD'S WILL"

She was born Anne Dieu-le-Veut in 1661 in Brittany, France. But she found herself in the Caribbean as one of the so-called "Filles de Roi," or "King's Daughters," a program that deported women, most of them convicted criminals, to French colonies where they were expected to take advantage of a fresh start. The idea behind the "Filles de Roi" program was for these deportees to marry French colonists, settle down to start a family, and live a good, redeemed life.

Anne landed on French Tortuga, a Caribbean island that forms part of Haiti. She did end up getting married—but it was definitely not to an upstanding French colonist, as the rehabilitation program hoped. Tortuga was a known pirate haven, and Anne married the buccaneer Pierre Lelong. After Lelong was killed in a fight, she married again; and again, not to a French colonist. This time, it was to another buccaneer she met on the island, a man named Joseph Cherel.

But bad luck followed her like a plague. After all, English novelist Daphne du Maurier once wrote that marriage and piracy do not go together. And that seems true, at least if Anne's tale gives us any wisdom on the topic. After a pirate named Laurens de Graaf killed Cherel, Anne challenged him to a duel. He refused to fight a woman, and—you probably weren't expecting this—he proposed to her as she pointed a gun in his face. Perhaps even more surprising . . . is that she accepted. Anne, WE HAVE QUESTIONS. As his wife, she shared command of the ship and fought alongside captain and crew—openly as a woman.

Her story, though, ends when she was captured after she and Laurens attacked a British ship off the coast of Jamaica, and she was held captive for three years. After her release in 1698, she retired to the echelons of legend and lore. ◆

SUDDEN MATRIMONY

Since Anne was from Brittany, where apple-flavored spirits are very popular, it would be fitting to use an apple brandy in her drink. This concoction is strong, but it has a surprisingly smooth flavor thanks to the almond flavor of the syrup. It's a way to balance the parts of Anne's story that showcase her bravado and badassery, while also acknowledging the softer parts of her later years during which she may have settled into a cozy phase with her husband, Laurens de Graaf.

INGREDIENTS:

- · 1 ounce apple brandy
- · 1 ounce bourbon
- · ½ ounce orgeat (an almond-based syrup)
- · Angostura bitters (optional)
- · Apple slice, for garnish

METHOD:

Add all components to a mixing glass, then drop in ice (this is an instance where a large ice cube, which won't dilute your drink as much, is a good option).

Stir together, then strain into an old-fashioned glass (again with a large ice cube).

Garnish with a slice of apple.

♦ MAKE IT A MOCKTAIL ♦

- · 1 ounce apple juice
- · 1 ounce black tea
- · ½ ounce orgeat (an almond-based syrup)
- · 1 drop vanilla extract
- · Apple slice, for garnish

Prepare as above.

JEANNE DE CLISSON
AND HER BLOODTHIRSTY REVENGE

Born Jeanne Louise de Belleville, Dame de Montaigu, in Belleville-sur-Vie in the Vendée, France, Jeanne de Clisson had a particularly unique background among her female peers: she was a noblewoman-turned-pirate.

Her story begins not unlike many other women born into fourteenth-century wealthy families. When she was twelve years old, she was married to nineteen-year-old Geoffrey de Châteaubriant, the heir to one of the key defensive estates in the region. Jeanne and Geoffrey were not married for love, but rather to solidify a strategic alliance between their families. But Geoffrey died not long afterward, and as a young widow with two children, Jeanne now found herself in control of a group of lordships just south of the Breton border.

Two years later, she remarried, to Guy de Bretagne de Penthièvre. But as luck would have it, shortly after her nuptials, she and Guy were granted permission by the Catholic Church to have their marriage annulled. How is this luck? Well, for Jeanne, she'd just met the love of her life. But that wasn't what actually mattered to the Church. Guy's family also lodged complaints with the bishops of Vannes and Rennes in an effort to protect their family's noble heritage—Jeanne was of nobility, but apparently *not* noble enough—and the pope granted the dissolution of their marriage. Jeanne's love, Olivier de Clisson, was a wealthy Breton, who held quite a bit of land himself. Thanks to Jeanne's inheritance from her first marriage, their combined assets essentially made them a fourteenth-century power couple. But what really made them an exception to many marriages at the time is that they were actually in love.

Just when everything seemed to be going steady, war broke out in the form of the Hundred Years War, which pitted England and France against each other. Like many other French nobles at the time, Olivier and Jeanne feared they could lose their land and other holdings to the English if England was victorious. Olivier sided with the French, but soon an influential nemesis became convinced that Olivier was actually an English sympathizer. Charles de Blois, Duke of Brittany, was as powerful as he was paranoid, which meant that his opinion *really* mattered. Consequently, Olivier was accused of being a traitor and imprisoned, and though no evidence of guilt was ever found against him, he was still sentenced to death and executed by beheading. But things didn't end there. As a warning to other sympathizers, his body and head were—separately—shipped to different regions of France and put on public display.

The desecration of his corpse was intended to be shameful and to instill fear in others; i.e., look what happens if you step out of line. Jeanne was not only grief-stricken over losing her husband but now also infuriated and humiliated at his treatment postmortem. She sold everything, from her jewels to the furniture that decorated the family's castles. She even sold all her land. Then, with the money she raised, she built up a pirate fleet of three black ships with red sails, known as the Black Fleet. Her motives couldn't be clearer; after all, she named her flagship *My Revenge*. For the next thirteen years, the Black Fleet struck terror into the hearts of French sailors, plundering French warships throughout the English Channel—and *no one* got out alive.

Jeanne is a particularly interesting pirate because she was not seeking riches or treasure. As a widow and a mother of seven, she was instead seeking her own kind of justice. Her revenge business focused specifically on terrifying three specific targets: Charles de Blois; the King of France; and, really pretty much France itself. As a woman, she developed a particularly menacing reputation for vengeance and cruelty, earning herself the nickname of the Lioness of Brittany.

During her time at sea, Jeanne never was able to get her revenge on Charles de Blois; alas, he was killed in combat when his troops were defeated in the Battle of Auray in 1364. But not everything ended badly for her. After ending her life of piracy, she married again, to Gautier de Bentley, who had been one of the King of England's military deputies. Compared to most other pirates, her final years were relatively peaceful; she settled with her husband in a castle on the Brittany coast, and it's there she died in 1359. ♦

RED SAILS

This Jeanne-inspired drink highlights her obvious fire; after all, she had to have had a great deal of passion to go on a thirteen-year revenge tirade. We're also throwing in something red, evocative of the red sails that enveloped the horizon as she pursued those who wronged her.

INGREDIENTS:

- ½ ounce simple syrup
- ½ ounce lemon juice
- 1½ ounces cinnamon whiskey
- ½ ounce Grand Marnier
- 4 ounces cranberry juice

METHOD:

Combine in a shaker and strain over fresh ice.

♦ MAKE IT A MOCKTAIL ♦

- 1 ounce cinnamon syrup (you can make this by simmering 1 cup of sugar with 1 cup of water and a few cinnamon sticks; let it cool and strain out the sticks)
- ½ ounce orange syrup
- ½ ounce simple syrup
- ½ ounce lemon juice
- 4 ounces cranberry juice

Shake and strain over ice as above.

PART 5

The Cauldron

Though there are plenty of deviations from the typically wicked stereotype (think: *Hocus Pocus* or Samantha from *Bewitched*), most fictional witches have some sort of tie with magic, mysticism, and/or the devil.

However, as far as actual history is concerned, the term "witch" didn't always equate to someone being evil—in fact, it was far from it. Many of these "witches" were healers, often called wise women (or men), who knew their way around botanicals and could help others in the community in time of need. Looking for something to help soothe a sore throat or improve fertility? Whatever you were looking for, chances were that you could go to your local "witch" and pick up an herbal remedy that would help. It didn't necessarily mean this same person was in league with the devil—well, that is, until one day when it did. Cue the wild accusations, witch hunts, and senseless executions.

Like witches, alchemists—those who combined medieval science and philosophy to better understand physical transformations (a.k.a. early chemists)— were also highly valued in their communities for their knowledge. Until they *weren't*. When it came to things that seemed unexplainable to the greater community, it was easier for the public to blame the witches and alchemists for their misunderstandings. What's more, religious leaders who felt threatened by these ideas poured extra fuel on the fire of public suspicion and animosity.

As you'll see in this upcoming selection of stories, many of the women and men who were accused of using the so-called dark arts to do their bidding— whether that bidding was a love spell or turning iron into gold—were shunned, condemned as heretics, and even executed for "crimes" they didn't even commit. And there's nothing darker than that. ♦

HERBALIST MATTEUCCIA DI FRANCESCO COULD FLY

icture it: one day, your neighborhood pharmacy is shuttered because your pharmacist—or maybe your doctor—has been arrested, accused of drinking the blood of infants and flying to an orgy involving the devil. Well, back in the fourteenth century, this is exactly what happened in the small village of Ripabianca, which sits in the Umbria region of Italy. Most people there lived in rural servitude. Most people were uneducated. Many were superstitious. And many relied on Matteuccia di Francesco for their health and well-being—at least, that is, before she was accused of fornicating with the devil.

Matteuccia was an expert on herbs and was probably an apothecary, or at least worked in a similar capacity, preparing ointments and herbal teas to heal ailments and injuries (maybe with the recitation of a few "magic" words for a sprinkle of good measure). It would have been likely for her to have been the local midwife and considered a wise woman in her village, though that is still just speculation. As word about Matteuccia's herbal remedies and potions spread, her client base grew quite sizable. Her advice and tinctures were mostly harmless, even if they seemed strange. Think: a salve made out of radish, garlic, wormwood, and a few other herbs thrown in; boiled in butter; strained; and then used to cure your headaches. Might seem odd, but hey, if it works, it works.

Most people in the medieval era never saw a doctor, but they absolutely went to visit their local wise woman. Unlike physicians, who at the time were a kind of haphazard group who studied philosophy and the stars and "trained" (we use that term *very* loosely) mainly to observe, wise women were able to apply more than six hundred plants for medicinal uses—largely thanks to Dioscorides, a Greek physician, pharmacologist, and botanist who shared his knowledge via multiple volumes about herbal medicine. Though the community benefited from her work, Matteuccia was accused of being "a woman of a bad life and reputation, public enchantress, sorceress, evil spell caster, and witch." The records of her trial detail the charms she used, and her specialties seemed to have consisted of mainly healing prayers and love spells.

We don't meet up with Matteuccia in history because of her apothecary skills, though; we meet her after she's accused by so-called reputable men of practicing witchcraft. Witch hunts were gaining popularity at the time because authorities were redefining the crimes of witchcraft. People could now say things like, "She has a wart and witches have warts, so we should kill her"; basically, it gave everyone a kind of checklist to determine whether someone was a witch or not. Frequently encouraged by priests, judges, and local authorities who may or may not have studied theology or law, these so-called experts believed that there were, absolutely, witches in their society and that their evil needed to be expelled.

Interestingly, Matteuccia's trial is one of the earliest Italian witchcraft cases for which a complete trial record survives—and what really makes it stand out is that it's also considered the first case where an alleged witch is accused of flying. She was charged with more than thirty counts of witchcraft in all, and among them were accusations she had drunk the blood of many infants, of being able to turn into a cat, and of having flown on a goat. According to court records, her accusers characterized her herbalist services as enchantment, claiming that she "enchanted the body, head, or other limbs of patients." It really didn't matter if her customers died or if she cured their illness, though; she would still have been held guilty of practicing witchcraft. Because "reputable men" said so.

We know Matteuccia confessed to the accusations against her, though it's unclear if her confession happened under torture, which was super common at the time and especially at witch trials. She confessed to having sold medicine, which she probably did, but she also confessed to having flown on the back of a demon after smearing herself with an ointment made of the blood of newborn children. We're a little less than convinced about that last one. Regardless, in 1428, she was burned alive at the age of forty. ♦

DIABOLICAL SPIRIT

It proved a little too challenging to make a drink inspired by a goat flight (imagine that), but we *did* fall in love with the phrase "diabolical spirit." This libation is a reference to the allegations that Matteuccia drank blood, but it's really quite delightful—not to mention, it has a beautiful red color with a surprisingly complex flavor. Looks like blood! Rich in taste! Full of antioxidants! It's practically a health drink.

INGREDIENTS:

- ¾ ounce grenadine
- ½ ounce lemon juice
- 1 ounce gin
- ¾ ounce Amaretto
- 3 ounces pomegranate juice

METHOD:

Shake together with ice and strain over fresh ice.

♦ MAKE IT A MOCKTAIL ♦

Skip the gin and use almond syrup in lieu of Amaretto. Garnish with fresh herbs like rosemary or lavender.

URSULA KEMP AND
THE ST. OSYTH WITCHES

Let's set the tone for what it would have been like in St. Osyth, England, back in the sixteenth century—that is, what it would have been like if you were accused of witchcraft. Going back as far as the eleventh century, the growing Christianity movement and citizens in general throughout the Western world began to associate witchcraft with things like heresy and pacts with the devil. By the fifteenth century, Pope Innocent VIII declared that accused witches were to be "corrected, imprisoned, punished, and chastised" by their religious peers—and that's also about the time when a frenzy of witch hunting began. Within that frenzy, the St. Osyth witches, as they're commonly called, were convicted of witchcraft in 1582—and among those alleged witches was a woman named Ursula Kemp.

In Ursula's lifetime, the passage of "An Act Against Conjurations, Enchantments, and Witchcrafts" marked the first time that indictments for homicide caused by witchcraft began to appear in the historical record. That's huge in and of itself, but it wasn't the only significant anti-witchcraft notion at play here.

There was also the influence of the *Malleus Maleficarum*, which was regarded as the "go-to handbook" for not only how to recognize and detain witches, but also how to interrogate them. The book targeted women, and specifically midwives, who were believed to kill infants in offering to the devil, among other blasphemous activities. Used well into the eighteenth century, the *Malleus Maleficarum* was the ultimate, legal witch-hunting manual, and it gave permission for anyone to do anything to stop a witch. *Anything*.

Unfortunately for Ursula Kemp, she was a midwife and possibly also an herbalist (cue dread-inducing foreshadowing music). She was well known in her community and frequently called upon by town residents to heal people who had become ill. But before long, her fellow villagers became suspicious: if Ursula could heal a person, maybe she was just as easily able to injure them, too.

Problems started when a woman named Grace Thurlow, also from St. Osyth, launched a few dangerous accusations against Ursula. Importantly, Ursula had once cured Grace's son with her incantations. However, just months later, Grace's infant daughter died after falling from her cradle—and it happened shortly after Grace and Ursula had argued about how to care for the baby. And that wasn't all. Grace had also developed a problem with her legs, and when she'd asked for Ursula's help, Kemp agreed, but for 12 pence. It's difficult to compare that to contemporary money, but, estimated, it's probably the equivalent of $10 to $15 today. Grace agreed to the price, but when healed, refused to pay. Again, the women argued. When Grace began to walk with difficulty again, she believed that it was because Ursula had cast a spell upon her. It was then that Grace filed a complaint with the magistrate, and an investigation into Ursula followed. This complaint, in turn, made Ursula a prime target for the village's witch hunter, Brian Darcy, who was *also* the local magistrate. Yikes. As things stacked up against her, she was arrested and charged, and as it so happened, Brian Darcy was also the justice at her trial. *SUPER yikes.*

The charges brought against her ranged from preventing beer from brewing to causing death through the use of sorcery. If found guilty, she would be punished by execution. After she was charged, Ursula was locked in what the villagers called "The Cage." The Cage was actually a two-bedroom cottage used as a medieval prison, and Ursula and a dozen other accused women (nicknamed the St. Osyth Witches) were jailed there while awaiting trial.

It will come as no surprise that Grace testified against Ursula. Another villager, Alice Letherdale, testified that after she and Ursula had argued about cleaning products, Alice's daughter, Elizabeth, fell ill and died. Alice claimed that she'd seen Ursula "murmur" in her daughter's direction and blamed Ursula for bewitching her daughter to death. Perhaps the most incriminating testimony, though, came from Ursula's own eight-year-old son, Thomas Rabbet. Thomas wasn't expected to take the stand, and it was likely a surprise even to Ursula, but during the trial, witch-hunter Darcy coerced him to testify against his mother. Too young to understand what was happening, he claimed that his mother kept familiars—these were their four cats—in their home, and he described how she used them to kill people. *Ooof.* It makes you wonder how much the witch-hunter groomed him to say.

But the most devastating part of her trial came from the witch-hunter-justice himself, who claimed that Ursula had made a full confession to him—but, conveniently for him and inconveniently for her, it had happened in private. There isn't any record of such a meeting, but Ursula allegedly confessed to Brian Darcy that she'd sent her familiars to cause Grace's condition, and that she'd also used them to kill Joan Thurlow and Elizabeth Letherdale. In this *alleged* private confession, she *allegedly* named the names of other so-called witches to redirect blame; and they, in turn, named more. In total, fourteen women in St. Osyth were tried for witchcraft. We know from trial records that at least two were executed—and Ursula was one of them. ♦

THE CAGE

This cocktail will trap you with deliciousness but is otherwise harmless, other than the fact that it includes a liqueur that's a *little* pricey, which is Chartreuse. The herbaceous (and secret) nature of the Chartreuse recipe is a mirror to Ursula's midwifery and the use of herbs in witchcraft. Once you start playing with Chartreuse, you quickly realize its complex flavor can be used to great effect in many drinks.

INGREDIENTS:

- 1 ounce vodka
- 1 ounce green Chartreuse
- 1 ounce black tea
- ½–1 ounce vanilla syrup

METHOD:

Shake and strain into a chilled coupe.

♦ MAKE IT A MOCKTAIL ♦

- 1 ounce black tea
- 1 ounce each two different herbal teas— your choice!
- ½–1 ounce vanilla syrup

Shake and strain into a chilled coupe.

THE FLOWERS OF BOTTESFORD
MAY HAVE BEEN FRAMED

The story of how Joan Flower and her two daughters, Margaret and Philippa, were accused of killing the two young sons, Henry and Francis, of Francis Manners, Sixth Earl of Rutland, was published in a pamphlet titled "The Wonderful Discoverie of the Witchcrafts of Margaret and [Philippa] Flower, daughters of Joan Flower neere Beuer Castle" as both a record of the events and a warning to other witches. Called the Belvoir Witches, the Bottesford Witches, and/or the Flowers of Bottesford, they were consequently executed at Lincoln, England, on March 11, 1618.

After initially being hired by the Manners family to help with preparations for a visit by King James I, the women had recently been let go from their jobs. During their employment, they were vaguely accused by other staff of stealing from the family, among possible other alleged indiscretions that only half-assedly made it through history. The real problem, however, was that the women just weren't well liked. Those who accused them of theft and those who believed it also suspected that the true motive behind the murders of the Manners' sons came from vengefulness.

The women were known in the community for their knowledge of herbs and herbal remedies. They were also rumored to know about the "dark arts," though there was no evidence that the women ever caused any harm with their herbal knowledge. Keep in mind: this was a time when it was believed that just a catch of a witch's eye or the point of their finger could curse you—and you might *die*. When it came to the deaths in the Manners family, the women were accused of having chanted "as the glove does rot, so will the lord" over a glove belonging to one of the Manners' sons—a glove that they later buried deep in the ground. (And thus the curse was, quite literally, planted. If you believe in such things.)

But newly discovered documents suggest the Flowers' case may have actually gone down a little differently than legend suggests. Here's the real scandal: they *may* have actually been framed by a member of the aristocracy. And that person *may* have been George Villiers, First Duke of Buckingham, who was a favorite of the king.

It was rumored that the duke wanted to marry the daughter of Francis Manners. But, because Manners had two sons, the duke knew that even if they did wed, he would not be in line to inherit the family's wealth. There's growing evidence to suggest that he upped his odds of inheritance by having Henry and Francis poisoned and then blamed it on the Flower women, since apparently no one liked them anyway.

Whether or not this is true, it was not public knowledge back then, and so the case went to trial. Joan died before arriving at Lincoln Castle, where she and her daughters were to be incarcerated before their interrogation. Margaret and Philippa, uneducated and unpopular, were left to defend themselves, and did so sometimes with conflicting stories—because they weren't guilty, they didn't really have a "story" to stick to, you know? But in many ways, it was over for them before it even started. Considering the average witch trial lasted only about twenty minutes, they didn't stand a chance. ♦

STRANGE MEDICINE

There are a *lot* of evocative elements to the story of Joan Flower and her daughters, Margaret and Philippa: the idea that they were healers; the accusations of murder; or the fact that Joan died suddenly after choking on a piece of bread she had asked to be given as a symbolic communion, to prove she wasn't a witch, and Margaret and Philippa telling differing stories once they'd arrived at Lincoln castle. But for the drink, we're going to focus on their work as herbal healers, though we're not going heavy on the herbal aspect. This drink is filled with refreshing fruit, so it's full of antioxidants. To your health!

INGREDIENTS:

- 2 large ripe strawberries, sliced into quarters
- ½ small tangerine, sliced into wheels
- ⅛ cup blueberries
- 2 ounces chamomile-infused gin (simply steep 4 ounces of gin with a chamomile tea bag for 30–40 minutes, then strain and pour needed amount)
- ¾ ounce lavender syrup
- ¾ ounce lemon juice
- 2–3 ounces Ginger ale
- 3 edible flowers, for garnish

METHOD:

Place your fruit into a large glass with ice.

In a mixing tin, combine the gin, syrup, and lemon juice. Shake and strain over the fruit.

Top with ginger ale.

Garnish with three small edible flowers to represent Joan, Margaret, and Phillipa—we recommend marigolds, violets, nasturtium, or a mix of all three!

♦ MAKE IT A MOCKTAIL ♦

Instead of gin, use chamomile tea and prepare as above.

HEINRICH CORNELIUS AGRIPPA, THE "SCIENTIFIC SWINDLER"

He was a lawyer, a physician, a theologian, a soldier or perhaps a mercenary, and an alchemist. He was also an influential and prolific occult writer, and now, more than five hundred years after his death, he is considered one of the most influential occult philosophers of the early modern period.

Occult philosophy studied the natural world, the celestial world. But back when German polymath Heinrich Cornelius Agrippa was alive during the sixteenth century, some considered him to be a scientific swindler. This wasn't because he was trying to get you to part with your money, but because he had ideas, big ideas, that sometimes made uneducated or undereducated people nervous and anxious. Plus, his ideas didn't always align with the religious-inspired beliefs of the time, either.

Despite the lasting legacy he left behind, not everyone in his lifetime was quite so pleased with his theories and experimentation. Even other alchemists and mathematicians struggled to accept his brilliant ideas, which explored the hidden causes of things and their manipulation by "magic." In his work, Heinrich tried to explain the philosophy, logic, and methods of magic and astrology, and how these concepts might work, generally speaking, in our universe and in our lives. But his writings were quickly condemned as heretical and blasphemous. Heresy doesn't have a complicated definition; if you're accused of it, it basically means that you hold a belief with which the Church disagrees. Being condemned as a heretic was to be banished, ostracized, and perhaps even executed. Despite the opposition—or perhaps because of it, funny how that happens—Heinrich's manuscript would go on to circulate among philosophers and alchemists (and then scientists) for more than a century.

Heinrich's goal actually sounds pretty noble in its ambition. He believed that if he could separate magic from baseless and irrational perception, it would make way for the restoration of humanity—and along with that, a reformation of Christianity. To that end, he penned philosophical critiques of every "science" known at the time. He wrote what is now considered one of the first testimonials to acknowledge the limits of human understanding and the uncertainty of human existence. And so, it really comes as no surprise that he began to develop a reputation as a man who "professed to overturn all the science."

Esteemed among his peers and scholars, his work still outraged the Church, and he was arrested, jailed, and denounced as a heretic. Fortunately, he was not, as many others were, executed for his crimes, and he died at the ripe old age of forty-eight in Grenoble, France. ♦

RESTLESS HERETIC

When we think of alchemy, and particularly alchemy in France, the idea of things bubbling comes to mind. So it seems only natural to include sparkling wine in Heinrich's drink. But let's also try something that isn't as commonly found in cocktails, to mirror the experimental nature of alchemists' work. As for the mead? Well, mead was likely something Agrippa would have encountered in his life and will help ground our flavors.

INGREDIENTS:

- 1 teaspoon blueberry jam
- 2 ounces honey mead
- 4 ounces champagne or sparkling wine

METHOD:

Put your jam and mead in a shaker and muddle or stir so the jam dissolves into the mead. Then, give it a shake with ice, and strain into a chilled coupe.

Top with champagne or sparkling wine.

♦ MAKE IT A MOCKTAIL ♦

- 5 ounces ginger ale
- 1 ounce honey syrup
- 1 teaspoon blueberry jam

Combine all components in a glass and stir until well-mixed, then add ice.

REV. GEORGE BURROUGHS WAS SO STRONG THAT IT *HAD* TO BE THE DEVIL'S DOING

Like a lot of witch trials, most people think the Salem Witch Trials centered around a group of accused women—and that's fairly true, since the percentage of accused women was significantly higher than men. But it's worth noting that the Salem trials *did* also include some accused men (and even an accused dog or two). Over the course of these trials, at least six men were convicted and executed, including George Burroughs, a nonordained, Harvard-educated Puritan preacher.

Not everyone in town liked George Burroughs. Falling on hardship after his wife's death, he'd once been forced to borrow money from another family in town, the Putnams; he had young children to care for and a funeral bill to pay, and he needed help. But when George moved literally *just* outside of town before repaying the loan, the Putnams, angry, had him arrested. Other accounts suggest he left when his parishioners stopped paying his salary. Possibly both were true. Eventually, he was able to repay the loan, but his reputation by that point was shot, and when locals began to accuse others of witchcraft and paranormal behavior, George was smack dab on their list.

Based on, well, *nothing* really, authorities indicted him on four charges of witchcraft. Upon his trial, he was found guilty of witchcraft and of conspiring with the devil. There were no good reasons to convict him, except that in the seventeenth century, accusations of witchcraft were easy to pick up and difficult to shake off. One reason that he was considered guilty? He was athletic, and that kind of physicality and strength was absolutely for sure a sign of diabolical intervention. A man his age with those abs? *No way.*

When George recited the Lord's Prayer before he was hanged, some in the audience called for his pardon—it was unfathomable that a witch would (or physically could!) recite a prayer. Nevertheless, he was hanged at Witches Hill in August 1692 because that's what you did with witches. ♦

MAN OF GOD

Because one of the pieces of "evidence" used to prove that George had supernaturally granted strength involved the lifting of a musket with one finger, it seems only right to pair his story with a drink that has a smokey note. This one involves playing with fire—so please be very cautious and perform the last step near a reliable water source!

INGREDIENTS:

- ½ ounce lime juice
- 1 ounce pumpkin syrup
- 1 ounce low-sugar apple juice
- 2 ounces mezcal
- Sprig of rosemary, for garnish

METHOD:

Combine liquid ingredients in a shaking tin with ice. Shake, then strain over fresh ice. Using a lighter, ignite the tip of the rosemary sprig briefly, then blow it out and use as garnish.

◆ MAKE IT A MOCKTAIL ◆

Build as above, but use 2 ounces of aloe juice combined with 1 drop of liquid smoke instead of the mezcal.

JANET HORNE, BURNED ALIVE
FOR WHAT WAS PROBABLY DEMENTIA

Janet Horne has the honor of being the last person to be executed legally for witchcraft in what's now known as the British and Irish Isles.

It was in 1727, in Dornoch, in the Scottish Highlands, that she and her daughter were arrested and jailed. Janet had been accused by her neighbors of turning her daughter into a "pony," summoning the devil to shoe the animal, and then riding the "pony" to her rendezvous with the demon himself. Her daughter, meanwhile, was arrested because she had a physical disability, which automatically meant she must be in league with the devil.

While she had once worked in domestic roles in her younger days in moneyed homes, Janet was elderly and frail at the time of her trial, and, today, experts believe that she was exhibiting signs of dementia. She was blamed for local crop failures and animal deaths, which were common accusations against witches. Confused, Janet went along with it all. Her crime, though? It certainly was *not* transforming her daughter into a pony. Today, it's believed that her daughter had a congenital disability affecting her hands and feet, a condition their neighbors incorrectly believed were hooves. Anything that could make you appear physically different, right down to a teeny tiny mole, made people wonder if you were a witch.

The day of the trial, Captain David Ross, the sheriff-deputy, found both women guilty, mainly because once you were accused of being a witch, *you were a witch*. Period. He ordered both women to be burned alive. Fortunately, before the executions, Janet's daughter was, somehow, able to escape. Sadly, Janet did not, and it's clear that she was suffering from confusion about the events and circumstances around her, and possibly even where she was. She received no help. Instead, she was stripped, tarred and feathered, and paraded through town in a barrel. Reaching the site of execution, Janet went about warming herself before the fire—the fire she'd been sentenced to die upon. ♦

APOLOGY

There are so many travesties associated with Janet Horne's story. We don't even know if Janet was really her name, since, according to historian Lizanne Henderson of the University of Glasgow, the name "Janet" was also used sort of generically to refer to women believed to be witches. Horne's accusation, trial, and execution are so obviously the results of what can happen when people let their own fear drive their behavior. So, let's make a drink that is cozy and scrumptious and has an association with times of good will and cheer as an apology to the Hornes and what they went through.

This one borrows from a drink that's very popular in Scotland, where the Hornes lived. The drink known as Whipkull likely originated in Scandinavia, but it's now something that's made during Scottish holiday season festivities, to celebrate the end of one year and the beginning of the new. Whipkull isn't difficult—it's similar to eggnog—but it does involve some extra cooking steps. Most recipes are made in amounts that would be for groups, so we thought we'd simplify the whole thing by adapting it to a flip that you can make just for one.

INGREDIENTS:

- 1 egg
- ¾ ounce demerara syrup
- 2 ounces rum
- ½ ounce Drambuie
- Sprinkle of ground ginger

METHOD:

Ideally, you'd use a frother to get your egg whipped in your shaking tin before adding additional ingredients. If you don't have a frother, no worries!

Your drink will still be yummy, but it may not turn out quite as velvety.

Combine egg, syrup, rum, and Drambuie in a shaker. Give it a dry shake (meaning without ice) first, then add ice and shake some more. The goal is to aerate the egg as much as possible.

Strain your drink into a chilled coupe and top with ground ginger.

♦ MAKE IT A MOCKTAIL ♦

- · 1 egg
- · ¾ ounce demerara syrup
- · 2 ounces low-sugar or no-sugar-added white grape juice
- · ½ ounce honey lavender syrup
- · Sprinkle of ground ginger

Combine all elements as above.

WHAT HAPPENED TO GEORG HONAUER
WHEN HE COULDN'T TURN IRON INTO GOLD

The first thing we learned about Georg Honauer was that he died wearing a gold-tinsel suit. Naturally, we needed to know more. Born around 1572, Georg was an alchemist—and most definitely a *fraudulent* alchemist—who made a lot of promises about gold. And when he found himself in the services of Frederick I, Duke of Württemberg, and couldn't fulfill the sensational promises he made, well—that's when he met his untimely end.

The sixteenth century was a time of rapid population growth across Europe, and there was also a rapidly growing demand for precious metals—in particular, gold. Gold and silver had been imported from what was then called the New World, but there wasn't nearly enough to satisfy the public demand. Mining for metals wasn't cheap or easy, so people turned toward another option: Why not just make it themselves? (Anyone have the recipe?)

Alchemists were early chemists, and some claimed to be able to "transmute" (convert) base metals, like iron or lead, into precious metals, like gold or silver. This was not a new idea. Ancient Egyptians, long before Georg's lifetime, were adept at doubling or even tripling the quantity of their metals, though it was all fake. For instance, if you add a small amount of gold dust to a base metal like copper, you create a metal that *looks* like gold, even though it's not. Alchemy had a bad rap when alchemists like Georg were still alive—they were all pretty much written off as fraudulent, and their transmutations were considered to be shams.

Even so, Georg promised Frederick I, Duke of Württemberg—first in writing and then in person—that he could make gold. For what it's worth, he also curiously referred to himself as the Lord of Brunhoff and Grabschutz in Moravia. Intrigued, when the duke asked to see an example of his work, Georg presented one small piece of gold and one of silver. And then, when the duke asked his assayers if Georg's small pieces of gold and silver were, in fact, real—

cross your fingers for him—he somehow passed the test. Well, he fooled them well enough to move on to the second round, at least. How? Your guess is as good as ours.

But Frederick wasn't about to back a man who couldn't produce more than a penny-sized piece of gold. And so, he asked Georg to produce two hundred thousand ducats worth of gold from the base metal, iron. There was a bit of haggling right from the start. Georg claimed that he only had enough materials involved in the process to produce thirty thousand ducats worth of gold. They agreed to the lesser amount. It took some considerable effort to move the iron from the duke's armory in Mömppelgart to Stuttgart for transmutation, but they did it. And then things got *very* real for Georg. When the iron arrived, knowing he was a total faker who couldn't pull this off, he panicked and fled. In response, the duke had portraits of Georg painted—similar to today's "Wanted" posters. Before long, *lots* of people were on the lookout for him—and it worked.

Once he was captured, he was forced to try the transmutation again. But Georg could only change iron into, well, iron. *Ah, yes.* The duke was unimpressed and greatly displeased. Georg was put on trial and convicted on the charge of fraud. His execution was to be by hanging, but Frederick gave the event an unusual and personalized touch. The gallows were erected on a stone foundation made from the same iron that Georg had promised to convert into gold and didn't. It's said this special treatment cost the duke around three thousand Dutch guilders. We don't know what that's equivalent to today, but we also imagine that he just didn't care. And for the cherry on top of his anger, on the day of the execution, Frederick ordered Georg, age twenty-five, the object of his derision, to be dressed in a golden garment covered entirely with gold tinsel for his hanging. ♦

SHAM TRANSMUTATION

The inspiration here is, of course, George's false claim that he could make gold from other things. This recipe also has a bonus second version! It's wonderful as written in the original, but if you want to go extra fancy, the addition of yellow Chartreuse will make it a more herbaceous sip.

INGREDIENTS:

- 1½ ounces vodka
- 3 ounces ginger beer
- 3 ounces pineapple juice
- 1 ounce Goldschläger

METHOD:

Combine the vodka, ginger beer, and pineapple juice in a glass with ice, then float the Goldschläger on top. The heavy liqueur will drop into the drink, leaving the cinnamon-flavored gold flecks on top.

Bonus kick-up: Add ½–¾ ounce of yellow Chartreuse to the mix before adding the Goldschläger.

♦ MAKE IT A MOCKTAIL ♦

Leave out the vodka, and combine:
- 3 ounces pineapple juice
- 3 ounces ginger beer
- 1 ounce cinnamon syrup

Use cinnamon syrup instead of Goldschläger—and if you want to add that golden touch, sprinkle a little edible gold glitter on top.

THE DAMNING EVIDENCE AGAINST THE PENDLE WITCHES, TOLD BY A NINE-YEAR-OLD

In 1612, ten people were charged with witchcraft and sentenced to death based on the testimony of a nine-year-old girl, Jennet Device, in a tragedy now known as the Pendle Witch Trials. What's more, three of the people accused and executed as a direct result of her testimony were her mother, Elizabeth; her sister, Alizon; and her brother, James.

For years, Demdike Sowtherns, Jennet's grandmother, had been known in the Pendle district of Lancashire, England, to be a local witch, and she'd never courted any trouble. However, things changed on March 21, 1612, when Alizon Device, her granddaughter, stopped to talk to a peddler named John Law whom she'd encountered on a road near Trawden Forest, just outside of Pendle. Initially, she asked to purchase—or maybe even tried to hustle—some metal pins he was selling; either way, he refused the deal. Angered, Alizon muttered something under her breath as she continued on her way, and he, surprisingly, fell down in the road just a moment later. Modern historians believe that John suffered a stroke, but locals believed that Alizon had cursed him. His injury was so surprising, in fact, that a remorseful Alizon *also* thought she had cursed him, accidentally—and she even went as far as to try to reverse a curse that she didn't know how she'd conjured in the first place. To neighbors and local authorities, this was taken to be an admission that she had committed the crime.

Still believing she had somehow accidentally cursed John Law, she confessed to Pendle's magistrate, Robert Nowell. But there was more context here that played a role in his reaction. In Robert's investigation, her brother, James, told Nowell that his sister, Alizon, had once bewitched a local child as well. He also stated that his grandmother, Demdike, had the mark of the devil, and also implicated his mother in practicing witchcraft. And then, Jennet confirmed her family's involvement with witchcraft to the magistrate, corroborating events described by James. She also implicated James. What about Elizabeth? Well, there is sadly no record of Elizabeth defending her children.

Perhaps in an attempt to take some of the heat off her own family (though that's just a guess), Alizon began accusing other local women of witchcraft. Among them were her neighbors Anne Whittle, known as "Chattox," and her daughter, Anne Redferne. Undaunted, they pointed a finger right back at the Devices.

Robert Nowell just had the biggest witchcraft case of his life fall into his hands. He apprehended Demdike and the other implicated family members, as well as their neighbors and all the others Alizon had accused—and sent everyone to the Well Tower at Lancaster Castle to await their trials. The accusations, though, quickly turned into a frenzy, and more and more women were being accused of witchcraft by their neighbors. Known collectively as the Pendle witches, they remained together in the tower for five months awaiting trial.

In the end, this is more a story of imagination, not of witchcraft. Demdike passed away before the trial even began. The chief witness against Elizabeth, James, and Alizon was Jennet, who delivered the same damning testimony against her family that she had told Robert Nowell—leading them all to be convicted and executed by hanging.

And it was all based on the testimony of a kid.

Today, depending on the state or country where you live, laws differ on whether or not children can testify in court; in some cases, children of any age can be called to give evidence if it's determined they're competent to do so based on their understanding of the situation, whereas in other places no children may be called as witnesses. In this case, though, the star witness was just nine years old, and her story, which was totally unverified, proved to be much more damaging than an average third grader's youthful indiscretions. ♦

CHILD'S WORDS

The fact that Alizon and the rest of the family were condemned to death based on the testimony of a single nine-year-old child is unsettling. And, as for Alizon's alleged "curse" of the peddler, who doesn't recall saying something biting as a teenager? The whole story swirls around kids saying things impulsively, and in this case, people died as a consequence.

All of this reminds us of the times as kids where we would play at drinking "grown-up" beverages by sipping grape juice and pretending to be worldly. So, to recapture some of that innocence of youth, we're using grape juice in this one.

INGREDIENTS:

· 3 ounces grape juice
· ¾ ounce lime juice
· 1 ounce ginger liqueur
· 1½ ounces gin
· Club soda, to taste (1–2 ounces)

METHOD:

Combine the grape juice,
lime juice, ginger liqueur,
and gin in a cocktail shaker
with ice. Shake and strain over
fresh ice, then top with club soda.

♦ MAKE IT A MOCKTAIL ♦

Substitute ginger syrup for
the liqueur and flat tonic
for the gin.

JOHN DEE WAS AN ANGEL WHISPERER

Think of the smartest person you know—and just know that John Dee was smarter. He was a Cambridge-educated polymath and royal advisor who also conversed with the angels—or at least, tried. John was genuinely curious about our world, and the possibilities beyond our world. His understanding of mathematics, chemistry, and physics was extraordinary, and it's said that he turned down multiple prestigious academic positions in the hopes that he would score an official position with the crown. And he actually *did*—that is, before he was arrested.

John was charged with the crime of "calculating," which was then considered an act of treason. What happened was that back in 1555, he'd cast horoscopes for Queen Mary and her younger sister, Elizabeth, who would become Elizabeth I. Interrogated by the Star Chamber, which was an English court that sat in the Palace of Westminster, he was exonerated; during the Renaissance, astrology was considered a science, not a blasphemous dark art, and that meant that he was off the hook. Occultism and similar types of practices were pretty normal for the period, and John spent most of his time focusing on alchemy, divination, and Hermetic philosophy. He didn't view any of his studies as heretical; rather, he saw the practices as a way to learn more about the world and the cosmos. But here's a problem that John and his peers ran into: mathematics made people back then suspicious. It's true. Many didn't understand it and, therefore, didn't like it or at least didn't trust it. John and his colleagues were studying in a society that considered their studies not just disreputable but often in league with the practices of witchcraft and the dark arts—and sometimes, they were arrested for it.

And it wasn't just math. Alchemy, too, was misunderstood and was frequently confused with witchery. When your work and interests fall into what's considered to be beyond our physical world, you start toeing the line between an afternoon discussion about horoscopes in the queen's court and being punished by death for heresy. Eventually, John left the queen's service to seek deeper knowledge of the occult and the supernatural. In doing so, though, he aligned himself with individuals who were, or who were once, considered to be con artists, charlatans, and frauds because of their work—in other words, far from the royal court.

John's gadgets and devices may have seemed magical to the untrained eye, but many were actually early mathematical instruments. The children near his home reportedly "dreaded him because he was accounted a Conjurer." But here's the thing: in many ways, John *was* a conjurer. In addition to his scientific and mathematical work, he spent time gazing into a crystal ball and obsidian mirror. And he also spent years scrying for angels and spirits, seeking "angelic conversations."

Many of his contemporaries tried to pin him down as a philosopher, or an astrologer, or a curious mathematician, or maybe even a magician. He was a fairly marginal character for most of the twentieth century, and it wasn't until the 1960s and 1970s that his story began to reemerge with a new focus placed on his contributions to subjects including mathematics, geography, astronomy, and navigation, deemphasizing his magical investigations and occult leanings.

During his lifetime, John was never rewarded for his intellectual achievements. Nor was he imprisoned for them. But his legend, ideas, and inventions live on in so many ways—through literature, comics, opera, songs, and even in video games. Angel conversationalist or not. Conjurer or mathematician. Maybe he was a bit of all of everything. As John himself once said, "Who does not understand should either learn, or be silent." ♦

ANGEL LANGUAGE

This is a beverage that shares some roots with the classic champagne cocktail from the 1850s but with a twist that gives a nod to John Dee and his unique communications with the beyond. As you sip, the marshmallow in the drink breaks down, splitting apart into little cloudlike formations. You could also, for fun, pretend to read the shapes like tea leaves in a nod to Dee's divinations!

INGREDIENTS:

- 1 blorp of marshmallow creme
- ½ ounce crème de violette (you can sub out another liqueur here if you prefer!)
- 1 ounce vanilla or whipped cream vodka
- 3 ounces champagne

METHOD:

This is one you build in the glass: a chilled coupe. Put the marshmallow in first, and pour the other ingredients over it one by one, adding the vodka and champagne last.

♦ MAKE IT A MOCKTAIL ♦

- 1 blorp of marshmallow creme
- ½ ounce violet syrup or other syrup of your choice
- 1 ounce cream soda
- 3 ounces ginger ale

As above, add the marshmallow creme to a chilled coupe, then pour over the syrup, the cream soda, and the ginger ale.

HOW ALICE SAMUEL'S HAIR APPARENTLY PROVED BEYOND A DOUBT THAT SHE WAS A WITCH

I n November 1589, ten-year-old Jane Throckmorton suddenly began suffering seizures. Doctors were aware of seizures by then, and they were no longer a sign of demonic possession (as it had once been assumed). However, after Jane's sisters and domestic workers in the home also developed the very same symptoms, locals started to worry that something evil was afoot.

As many as twelve domestic workers and five daughters fell sick in the Throckmorton house, in the small village of Warboys, England—falling ill not at the same time but over several years. Finally, Jane confessed to her father, Richard, that she'd been cursed by a local woman named Alice Samuel. Richard contacted his wealthy and powerful landlord, Sir Henry Cromwell. Henry sent the Lady Cromwell to speak with Alice on the Throckmorton's behalf. Alice Samuel poured out her heart to the woman, believing that they were having a real conversation about these terrible accusations against her, but, as she spoke, Lady Cromwell snipped a piece of Alice's hair. Odd? Most certainly. But only *kind* of odd. There was a folk remedy suggesting that burning a witch's hair reduced the impact of any spells they'd cast. Lady Cromwell gave the lock to the mother of the sick children to perform the task.

That night at home, Lady Cromwell woke from nightmares and fell gravely ill. She eventually died from her pain and sickness, but her illness lasted two years. That was bad news for Alice, whom locals blamed for bewitching not only the Throckmorton home, but now also Lady Cromwell. Alice, her husband, and their daughter, known as the "Witches of Warboys," were all publicly hanged in April 1593.

As for those ill in the Throckmorton household, they were all miraculously "cured" after the Samuel family execution. ◆

LOCK OF HAIR

Lady Cromwell cutting off a lock of Alice's hair to rob her of her powers is an image that's hard to shake. There was just no space for bodily autonomy in the sixteenth century if you were a suspected witch. While we can't know what Alice's hair smelled like, we do know that in the sixteenth century, hair care routines mostly consisted of items that were easy to track down. To wash your hair during this time, you might have used just plain water, or perhaps a mixture of water, herbs, flowers, and egg whites. So today, we're using that as inspiration for a drink made in honor of Alice's lost locks.

INGREDIENTS:

· 4 basil leaves
· 1 ounce lemon juice
· ½ ounce rose syrup
· 1½ ounces bourbon
· 1 egg white

METHOD:

Put three of the basil leaves and the lemon juice into a shaker and muddle. Add the rose syrup, bourbon, and egg white, and dry shake (without ice) then add ice and shake again.

Strain into a chilled coupe (if you don't like basil flecks in your drink, double strain).

Garnish with remaining basil leaf.

♦ MAKE IT A MOCKTAIL ♦

Make as above using black tea in lieu of bourbon.

PART 6

Embalming Fluid

Unlike in the famous 1954 film *Invasion of the Body Snatchers*—or its 1978 remake—when we talk about body snatching, we're not spinning science fiction tales of human beings replaced by alien duplicates (*if only*).

Real body snatchers stole bodies from graves—and then sold them, usually for a good chunk of change.

Up until the eighteenth century, there wasn't a ton of formal medical education for people who wanted to learn about the human body. In fact, communities typically relied on a hodgepodge of professions to help those suffering from various ailments, and without standardized education, the results could be very mixed. By the mid-1700s, however, it became clear that the best way to teach medicine was to formalize the way practitioners were taught. And so, over the course of the next century or two, dozens and dozens (and *dozens*) of medical schools popped up across the Western world, with more and more students eager for instruction.

Of course, the best way to study anatomy is through the dissection of an actual human body, but both American and European laws set strict limits on cadavers that could be used for such a lesson (i.e., the bodies of criminals were fair game, but regular civilians, not so much). With the sudden influx of schools, there just weren't enough cadavers readily available for use, and so institutions often had to resort to less-than-legal ways to find enough bodies to accommodate the rising demand.

Enter the body snatchers (also called "resurrectionists"). In this next section, you'll learn all about the people who didn't mind getting their hands dirty (quite literally) in order to either advance the study of human anatomy, make a quick buck—or both. ♦

WHY JOHN HUNTER IS KNOWN AS
THE PATRON SAINT OF BODY SNATCHERS

Scottish surgeon John Hunter was involved in the dissection of thousands of bodies. Yes. *Thousands*. And that's why he's considered the patron saint of body snatchers today. Quite an honorary title to hold.

John devoted his life to unraveling the complexities of the human body. During the late eighteenth century, he explored the role of inflammation in the healing process. He demonstrated the circulation of the lymphatic system. He's the one who set up the foundations for performing bypass surgeries. He revolutionized the practice of dentistry. We could go on. But we're not here to give him more gold stars.

John was a born observer and began dissecting bugs and other little critters when he was a kid. His brother, William, who was ten years older, had opened an anatomy school in Covent Garden, and John left the family farm in his late teens to attend. It was also where he got into body snatching. As he grew older, he wanted to pass along the knowledge he'd obtained to the next generation. In other words, John almost certainly led medical students from his brother's school on nighttime trips to snatch bodies from nearby churchyards and burial grounds—all for the "greater good," sharing his expert snatching techniques with new students along the way. He wasn't shy about doing business with local body snatchers, either, and he was in charge of the school's relationships with those working throughout London. He was good at what he did, snatching and surgery, and consequently, there were enough cadavers to go around at William's school.

In the twelve years that the brothers worked together, John was involved in the delivery and dissections of more than two thousand cadavers. That's right, *two thousand*. John stole corpses, yes, but he also instructed students on anatomy, experimental treatment methods, and surgical techniques. Known to use himself in his own experiments, we were horrified to learn that he once infected himself with gonorrhea . . . *on purpose*. However, as John became more adept at both surgery and at snatching, his relationship with William became contentious. After all, John had new and innovative ideas, and, while we don't want to say his brother wasn't enthusiastic about his work, John had a special and rare curiosity and excitement about the human body that most did not. After John was commissioned as an army surgeon during the Seven Years' War between Great Britain and France, they eventually stopped talking to each other altogether.

After the war, John didn't return to Covent Garden. Instead, he carved out a niche for himself in dentistry and then refocused on his private surgical practice and lecturing. And from there, he goes on and on, racking up more anatomical achievements.

But we don't mean to bury the gnarliest detail. When it came to body snatching, John's home was more interesting than his scorecard because his house had a secret: it was two-sided. The front of the house was well-appointed and welcoming—it was where his wife entertained. However, the back, which was technically a different building, was *none* of those things. The two buildings backed up to each other with a sort of makeshift drawbridge connecting them, and the back housed everything John needed for surgical and scientific work, including dissection, plus a collection of specimens. Nightly deliveries of fresh corpses went to the back entrance.

Modern historians consider John to have legitimized the performance of autopsies. He didn't invent the procedure—the first recorded autopsy dates back to 44 BCE—but he definitely brought it into the mainstream. When he died of a heart attack at age sixty-five, his own body was dissected—according to his wishes—by his students. Admittedly, we would have been disappointed if it hadn't been. ◆

POSTMORTEM

Deconstructed cocktails are currently having a moment. And that may sound kinda silly—handing people the ingredients for a drink, unmixed. But sometimes, these can be really fun. They're meant not so much for when you're making yourself a drink but for when you're serving a special guest. In particular, it allows the guest to regulate the strength of the drink, something that most folks would probably appreciate!

This is sort of a very stripped-down variation on a rum punch—it's only got three ingredients, so it's simple to make.

INGREDIENTS:

- 1½ ounces white or silver rum—you want one that's clear with a fairly neutral flavor (not the time for spiced)
- ½–¾ ounce grenadine
- 4 ounces ginger beer

METHOD:

To make the Postmortem, you need two serving vessels—a small glass like a shot glass, and a larger glass for the chaser.

In the smaller glass, pour a good white rum over ice.

In the larger, chilled glass, mix the grenadine with the ginger beer. Add ice after mixing.

THAT'S IT. Serve together, and your guest can either alternate sips of spirit and chaser, or do it as a shot and then enjoy the chaser on its own afterward. Or dump the shot in! Drinker's choice!

♦ MAKE IT A MOCKTAIL ♦

In this case, the drink without the shot is a mocktail on its own, but if you or your guest would like to have it served the same way as the cocktail, a little white grape juice with a splash of apricot nectar is great for the shot.

MEET BODY SNATCHER WILLIAM JANSEN
AND HIS TICKLISH ASSISTANT

H e was most certainly not the only professional body snatcher in Washington, DC (or "resurrection man" as the press liked to call them in the late nineteenth century), but he was for sure one of the most colorful. And during his glory days in the 1880s, William M. Jansen was one of the most famous—infamous?—body snatchers along the East Coast of the United States.

William stole bodies from graves in burial grounds around Washington, DC, and then sold these stolen corpses to local medical colleges. And because there were several medical schools in the District of Columbia, the city had become a kind of hub for such activity. With that increase in demand came an increase in price—the city had a finite number of graveyards with corpses to be disinterred, after all, which meant each corpse was a hot commodity. William himself once said there was no better business to be in for making money.

Luckily for him, until the very end of the nineteenth century, laws about grave robbing and body snatching were fairly lax in Washington, DC. And by fairly lax, we mean: there was no law against body snatching in the District of Columbia until the 1890s. As long as a resurrectionist left the victims' clothing and any other items behind, they couldn't be prosecuted for larceny. As a result, police who caught a body snatcher—even in the act of snatching a body— could only charge them with some kind of obscure and unrelated violation that resulted in nothing more than very minor penalties.

Resurrectionists were a bold sort; you needed to be for the kind of job that you were trying to pull off every night. But William was *BOLD*—all caps intended. Sometimes, to get a leg up on the competition, he dug up graves in the daytime, when anyone and everyone could see. He simply didn't care. Once, he sold the same body *twice*, though he was arrested for that one, charged with transporting a human corpse through the streets without a permit and convicted of malicious trespass. William spoke to the press at length defending his profession, explaining how important it was to the medical community and to the health of the community at large. Following his release from jail, he retired, though there's also speculation that maybe he just lost interest, or perhaps he'd become too recognizable to be successful anymore.

Instead, he planned to lecture about the most interesting thing he could think of: himself. His dramatic debut was described as half lecture and half demonstration of the life of a body snatcher, and it failed on *many* levels. The first problem was that William suffered from stage fright. The second? Attendance was sparse—in fact, he may have performed for just one night, but accounts vary. Things didn't go well on opening night. During the show, William spoke about the benefits of resurrectionists, and he closed with a bit of a reenactment, a kind of pantomimed performance of his work, in which he brought an assistant on stage as a stand-in for a corpse along with several piles of soil—you know, to make it seem like you were right there in the cemetery with him. But, in a stroke of bad luck, his assistant was ticklish—and burst into laughter every time he was picked up from his "grave." The *Washington Post's* theater critic reported jeers and catcalls from the audience, who yelled things like, "What kind of a show is this, anyway?"

After William's death, reporters from the *Washington Post*, who knew him well from all his talks with the press, eulogized him in a long and sincere obituary. They called him "most happy in the companionship of corpses," and that he "grimly lamented his inability to rob his own grave . . . because no one could do such things as well." ♦

TICKLISH ASSISTANT

The only name that would serve a drink about Jansen was the Ticklish Assistant. We know from accounts that Jansen drank whiskey, so that had to be included, and we also wanted bubbles because of the way they tickle the palate. Because this combination of ingredients masks most of the alcohol flavor, we hope it tickles your palate—just like Jansen's assistant.

INGREDIENTS:

- Sprig of fresh rosemary, plus additional sprig, for garnish
- ¾ ounce limoncello
- ¾ ounce whiskey (we used Irish, but it's drinker's choice on this one)
- ¾ ounce gin
- Splash of simple or vanilla syrup (optional)
- 1 drop liquid smoke
- 1 egg white
- 2 ounces ginger ale

METHOD:

Put the sprig of fresh rosemary into your shaker and give it a press with your muddler—you just want to break the surface of those fronds so the flavor and oils can join the party. Then add the limoncello, whiskey, gin, simple syrup, liquid smoke, and egg white.

Dry shake (without ice) for a while, then shake with ice and strain over fresh ice.

Top with ginger ale—your egg white will bubble up and take on an almost meringue-like airiness. Garnish with a sprig of rosemary.

♦ MAKE IT A MOCKTAIL ♦

Press the rosemary as above, then add:

- 2 ounces cold coffee (if you want, you can make this a combo of a coffee and a flavored tea)
- 1 ounce lemon juice
- ½ ounce simple or vanilla syrup
- 1 drop liquid smoke
- 1 egg white

Shake, pour, top, and garnish as above.

ANDREAS VESALIUS PROVED WOMEN HAVE JUST AS MANY TEETH AS MEN

A ndreas Vesalius revolutionized the study of the human body—and he was able to do so because his hands-on observations empowered him to publish groundbreaking, forward-thinking works about how our bodies function. He was a sixteenth-century Flemish anatomist and was one of the first physicians to accurately record and illustrate human anatomy, all based on his own findings from autopsies and dissections of human bodies. This even earned him the nickname Father of Modern Anatomy.

But it wasn't a squeaky-clean road to success. As a side gig, Andreas also worked as a body snatcher. He felt strongly that hands-on experimentation and experience should take precedence over textbooks. Before he came on the scene, learning anatomy looked a lot like this: a professor sat in a chair, consulted their notes, and lectured to their class from a book. Concurrently, a surgeon would perform the dissection in front of a classroom, but students could observe whatever he was doing only from a distance. Andreas, however, worked very differently. He didn't just read books; he snatched bodies from local graves and studied them up close. He led students right into the graveyard, imparting knowledge along the way. It was smart, he explained, to keep an eye on any terminal patients in public hospitals—*juuuust* in case. Always thinking two steps ahead, he successfully negotiated with judges and authorities to convert criminals' life sentences into death sentences—and then, once the prisoner was executed, their body would end up on his dissection table. As he saw it, he just needed the right tools for his job, and those tools included corpses. Despite the illegality of body snatching and public dissection, crowds packed into lecture theaters whenever his demonstrations were held.

By the time he reached his mid-twenties, Andreas had assembled a collection of anatomical information large and detailed enough upon which he could—and did—base illustrations on the human body's parts and organ systems, from head to toe. He drew detailed, composite illustrations of the human anatomical structures, including everything from the skeletal system to the nervous system. Based upon research extracted from the dissections he'd performed himself, he wrote and illustrated the first comprehensive textbook of anatomy, including fully illustrated anatomy of male and female bodies; in all, the tome contained more than 270 detailed illustrations of both full bodies and body parts. This was *huge*. Yes, a physically huge book, but also huge because nothing like this existed, and it was an absolute game changer.

Previously, Claudius "Galen" Galenus, a renowned ancient Greek physician, was considered the most influential physician and the most important medical scholar of classical antiquity. Galen's works, which were published thirteen hundred years earlier, were still considered the authoritative texts in medical education in Andreas's time, but there's a troubling kicker: all of Galen's anatomical observations came from animal dissections, primarily primates— and never from actual humans. It was forbidden under Roman religion to study the human body itself. To be fair, it wasn't exactly legal to study it during Andreas's time. Christians believed in the resurrection of the body after death, so to interfere with the dead was pretty problematic.

Andreas didn't see himself as challenging the theories of Galen; in fact, he praised Galen throughout his writing—but he did so while *also* correcting him, and that had never been done before. Many scholars considered it an attack on accepted doctrine, but that so-called attack allowed Andreas to correct some very mistaken assumptions that had been passed down over the centuries. Because of his observations on *human* cadavers, he disproved, for example, a whole bunch of things that we take for granted today. And that included debunking wild ideas like the two-horned uterus, the five-lobed liver, the seven-segmented sternum, the bone at the base of the human heart, and the strangest assertion of all: the idea that men have more teeth than women. ◆

GALEN'S GULP

This is a choose-your-own-adventure cocktail! Vesalius's Flemish origins inspire us to drift closer to something inspired by Belgium: beer. We will admit that we're not big beer drinkers, but as beer cocktails have gained in popularity as a way to have a lighter mixed drink, this could be the perfect opportunity to give it a try. A shandy is a drink that's usually made with equal parts beer and something else; that something else is disputed depending on who you ask. But we went with ginger beer, to add a little bite.

INGREDIENTS:

- 3 ounces pale ale
- 3 ounces ginger beer
- ¾ ounce syrup or liqueur of your choice

POSSIBILITIES:

- Mango syrup
- Grenadine
- Rose syrup
- Habanero syrup
- Pumpkin syrup

METHOD:

Combine your prechilled pale ale, ginger beer, and room-temp syrup or liqueur into a chilled glass. Stir gently and enjoy.

♦ **MAKE IT A MOCKTAIL** ♦

Sub out lemonade for the pale ale, and stick with a syrup instead of a liqueur.

WHY THE MAYO CLINIC APOLOGIZED FOR CUT-NOSE'S SKELETON

William Mayo was an internationally acclaimed surgeon and physician and one of the doctors who founded the famous Mayo Clinic in Rochester, Minnesota. He was considered an ambassador of the medical profession, which is likely a reputation he'd be happy to hear he maintains to this day. But the story you might not have heard of him is the one concerning his disrespectful treatment of the dead body of an indigenous man.

Marpiya Okinajin, or "He Who Stands in the Clouds," was a Dakota man and prominent warrior who was better known to the nonindigenous inhabitants of North America as "Cut-Nose." In the mid-1800s, the Santee tribe were fighting to restore Santee Dakota sovereignty in Minnesota, which were tribal lands before they were taken by white settlers. During this uprising, a group of Santee was apprehended by white officials when they surrounded a group of white settlers near Fort Ridgely—and the American government decided to make an example of them.

On December 26, 1862, in Mankato, Minnesota, thirty-eight people from the Santee tribe, including Cut-Nose, were executed by hanging under orders from President Abraham Lincoln in what was, and still is, the largest mass execution on a single day in US history. The bodies were placed in a shallow mass grave, and the next day, many were removed and sold for use as cadavers in medical schools. Cut-Nose's remains were sold to William Mayo for dissection and anatomical research.

Initially, William kept the bones at his private residence. He used the skeleton primarily as a teaching tool for his sons and allowed them to play with it like a toy. The skull went on to be displayed at the Mayo Clinic until 1998, meaning that it took more than a century before Cut-Nose's remains were properly returned to the Santee and properly buried. And it wasn't until 2018 that the Mayo Clinic publicly acknowledged their misdeeds and issued a formal apology, in a casino conference room in Santee, Nebraska. ♦

REGALED WRONGDOER

It's difficult to think of a drink that might pair well with a tragedy on par with William Mayo's disrespectful treatment of a human body. So, instead, let's consider this story for its place in time. The year 1862, when Mayo took Marpiya Okinajin, was also when Jerry Thomas released his famous *Bar-Tender's Guide*, the first cocktail book in the United States. It is full of interesting recipes, many of which are absolutely foundational to modern cocktail culture. But some are also impractical—for the simple reason that they're made in very large batches. So, we are going to take inspiration from his recipe for "Ginger Lemonade"—which is a large-batch mix that involves, among other ingredients, 12.5 pounds of sugar, and two tablespoons of yeast. It's actually listed among his temperance (i.e., nonalcoholic) recipes. Our version is much easier—and scalable.

INGREDIENTS:

- 1 ginger tea bag (or a nub of thinly sliced ginger root)
- 4 ounces gin (you will use only 2 ounces in your drink)
- ½ ounce ginger liqueur
- 4 ounces lemonade
- Thin slices of ginger and lemon peel, for garnish (optional)

METHOD:

Combine the ginger tea bag and gin in a small airtight container and give it a good shake. Let it steep for 30–40 minutes, then strain the mixture into a clean container.

Glaze the interior of a chilled glass with ginger liqueur and pour out any excess.

Add the gin to the glass, then pour over the lemonade. Give a gentle stir and add ice. Garnish with the ginger and lemon peel, if desired.

♦ MAKE IT A MOCKTAIL ♦

The only change for this drink is that you will make ginger tea instead of using gin. This will work best if you heat 1 cup of water and steep it with the ginger, allow it to cool before straining, and then build as above.

PERCY AND MAUDE BROWN, THE GERIATRIC GRAVEDIGGERS OF THE DISTRICT OF COLUMBIA

This may sound harsh, but that doesn't mean it's not true: lexicographer Ambrose Bierce once called a body snatcher someone who "supplies the young physicians with that which the old physicians have supplied the undertaker."

In the late 1800s, the District of Columbia was packed with professional body snatchers; in a city with a total area of about sixty-eight square miles and roughly 170,000 residents, there were four separate medical schools, each willing to pay a pretty penny for cadavers for their anatomy classes. Corpses often went for $15 to $25, though sometimes way more or way less, and even individual body parts were also worth some cash. Estimating what that amount translates to today is a dicey game, but probably between $300 to $400 per body. There were roughly fifty or so cemeteries that body snatchers used to meet that high demand—a demand that far outpaced the legal supply because most available corpses were those of executed criminals. In the cemeteries, though, *anyone* could be a potential corpse for sale, not just criminals, and all you needed to get the job done was a shovel, a sack big enough to fit the remains, and a foot-long metal hook attached to a length of rope for pulling a body from its grave.

In that lucrative grave-robbing business was the brother-and-sister team of Percy and Maude Brown. It's said that Percy and Maude were, very likely, the oldest body snatchers still working at the trade—some accounts report them working into their eighties, but we can't confirm just how old these two actually were. An 1888 *Washington Post* account describes "Maudie," as her brother called her, as a woman dressed in black, with a wide white ribbon tied in a bow around her neck. She once was in charge of finding fresh graves but was forced to stop when she lost her sight. Percy would then follow up on those sites and snatch the body.

Another *Post* article claimed that Maude and Percy were responsible for more than five hundred body snatchings throughout their career. One story that follows them around is that one night in 1878, they may have once accidentally delivered a fresh corpse not to a buyer, but to the building next door. If not Maude and Percy, then *someone* sure did—and who are we kidding, you know that must've happened more than once.

The pair are most often tied to what's known as the Mount Olivet Mystery: a body they'd taken from the Mount Olivet cemetery was later found on the dissecting table at Columbian College, which later became National Medical College. Eventually, the missing corpse was tracked down by the superintendent of the cemetery, and reinterred. Maude and Percy, who had snatched it, weren't apprehended, nor did they give a refund after the body they'd sold the school was confiscated. After all, body snatching has no money-back guarantees. ◆

WRONG DOOR

The Browns certainly seemed to consider crime a family affair. The incident that really captured our attention was the night when they accidentally delivered a fresh corpse not to a buyer, but to the building next door. Imagine the shock of opening a door to have a dead body thrust upon you! So, let's craft a drink that also comes with a surprise, but a fun one. In this concoction, the initial drink is a bit more spirit forward—like an initial shock—and grows smoother and more sippable as you go. It also transforms from an espresso martini into something closer to a white Russian.

INGREDIENTS:

- 1 ounce cream
- 1 ounce coffee liqueur
- ½ ounce vanilla liqueur
- 2 ounces vodka
- ½ ounce cold espresso

METHOD:

First, stir together your cream and coffee liqueur and pour into an ice mold. (It's easy to make multiples! Just multiply the ounces. But note that the longer you leave cream frozen, the less creamy its consistency will be when it melts, because ice crystals can form that separate the water from the fat.)

Once your ice cubes are frozen, glaze a prechilled glass with vanilla liqueur, pouring out any excess.

Put the vodka and espresso into a shaker with plenty of ice, and shake until it is VERY cold. Strain into your glazed and chilled glass, and drop in your cream and liqueur ice cube.

♦ MAKE IT A MOCKTAIL ♦

- 1 ounce cream
- 1 ounce coffee-flavored syrup (you can make this by simmering 1 cup of coffee with 1 cup of sugar until the sugar has fully melted; let it cool before use)
- 2 ounces cold chamomile tea
- ½ ounce espresso
- ½ ounce vanilla syrup

Build as the cocktail.

UNIVERSITY OF MARYLAND'S
"FRANK" COULD STEAL A BODY IN A JIFFY

It's said that he was able to steal a corpse in just thirty minutes, and while we don't know how long it took other grave robbers, that seems pretty damn quick. His method went like this: he would typically follow a funeral procession, scout the situation, and return that night to snatch up the body. He would dig at the head end of the coffin, break it open, and then, using a large meat hook, he would hook the body under its chin and yank it out. After refilling the grave with dirt, he'd throw the bagged body over his shoulder and head out, eager to make his delivery.

Frank, whose surname has been lost to history, was an active body snatcher for the University of Maryland Baltimore's School of Medicine, which (just like every other medical school in the United States in the nineteenth century) had a problem: there weren't enough cadavers to go around. As of 1814, he was on the books as a "janitor"; but his *actual* job was robbing graves for the university. He stole corpses in and around Baltimore, and he charged $2.50 for small corpses and $5 for larger ones—though some numbers suggest this could go as high as $10. Though it's hard to be precise, that would be about $200 today.

At first, he primarily worked the four cemeteries closest to the university, but as his reputation grew, his territory spread out across not just the city but the northeast. A University of Maryland professor of surgery, in correspondence with a doctor at Bowdoin College in Maine, wrote, "It will give me pleasure to render you any assistance in regard to subjects…I shall immediately invoke Frank, our body-snatcher (a better man never lifted a spade) and confer with him on the matter. We can get them without any difficulty at present." Unpreserved bodies that weren't immediately delivered were stored in whiskey-filled barrels—sometimes rum—before being shipped out of Baltimore. Pricing for bodies stored in whiskey was expensive, about $50, including $1 for the barrel and an additional 35 cents per gallon of whiskey. Today, that would be almost $1,000 a body, roughly. Once they removed the bodies, medical students (cue shudder) were known to sell the liquor to make a few bucks. (Don't worry, we'll hold your hair back while you retch.)

As Frank's true knack became little more than an open secret, protests about the rampant desecration of graves became so commonplace that the University of Maryland built secret passageways around campus to allow students and faculty to escape angry neighbors. It's worth noting that these secret passageways could've easily shared a double function: enabling the secret delivery of fresh corpses. ♦

ALREADY PRESERVED

One detail that kept coming up in accounts about Frank was the way he started stashing bodies in barrels of whiskey or rum for transport once his bosses at the University of Maryland decided to share their resource with other medical schools. If you drink enough of this one, you'll be well preserved before any body snatchers ever try to snatch you. (So please drink responsibly!)

INGREDIENTS:

- 2 ounces dark rum
- ½ ounce Campari
- ½ ounce demerara syrup
- 4–5 ounces lime-flavored sparkling water

METHOD:

Combine rum, Campari, and syrup in a shaking tin with ice, shake, and strain into a glass over fresh ice. Top with the sparkling water.

♦ MAKE IT A MOCKTAIL ♦

- 2 ounces white grape juice
- ½ ounce blood orange syrup
- ½ ounce demerara syrup
- 4–5 ounces lime-flavored sparkling water

Make the same way as the cocktail.

WILLIAM CUNNINGHAM, THE "BOGEYMAN" OF CINCINNATI

He had a "villainous bald head." He dressed up the bodies he stole. And he once returned to his "task" at the same grave site in which he had been caught digging earlier—after he'd bought those who had detained him a few drinks. Meet William Cunningham.

No one seems to have called William by his given name. Those who didn't call him "Old Man Dead" called him "Old Cunny." He was known as the local "Bogeyman" and "the Ghoul of Cincinnati," and tales of him coming to snatch up bodies were used to frighten badly behaved children into shaping up. He appeared in local folktales, but unlike many characters spoken of in folktales, William actually existed.

A man named Daniel Drake established the Medical College of Ohio in Cincinnati, which welcomed its first class in 1819—and it kicked off the Cincinnati body-snatching scene. The city quickly became a center for medicine; thirteen medical schools were operating there between 1820 and 1880, which meant there was a steady demand for bodies to dissect. William actively stole—and sold—bodies from grave sites around Cincinnati smack in the middle of that heyday, from 1855 to 1871.

During the day, William drove an express wagon, which was essentially a delivery vehicle. At night, however, he snatched and sold fresh corpses; it's estimated that he snatched and sold at least one hundred bodies. Rumor had it that William was fearless not just digging up but also transporting bodies. Fresh from the grave, he would dress corpses and seat them next to him on his wagon while he drove through town. There are anecdotes of him conversing with his dead passengers, laughing that they'd had too much to drink. ("Nothing to see here, officer!")

Unlike most body snatchers who stayed local, he didn't let something like location hold him back from making money—and there was a *lot* of money to be made, if you were willing to do the dirty work. He extended his customer base beyond just one city and shipped bodies to out-of-town and out-of-state physicians, including as far away as Kansas and possibly beyond.

After evading arrest for more than a decade, William was finally caught, and on September 12, 1871, he was officially indicted. He entered a plea of not guilty, paid $300 bail, and was released; he was also instructed to answer to the charge of illegal possession of dead human bodies at the next session of the Common Pleas Court. But he didn't. About a month after his indictment, William was admitted to the hospital, suffering, as reported by the *Cincinnati Enquirer*, "temporary derangement of his system" from his well-known heavy alcohol consumption. He promised the press he'd be out in a few days, and he'd be back to business. But he couldn't keep that promise, and William died on November 2. Before his death, he sold his body to the Medical College of Ohio for $50, which is roughly equivalent to $1,200 today. And after students were done practicing on it, the faculty put the skeleton on display. One reporter remarked that the only things missing from the exhibit were William's gray horse and his express wagon. ♦

CORPSE JUICE

OK, this name is a little horrifying, but stick with us. We're playing with the idea of a person who would play-act an entire scenario with a corpse he was transporting as he drove along in his wagon. Both hilarious and grisly—our favorite. So this is a drink that sounds and even looks a little unsettling, but it is, in fact, delicious and refreshing.

INGREDIENTS:

- 1½ ounces vodka—if you have fruit-infused, great!
- 4-ish ounces ginger ale
- ¼ cup watermelon, roughly chopped into small pieces and retaining any resulting juices

METHOD:

Build in the glass over ice: pour in the vodka and ginger ale, then dump in your watermelon and its juice and slurry—it looks like viscera, but tastes like summer!

♦ **MAKE IT A MOCKTAIL** ♦

For the mocktail, simply omit the vodka!

WHY JOHN SCOTT HARRISON WAS BURIED UNDER CEMENT (AND WHY IT DIDN'T MATTER)

John Scott Harrison never held the office of president of the United States himself, but he was both the son and father of US presidents. He was also a distinguished politician in his own right, serving from 1853 to 1857 as a member of the US House of Representatives from Ohio.

After John died in his sleep at age seventy-four, in May 1878, at his farmhouse in North Bend, Ohio, the Harrison family took what may seem to be a surprising number of precautions to keep his body safe in the afterlife. To be fair, grave robbing and body snatching were big problems in those years, and a very valid concern. To make matters even more tense and very real, shortly before his father's funeral his son, Benjamin, noticed that a nearby grave—the grave of Harrison's nephew, Augustus Devin, it turned out—had been disturbed, and Augustus's body had been stolen.

Alarmed, additional precautions were taken. John's body was interred in a metal-encased casket, in a reinforced brick-vaulted grave dug down a depth of eight feet (industry standard then, like now, was six feet). Three stone slabs were placed over the casket, and cement was poured on top to seal the whole thing. Harrison's sons even went so far as to hire a watchman to guard their father's grave—it was to be his sole duty for a month after the burial (after that, the remains would be considered useless to anatomists). It's also said that they paid him . . . in advance. Red flag!

While in town to address his father's death, another of Harrison's sons, also named John, decided to search the local medical schools for Augustus's body. He started with Ohio Medical College after hearing a tip that they'd just received a delivery of fresh corpses. It was when he was leaving the school, thinking it was a bust, that John was horrified to find his father, buried just the day before and with all those safety measures, hanging from an air vent rigged with a windlass. Horrified, indeed—*YIKES*. Someone had transported the corpse to the school less than twenty-four hours after the funeral. (*This is why we don't pay in advance.*)

Calls were quickly placed to detectives, and a janitor at the school was arrested. When the school immediately paid his bond, the community erupted in anger over the seeming acceptance of the practice. Though the search for Augustus continued, John Scott Harrison was reinterred, this time in the vault of a family friend, rather than the Harrison family tomb, just outside of Cincinnati. ♦

EVERY PRECAUTION

How does one commemorate such a sad tale—of a family so desperately trying to right a wrong, only to have something even more horrible shoved in their faces—in cocktail form? The best thing we can come up with is a drink in the trend of so-called medicinal cocktails—things that have healthy ingredients—in the hopes that it staves off the grave, and thus, grave robbers. At least for a little while.

INGREDIENTS:

- · 1 green tea bag
- · 4 ounces gin (you will have extra)
- · ¾ ounce curaçao
- · ¾ ounce lime juice
- · ½ ounce simple syrup
- · 2 ounces low-sugar cranberry juice

METHOD:

Steep the tea bag in the gin in an airtight container for 30–40 minutes, giving it an occasional shake. Remove the tea bag, then combine 2 ounces of the gin with the remaining ingredients in a shaking tin with ice. Shake, then strain over fresh ice.

♦ MAKE IT A MOCKTAIL ♦

Make as above, but use water-steeped green tea instead of gin and orange syrup in lieu of curaçao.

THE MEN WHO WERE
HARVARD'S SECRET "SPUNKERS"

In July 1999, a construction crew working inside the Holden Chapel in Harvard Yard found human remains in the walls of the building's basement. That may sound super suspicious, but they hadn't been hidden there by a serial killer or any sort of murderer. They'd been put there by the faculty, staff, and students of the school—on purpose. These were the bones of the many people whose corpses had been snatched from local cemeteries during the eighteenth and nineteenth centuries to be used as cadavers by those learning anatomy at Harvard.

Laws regarding cadavers for dissection were getting increasingly restrictive, and Harvard, for instance, was legally allowed only one cadaver each year. To make things worse, the school had recently adopted a more hands-on study of anatomy, known as the Paris Method, under which each student learned by dissecting their own assigned cadaver instead of one per class. While that would provide a more intense and valuable hands-on training experience than simply observing one's teacher perform a dissection, it also put the school in the position of needing to obtain a *lot* more bodies. So, they started looking to less-legal means of securing them: the body snatchers.

Around 1770, a group of Harvard's own faculty and students took matters into their own hands. Dr. Joseph Warren, along with his brother, Dr. John Warren (the founder of Harvard Medical School), and some other well-known legacy students, including the sons of both Samuel Adams and Paul Revere, were part of a controversial secret society known as the Anatomical Club—better known as the Spunker Club, appropriately featuring a shovel as its representative symbol. When it came to secrecy, the Spunker Club was like *Fight Club*: the first rule of being a spunker was that you didn't talk about being a spunker. The second rule of being a spunker was that you didn't write or speak the name of the club. You get the idea. Except some of them didn't, which is why we can talk about them today. The purpose was straightforward: make anatomic dissection possible with cadavers they themselves had procured from local cemeteries.

But by 1815, Massachusetts said enough was enough with all the body snatching and passed the Act to Protect the Sepulcher of the Dead, making it a felony to disturb a grave or steal a corpse. You can imagine this received a lot of pushback from the Massachusetts Medical Society. WHERE were they going to get fresh corpses now? In response, Massachusetts passed another law, the Anatomy Act, which allowed medical professionals to legally obtain the corpses of those who'd been imprisoned, those who had been determined to be mentally ill before their death, and those who had died in poverty. Not good enough for Harvard, the school began moving to a new supply chain: bribing New York City officials to ship corpses from New York to Boston.

By 1842, Harvard Medical School employed Ephraim Littlefield to supply the school with fresh corpses—and they paid him $25 per body (somewhere between $700 and $900 today). It's unclear if Ephraim himself snatched the bodies or if he was a go-between (or both), but amid those changes, the body-snatching Spunker Club wasn't really needed anymore—although no one is exactly certain when they shuttered, what with it being a secret club, and all. ♦

SECRET SOCIETY

Our cocktail in honor of the Spunker Club is related to the time and place this story happened. Hard cider was very popular back in the Revolutionary era, and a lot of the Founding Fathers were distillers as well, including George Washington, who famously distilled whiskey. This drink combines those elements with other tasty ingredients.

INGREDIENTS:

- · 10 fat blueberries
- · ½ ounce lemon juice
- · ½ ounce simple syrup
- · 1 ounce whiskey (drinker's choice!)
- · 4 ounces hard cider

METHOD:

Muddle the blueberries, lemon juice, and simple syrup in a tin, then add your whiskey and ice. Shake, then strain over fresh ice and top with hard cider.

♦ MAKE IT A MOCKTAIL ♦

Sub out strong tea for the whiskey, with a dash of jalapeño syrup. And use nonalcoholic cider instead of hard cider.

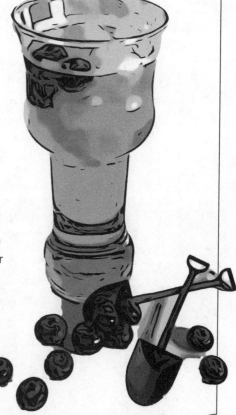

PART 7

Perfidy Pours

In American popular culture, the name "Benedict Arnold" is synonymous with treason. Benedict Arnold was a patriot and an American military officer who served with distinction for the American Continental Army, rising to the rank of major general during the Revolutionary War. He was even a celebrated military hero—that is, before he defected to the British side of the conflict in 1780. And with this decision, he cemented the legacy that would follow him indefinitely—as one of the most infamous traitors in the history of the United States. As his contemporary Benjamin Franklin put it, comparing him to an often-referenced betrayer from Christian theology, "Judas sold only one man, Arnold three million." *Ouch.*

Of course, one side's traitor can be the other side's secret weapon, and so in this section, we're including a wide swath of double-crossers from all angles—including the spies, revolutionaries, and scrappy local heroes who changed the course of history.

As historian Andro Linklater once told NPR's Steve Inskeep, "Some people are born to treachery." What kind of people, you may be wondering? Well, you'll just have to keep reading to find out. ♦

WHEN THE COAL MINERS
WENT TO WAR

In 1921, the conflict between West Virginia coal miners and coal mining companies escalated to a level of violence not seen in the United States since the Civil War. Long-standing grievances between the two culminated in a cataclysmic event known as the Battle of Blair Mountain, and by its end, hundreds of miners and union sympathizers were arrested, and some were even killed.

At the time, miners residing in three of West Virginia's counties lived in what's called a company town system. A company town is a place where all of your needs are taken care of by the company you work for. In theory, anyway. Basically, you lived in a company-owned house. You bought your food at the company store. Your pay was docked for things including the costs of the tools you used for your job. You get the point. And because the companies controlled essentially every single aspect of your life, they could do whatever they wanted with it. Pay you low wages? Limit supplies? Upcharge you for necessary resources? They sure did. It's not hard to see how miners and their families were trapped in a cycle of inescapable poverty. Mining, itself, was dangerous, too, with *deplorable* conditions. Fatal on-site accidents such as collapses, explosions, and fires were frequent.

Because of all that, the United Mine Workers of America wanted larger representation and union membership in that region. For the miners, though, organizing was grounds for immediate termination, and because they lived in company towns, immediate termination also meant immediate eviction from your home. As a miner living in a company town, you owned nothing. You *had* nothing.

At the Battle of Blair Mountain, roughly ten thousand West Virginia coal miners marched in protest of these perilous work conditions, squalid housing, and low wages. Led by union organizers, miners planned to confront the coal companies. But deputized forces who were put in place to quell the miners were *ridiculously* well-armed—since they'd all been supplied by the Coal Operators Association.

The results were catastrophic. Between fifty and one hundred miners were killed in this incident and more were displaced. Another 985 were arrested. Between ten and thirty local deputies were killed. Three soldiers in the National Guard were killed. The battle only ended when President Warren G. Harding sent federal troops from Fort Thomas, Kentucky, directly to the scene. When faced with fighting the arriving infantry units—upward of twenty-seven thousand soldiers—many miners simply surrendered; they'd signed up for change, not for a battle against the US military. And because the union had been stopped from entering, Blair Mountain was considered a tactical victory in the eyes of the coal mining companies.

The West Virginia governor initially sought federal charges against all miners who had surrendered to federal troops. However, the federal government declined to pursue these and instead moved ahead with a separate investigation of conditions in American coal mines. In response, the state decided to prosecute them itself and indicted more than five hundred people on charges including murder, conspiracy to commit murder, accessory to murder, and treason. The charge that caught the attention of, well, *everyone*, was treason—and it was leveled against twenty union members, including union organizer, thirty-year-old William H. Blizzard. Bill had been a coal miner since he was only ten years old, and he was considered by the coal operators to have been the leader of the march that sparked the battle.

A treason trial like this was high stakes for the person on trial, but also for the growing—and struggling—labor movement in the country. If the prosecution won, punitive anti-union tactics used by coal companies would likely become legitimized—and could be used by other anti-union companies in the future across all kinds of industries. So this was *BIG*. It was standing-room only in the courtroom during Bill's trial, and the media attention was intense—which allowed the regional conversation of labor issues to move into a nationwide conversation. The question about Bill was: If he was in fact the leader of the march, was he *actually* leading when the miners reached Blair Mountain, and had what the coal operators considered outright war against them been premeditated? The prosecution claimed that Bill had shadowed the miners as they marched. Witnesses for the defense, though, testified that while the march was happening, they'd actually seen him in Charleston, about sixty miles away. And the defense's star witness, an army infantry captain, stated that he hadn't heard any miners talk of going to war against the government; rather, they talked about how to best "protect the women and children" from the violent sheriff's deputies.

Four weeks later, without any evidence of his guilt, Bill was acquitted of the charge of treason. ♦

COAL DUST

We don't make many shots, but here we are! Apple orchards are very common in West Virginia, so it seems natural for apple to be involved in this drink. Plus, it's easy to imagine men about to go into a war taking a swig of whiskey for courage. And because coal dust covered EVERYTHING in this area at the time, we have a little sprinkling that will mimic the effect. We very much like the idea of shots that are small mixed drinks rather than simply straight alcohol.

INGREDIENTS:

- 1 ounce bourbon
- ½ ounce Amaretto
- ½–¾ ounce apple juice
- Sprinkle of black pepper

METHOD:

Stir the bourbon, Amaretto, and apple juice together with ice in a cocktail glass, then strain into a chilled shot glass. Sprinkle with black pepper.

Not a fan of shots? Use a larger glass with ice and top it with club soda or ginger ale!

♦ MAKE IT A MOCKTAIL ♦

Substitute black tea for the bourbon, and substitute almond syrup for the Amaretto.

Note: If a shot is delicious, there's no need to chug it in one go. Pressuring people to do so is not our jam. So though we offer this as a shot, it is FINE to drink it however you wish, including topping it with soda to make a mixed drink as mentioned above. It's all about making what YOU want, the way you will most enjoy it.

WHAT HAPPENED WHEN AN ENSLAVED MAN WAS CONVICTED OF TREASON

Not much is known about the man named Billy from Virginia who was charged with treason during the American Revolutionary War, and that's because he was an enslaved Black man. Billy, whose last name is lost to history, was probably born in or about 1754, maybe in Richmond County, Virginia. By 1781, he was enslaved on the estate of John Tayloe, a wealthy planter and member of the Virginia governor's council.

In May 1781, Billy was arrested, accused of fighting alongside the British against the Continental Army. It's important to note here that the British Army had promised any enslaved person their freedom in exchange for their service in His Majesty's army—*against* the Continental Army. And while some took them up on that offer, Billy held firm that he had *not*.

He was tried on May 8. His defense was that he'd been forcibly taken aboard a British ship, but that he had not actually taken up arms against the Americans. He was convicted—by four judges out of a panel of six—for treasonous acts, concluding that he must be a traitor. And so, he was sentenced to death by hanging.

Luckily, this did not come to pass. The two dissenting judges, plus his enslaver John Tayloe, wrote to Governor Thomas Jefferson, arguing that since Billy was enslaved, he could not be guilty. How so? Enslaved people were considered property—not people. Because Billy was not considered a citizen, he was unable to commit treason against the state. To back up this defense, they even restated the law that an enslaved person "not being Admitted to the Privileges of a Citizen owes the State No Allegiance and that the Act declaring what shall be treason cannot be intended by the Legislature to include slaves who have neither lands or other property to forfeit."

Perhaps ironically in this instance, this dehumanizing law actually saved Billy's life. Governor Jefferson delayed Billy's execution until the end of June that year, and that same month, the Virginia legislature pardoned him. ◆

THE LOOPHOLE

While Revolutionaries and Tories were fighting over what the best form of government was, Billy and people like him weren't included in the idea of liberty. But that very lack of freedom was what saved Billy from the gallows, though his life after his pardon is unknown.

A popular drink in the colonies at the time of this trial was Whistle-Belly Vengeance, which combined skunky beer, molasses, and breadcrumbs. Not our taste, but we *do* like molasses as a mix-in for another popular Colonial era drink—hard cider. And chamomile represents perseverance through adversity, perfect for raising a toast to Billy.

INGREDIENTS:

- 1 chamomile tea bag
- ½ cup molasses
- 1 ounce ginger liqueur
- 5–6 ounces hard cider

METHOD:

Simmer the tea bag with 1 cup of water for 5–10 minutes. Remove the tea bag and add the molasses; stir continuously on low heat until the molasses has dissolved into the water. Allow to cool.

Stir 1 ounce of the chamomile-molasses syrup into the ginger liqueur.

Pour the hard cider into a prechilled glass with ice and drizzle the ginger and molasses mixture into it.

♦ MAKE IT A MOCKTAIL ♦

Use nonalcoholic cider instead of hard cider, and ginger syrup instead of ginger liqueur. You may need to thin the ginger-molasses mixture with a little water to achieve a good drizzling consistency.

CHIDIOCK TICHBORNE, THE POET WHO FELL IN WITH A REGICIDAL CROWD

History hasn't left us with a ton of solid information regarding Chidiock Tichborne's life story, but what we do know is that he was a poet who was raised as a Catholic and found himself charged with committing an act of high treason. Chidiock surfaces because of his involvement in what's known as the Babington Plot.

After Elizabeth I was crowned queen in January 1559, she restored England's official religion to Protestantism, rendering Catholicism illegal. This was a total 180 from the previous five years, when her sister, Queen Mary I (also known as Mary Tudor), had been hell-bent on restoring the Catholic Church's preeminence in England, following the death of their Protestant father, the infamous Henry VIII.

The Babington Plot was a plan to reinstate the powers of the Catholic Church in England by assassinating Queen Elizabeth I, and then installing Mary, Queen of Scots (a.k.a. Elizabeth's Catholic cousin), to the English throne. In 1586, the plot failed, and in its wake, more than one person was executed for treason—including Mary, Queen of Scots, herself.

Most Catholics under Elizabeth's rule believed that Mary, Queen of Scots, was the rightful queen of England—but the truth was actually a lot more complicated. Mary was the legitimate claimant to the English throne through her Tudor grandmother, Margaret, who was Henry VIII's older sister. Elizabeth's line to the throne, on the other hand, wasn't quite as straightforward, even though she was the daughter of King Henry VIII (and his second wife, Anne Boleyn). Henry had notoriously broken allegiance with the Catholic Church after the Pope refused to validate his marriage to Anne. Since he was previously married, the Catholics refused to legitimize his second marriage while his first wife was still alive. Elizabeth was thus considered by Catholics, the court, and much of the general public to be the "bastard child of a whore." Even after she assumed the crown, she felt like her legitimacy was constantly being threatened, and that's how Mary ended up as a prisoner in England.

Years prior, while trying to escape political unrest and possible imprisonment, Mary had actually sought the protection of her cousin, but Elizabeth took the opportunity to instead imprison Mary, under house arrest, for nineteen years. During that time, Anthony Babington, who was raised in the Catholic Church, served as a page in the household where Mary was kept during her imprisonment. Over the years, Anthony became completely devoted to her, and conspired to restore Mary's place to the throne he thought she deserved.

Anthony did not come up with this assassination plan himself, but rather, he was inspired by a Catholic priest named John Ballard. The two even had an assassin lined up: a man named John Savage. It was at Ballard and Savage's request that Anthony organized and rallied fellow young Catholics to the cause—young Catholics like Chidiock Tichborne. Chidiock had been harassed, arrested, and interrogated by authorities about "Pope-ish relics" that he and his father had brought home from travels abroad. Neither was charged, but records suggest that this was not the only time they were harassed by the authorities over their religion. Frustrated and perhaps craving change, Chidiock agreed to take part in the plot.

Writing in cipher, Anthony exchanged letters with Mary, Queen of Scots, outlining the group's plans to rescue her. This five-word reply triggered her so-called "treasonous" act: "Let the great plot commence." Unfortunately, the plot did *not* go off without a hitch; the letter was intercepted and decoded, and Elizabeth I's authorities felt they had all the evidence they needed to prove that Mary was plotting to steal the British throne. Most accounts, though, suggest that in the greater letter, she'd simply asked for more detail. On trial, Mary noted there were no letters in her handwriting talking about assassination; however, her loose-lipped secretary confessed to taking Mary's dictation, and Mary found herself convicted of treason and executed by beheading.

Meanwhile, Anthony Babington and his co-conspirators were also arrested. When John Ballard was taken into custody, Anthony panicked, and decided they could still execute the plot but needed to do so immediately. Because of court records, we have a little insight into their back-and-forth.

Anthony Babington: Ballard is taken, all will be betrayed, what remedy now?

John Savage: No remedy now, but to kill her presently.

Anthony: Very well, then go you unto the court tomorrow, and there execute the fact.

John: I cannot go tomorrow, for my apparel is not ready, and in this apparel shall I never come near the Queen.

Anthony: Go to. Here is my ring, and all the money I have, get the apparel and dispatch it.

Sadly, a fashionable appearance didn't save anyone in the end. Babington, Savage, and Tichborne were apprehended and held in the Tower of London, waiting to be executed by hanging for high treason. Anthony, in his desperation, tried to offer a bribe for his pardon, but it was rejected. Each man was consequently interrogated, upon which they all confessed. In the end, all three were disemboweled while still alive at the gallows, after which the executioner distributed parts of their bodies to prominent locations around the city, to serve as a stunningly brutal warning for the public. ◆

UNREADY APPAREL

Listen, the Bloody Mary is the obvious choice here. Which is why we're *not* gonna do that. At first, we considered a variation on the posset—that's a warm, milk-based drink that was commonly imbibed during this time. If you know your Shakespeare, you may recall possets being mentioned in the Scottish play as the thing Lady M drugs King Duncan's guards with. And we noodled around with those for a while and didn't come up with anything we liked.

So, in a run to the grocery store, there—like it had a halo of light shining around it—was the ingredient that seemed like the obvious solution to this drink's dilemma. We promise this drink is worth it, but we know that we may lose some of you with this because it's an ingredient people have FEELINGS about: beets.

INGREDIENTS:

- 2 ounces vodka
- 1 ounce simple syrup
- 1 ounce lemon juice
- 2 ounces beet juice
- About 1 ounce club soda

METHOD:

Combine the vodka, simple syrup, lemon juice, and beet juice in a shaking tin, shake with ice, and strain over fresh ice.

Top with club soda.

♦ MAKE IT A MOCKTAIL ♦

Omit the vodka, and use 1½ ounces of lemon juice, and just ½ ounce of simple syrup. Mix as above.

JOHN WILKES BOOTH'S INVOLVEMENT IN THE EXECUTION OF MARY SURRATT

To this day, more than one hundred years after the events unfolded, there continues to be debate as to whether or not a woman named Mary Surratt was involved in the plot to assassinate the sixteenth president of the United States, Abraham Lincoln. Regardless, Mary was hanged for treason in the summer of 1865.

Mary Jenkins married John Surratt in 1840, and the couple then bought 287 acres of land, which they dubbed Surrattsville, in Maryland. Back in Mary's day, this was a tobacco-growing region with a long history of slavery. There, John opened a tavern that also served as a polling place, post office, and part-time lodging. The couple had at least half a dozen enslaved persons working on their land. Because it straddled the North and South during the American Civil War, Maryland was known as a border state; it never officially seceded from the Union, and so there were a number of enslaved people there. It was no secret that the Surratts favored the Confederacy, and their tavern became *the* destination for the similarly-minded to discuss politics. And after John died in 1862, Mary became the proprietor of the whole establishment.

When Mary found herself with financial challenges, she rented out her properties in Surrattsville and moved to the now-infamous townhouse in Washington, DC, that she'd inherited from the Surratt family upon John's death. She ran it as a boarding house from the time she moved in through April 1865, when she was arrested. It's widely accepted as fact that she hosted and attended conspiratorial meetings to remove Lincoln from office, meetings frequently held at her home and led by John Wilkes Booth.

Booth enlisted help to carry out his plot to kill the sitting president, and one of those people was Mary's son, John Jr. The initial plan wasn't murderous at all. Booth simply wanted to remove Lincoln from office by kidnapping him, after which he'd exchange him in return for the release of a number of

Confederate soldiers who were rotting away in Union prisons. Even though murder wasn't on the original agenda, the men he'd recruited knew that Booth was open to a presidential assassination, since he'd floated the idea during an earlier meeting (his cohorts quickly shut it down). On the evening of April 14, 1865, however, Booth and his co-conspirators *did* end up carrying out an assassination, shooting Lincoln during a performance of *Our American Cousin* at Ford's Theater. The president died from his wounds the next morning.

Less than five hours later, Booth had fled the city, and federal investigators, following up on an anonymous tip, paid a visit to Mary's boarding house. Mary didn't have much to say, and her answers to their questions were generally vague. In the two weeks immediately following the assassination, hundreds of people were detained and questioned—many who were known associates of Booth—while federal agents tried to whittle the suspect list down. John Wilkes Booth and John Jr. were the two most well known suspects, but there was a big problem: Booth had already been killed by Union soldiers in a barn in Virginia, and John Jr. had fled the country.

When investigators interviewed Mary and her boarders again, authorities uncovered potentially incriminating evidence in her home, including a photo of Booth (which is just as strange as it sounds) on her mantel. As a result, Mary was arrested for conspiring to assassinate the president. Testimony from a total of 366 witnesses made for a long trial. Most of the case against Mary rested on the testimony of two men in particular: John Lloyd and Louis Weichmann. John Lloyd was a former police officer who leased Mary's properties in Surrattsville. Louis Weichmann had attended college with John Jr., and he resided at Mary's boarding house during the period in which the conspiracy plot was conceived. Both testified that they had witnessed and overheard incriminating conversations among Mary, her son, and Booth regarding removing Lincoln from the presidency. *The end.*

Mary was executed by hanging on July 7, 1865, for "treasonable conspiracy." A crowd of nearly a thousand people came to witness the event. Executions often drew crowds, but this one was very high profile—*so* high-profile, in fact, that the same afternoon, the Surratt boarding house was attacked by souvenir seekers, who had to be stopped by police. ♦

DUBIOUS HONOR

Mary Surratt was the first woman to be executed by the US federal government, which is, as the drink's name suggests, a pretty dubious honor. Mary's story also takes place around the same time that Jerry Thomas was working—as you'll recall, his first cocktail book came out in 1862. One section that really got us thinking was whiskey punches, because court testimony alleged that Mary specifically mentioned having whiskey ready for the co-conspirators she hosted. This led us right to Jerry's revered vanilla punch, which was originally made with brandy. We chose to impart our own spin on it, but that's where the inspiration for this beverage came from.

INGREDIENTS:

- 1½ ounces bourbon
- 1 ounce limoncello
- A couple of drops of vanilla extract
- 2 ounces ginger beer

METHOD:

Combine the bourbon, limoncello, and vanilla extract in a shaking tin, shake with ice, strain into a glass with a large ice cube, and top with ginger beer.

◆ MAKE IT A MOCKTAIL ◆

Sub out the bourbon for a combo of black tea and ginger. (Just throw a slice of ginger in the cup while the tea steeps, or simmer it all together and strain.)

Use lemon juice instead of limoncello and know that you may want to add a little simple syrup to make up the sweetness. To your taste, as always!

WHY THE KING HATED THE "FALSE, FLEETING, PERJUR'D" DUKE OF CLARENCE

Though George Plantagenet, Duke of Clarence, never became king, you might recognize his name anyway, since he later became a character in two of William Shakespeare's famous plays, *Henry VI, Part 3* and *Richard III*, in which Shakespeare referred to him as the "false, fleeting, perjur'd Clarence." In real life, he was the younger brother of English kings Edward IV and Richard III. After their father was killed in battle defending England's crown, Edward took the throne and assumed the title of King Edward IV. Richard would follow. George himself was never crowned king, in part because his brothers had first rights, but also because he was executed for treason against his king-brother Edward before he turned thirty.

Feeling dizzy? You're not alone. The dynamics among these brothers were . . . crazy complicated, to say the least.

In the spring of 1477, George accused Ankarette Twynho, a lady-in-waiting in his home, of poisoning and killing his wife, Isabel, and, possibly, their infant son as well. He was outraged, but he was also mistaken. Isabel had actually died of complications from childbirth, and their son's death quickly followed. Still, George's allegation led to Ankarette's execution by hanging for the crime that April, and it probably wasn't a coincidence that George was in charge of the court that had ruled in his favor. Edward, however, posthumously pardoned her.

Only about a month or so later, another member of George's household, Thomas Burdett, was charged with "imagining the king's death by necromancy" and was accused of writing notes foreseeing the downfall of King Edward IV's family. Thomas and yet another member of George's household, John Stacy, who'd also been accused of witchcraft, were then executed on charges of high treason. George became irate. How could these executions of innocent people in his home be happening under his brother's reign?! He appeared at the council chamber at Westminster to express his displeasure. George was known to be volatile, and he was particularly hot under the collar about these deaths. Yes, he was responsible for accusing at least one of them, and in error—but to George, that was not the point. But his arguments were not welcomed. For the disturbance to the council, he was arrested on the orders of the king for being "in contempt of the law of the land." And in reply to this public outburst against the king, Edward IV threw down the gauntlet and accused his brother of treasonous acts against the crown.

It's clear that the king considered his little brother to be a royal pain in the ass. It wasn't just the executions; these brothers had *a lot* of sibling history to work through. Younger brother George always seemed to take things too far, as far as Edward was concerned. And George didn't like his older brother Edward telling him what to do, either. When George and the heiress Isabel Neville wished to marry, for instance, the king had given the match a thumbs down, but they defied his order and were wed in Calais in 1469, anyway. Now, there were accusations of murder in George's home . . . *and* there was a hot rumor that George was secretly orchestrating and arming an uprising against him. (Edward wasn't totally paranoid here; following his marriage, George *did* help plan and lead with his new father-in-law a revolt that, briefly, reinstalled Henry VI to the throne, though Edward got it back in the end. Still, just how much is a king-brother supposed to endure?)

In January 1478, Edward officially brought a charge of high treason against George for plotting against the king, the queen, and their heirs. George was also accused of sowing the seeds of sedition and inciting rebellion against the crown. He was immediately imprisoned in the Tower of London. Edward was so angry and so over his brother's increasingly difficult behavior that he had an act of a legislature created—a bill of attainder—just to declare George guilty and sentence him to be executed, all without a proper trial. No one knows exactly how George met his untimely end because it was a private execution, but there were rumors that Edward had him drowned in a butt of Malmsey wine. Who among us hasn't imagined drowning a sibling at one point or another? No one else? Liars! ♦

DOWNRIGHT SHAKESPEAREAN

George's life was so epically embroiled in the intrigues of the Plantagenets that he ended up being mentioned in not one, but *two* Shakespearean plays. That got us thinking about the drinks that are mentioned in the vast expanse of Shakespeare's writings. And the thing mentioned the most is, without a doubt, wine. That's fitting, since George was rumored to have been drowned in wine. Taking a little inspiration from both the Bard and rumors of George's end, we're gonna cheat a little and use a sparkling wine. It's prosecco time! Because Malmsey wine, the alleged execution weapon, is a dessert wine, this is a sweet drink—if it's too sweet for your taste, you can always increase the lemon juice to balance it out.

INGREDIENTS:

- ½ ounce lemon juice
- 1 ounce elderflower liqueur
- 1 ounce cognac
- 2 ounces prosecco

METHOD:

Combine the lemon juice, liqueur, and cognac in a shaker with ice. Shake, strain into a chilled flute or coupe, and top with prosecco.

♦ MAKE IT A MOCKTAIL ♦

- ½ ounce lemon juice
- 1 ounce elderflower syrup
- 1 ounce pear juice
- 2 ounces light ginger ale

Make as above, but this one can really, really get sweet. One great way to lighten up the sweetness is to use a ginger sparkling water instead of ginger ale.

THE COMPLICITY OF MAGDALENA RUDENSCHÖLD IN THE ARMFELT CONSPIRACY

◆

Magdalena "Malla" Rudenschöld was a Swedish countess and lady-in-waiting who was considered a triple threat thanks to her lively spirit, intelligence, and beauty. It's no surprise, then, that she had a *lengthy* succession of admirers and suitors. She never married, but she did fall in love—*HARD*—for a Swedish courtier and diplomat named Gustaf Mauritz Armfelt. Gustaf happened to be one of Malla's many admirers, but unfortunately, he also happened to be married. Though their affair lasted for years, Gustaf claimed that he never had serious feelings for her. But Malla? Girl was in *loooove*.

Importantly, the object of her affection had the ear of King Gustav III, who'd taken the Swedish throne through a bloodless coup d'état in 1777. As devoted as Malla was to Gustaf Armfelt, Gustaf was to Gustav III. However, after the king was assassinated in 1792, there was an ensuing struggle between various political parties, and Gustaf lost his social position within the ruling elite. On his deathbed, Gustav III had appointed Gustaf to the council of regency, which was the group that would rule Sweden until Gustav III's son was old enough to take the throne. Gustaf was also appointed Överståthållaren of Stockholm, the highest official for the city. But neither of those appointments ended up happening.

Instead, a new government, *not* preapproved by Gustav III, essentially exiled Gustaf Armfelt to Naples, Italy, under the guise of sending him there as a Swedish ambassador. Enter the Armfelt Conspiracy: a plot to depose this new anti-Gustavian government and to instead install Gustaf Armfelt, the man favored by King Gustav III, on the throne. The plot was instigated by, you guessed it, Gustaf Armfelt, but because he was living in Naples, it was managed and carried out by his agents in Sweden. Among them, most notably, was Malla Rudenschöld.

Malla and Gustaf communicated strictly through letters during his time in Italy, but neither knew or even suspected that their correspondence was being monitored. During Gustaf's first six months in Italy, Malla sent him at least seventy-five letters, which were all strictly personal. Initially, the confiscated letters revealed nothing more than some criticism of the government and vague mentions of conversations with Russia. In other words, they were fairly benign and certainly nothing to get litigious about. Four months later, however, a new pile of letters arrived from Naples; the tone had now shifted into reports about how things were for Gustavians in Sweden, and the letters were decidedly *not* benign. And so, Malla was arrested.

When authorities confronted Malla, she confessed to a planned coup. She admitted her involvement and also said that she had made no attempt to stop it. There was really no way she could deny her actions, since they were able to read her own letters back to her. She was thus charged with treason against the Kingdom of Sweden.

Many in her social circle petitioned for her pardon. However, her arrest coincided with the rise of Baron Gustaf Adolf Reuterholm, one of the regents of Sweden during the council of regency set up for the former king's son, Gustav IV. Baron Reuterholm wanted to strengthen the prosecution's case by publicly discrediting anyone involved in Gustaf Armfelt's intrigue. In the summer of 1794, those charged with taking part in the Armfelt Conspiracy, including Malla, were all sentenced. Sentences ranged from execution to the loss of noble status, loss of property, pillorying, imprisonment, and forced labor. Malla was sentenced to death; she ended up serving two years in prison for treason and was also pilloried in central Stockholm. Among her co-conspirators, one said of Malla that her true mistake was "love, this violent passion, which among so many people of all ages overwhelms reason." Pretty spot on, if you ask us.

And let's not forget about the man at the center of this plot. Gustaf, too, was condemned as a traitor and sentenced to death in the Swedish court; because he remained out of the country, though, he was able to avoid capture and punishment. In fact, Gustaf isn't much remembered at all for the conspiracy named for him. Instead, together with Göran Magnus Sprengtporten, he's regarded as one of the fathers of Finland, who helped the small country become its own autonomous nation. ♦

OVERWHELMED REASON

We want to work with a Scandinavian spirit you don't come across all that often in the United States unless you're really seeking it out: aquavit. It often gets shelved with liqueurs, but it actually has an ABV of about 40 percent, so in practice, it's pretty close to spirits like vodka or gin. Aquavit dates back at least to the 1530s, and it's often compared to gin because it is flavored with botanicals—the dominant flavor is caraway or dill. Its really unique flavor profile is very fun to play with, so we hope you experiment with it some more after taking a taste of this drink.

INGREDIENTS:

- 5 very ripe blackberries
- 1 ounce lemon juice
- 1 ounce simple syrup
- 2 ounces aquavit
- Club soda, to taste (1–2 ounces)

METHOD:

Muddle the blackberries in a shaking tin pretty aggressively; you want those babies *juicy*!

Add the lemon juice, simple syrup, and aquavit, and give it all a VERY thorough shake with ice. Strain out the blackberry pulp and let the juice flow over ice into a chilled glass.

Top with club soda, and you are all set. The amount of club soda is up to you; use just a little soda to get a more robust taste of the aquavit, or more to dilute it. Your call!

♦ MAKE IT A MOCKTAIL ♦

You're gonna make caraway seed tea: Coarsely crush a teaspoon of seeds and add to 1 cup of boiling water. Let it steep for about 8 minutes and use in lieu of the aquavit.

HOW ROBERT WILLIAM KALANIHIAPO WILCOX
TRIED TO STOP THE THEFT OF HAWAII

Robert William Kalanihiapo Wilcox tried to incite rebellion on not one, but two separate occasions. Yet what's *particularly* interesting about Robert's story is that he was arrested on charges of treason against an illegitimate Hawaiian government. (Can you even *do* that? Apparently, yes.)

Born on the island of Maui in 1855, Robert's mother descended from Hawaiian royalty, and his father was an American from New England. He was well educated and worldly—and, it's said, *maybe* a bit rash. Robert was also very pro–Native Hawaiian and supported King David Kalakaua, who at the time was working to reduce the local power of a group of white and mostly American men known collectively as the Missionary Party (and later, the Reform Party). Angered by this resistance, the party drafted a new pro-American constitution. They'd previously forced the king into signing legislation that guaranteed a duty-free market for Hawaiian sugar in exchange for special economic privileges for the United States, privileges that had already been denied to other countries. Their new legislature now undermined the king's authority; it removed Native Hawaiian land rights and gave the right to vote to whites and other foreigners, while at the same time restricting access for Native Hawaiians through things like land-ownership and literacy provisions. Under intimidation—and at gunpoint—the party forced the king to sign a document that became known as the Bayonet Constitution, which provided them with a financial and political windfall.

Amid growing frustrations from Native Hawaiians regarding the questionable new legislature, Robert formed an organization that aimed to revoke the Bayonet Constitution. He and his allies planned to have the king sign *another* new constitution, one that would either restore power to the original throne or supplant the king with his sister, Lili'uokalani. Robert led between 100 and 150 Native Hawaiians to the palace in an attempt to reestablish a native republic, but when they came up against new government forces and their weapons, the group surrendered the same day. Robert was then apprehended and charged with treason.

There was one key catch—and it was in his favor. By law, Robert was to be judged by a jury of his peers, which meant Native or part-Native Hawaiians. Knowing no all-Hawaiian jury would convict him for his pro-Hawaiian actions, the treason charge was dropped before his trial even started. Instead, he was tried for conspiracy; two juries heard the case and both found him not guilty. Afterward, Robert immediately became a Native hero.

When the king died in early 1891, his sister Lili'uokalani succeeded him as the first woman ever to rule the Kingdom of Hawai'i. She also became the kingdom's last reigning monarch and the target of a group called the Committee of Safety, whose members were mostly white businessmen in the sugar industry concerned about their trade agreement with the United States. Two years into her reign, Lili'uokalani was overthrown by the committee and forced to sign a formal abdication. After a non-Hawaiian provisional government was established, the new leaders sought annexation to the United States. US President Grover Cleveland, however, opposed it and called for the queen to be restored to power. Those who were part of that non-Hawaiian committee were adamant that they would keep their hold and power, and refused to pull back.

Robert formed an alliance with others who were similarly outraged, with the goal of removing the illegitimate government. The revolt, though, was suppressed, and both Robert and Queen Lili'uokalani were imprisoned. Robert was charged with treason, but all involved were pardoned, eventually—all, that is, except for the queen, who remained a prisoner in her palace.

When William McKinley became president of the United States in 1897, he was super-pro-annexation, whether the Native Hawaiians wanted it or not. Within a year, the American flag flew over Hawaii, and within three, the US Congress had officially voted Hawaii in as a US territory. As a territory, Hawaii sent one non-voting delegate to the US House of Representatives, and though the non-voting part wasn't ideal, a Territorial Delegate could introduce legislation. Robert, a natural choice, won the seat, which he used to introduce (and advocate for) Native Hawaiian concerns and legislature.

In 1959, more than fifty years after Robert's hard work and his death, Hawaii officially became the fiftieth state of the United States. It wasn't until 1993 when a joint resolution of Congress was signed by President Bill Clinton—informally known as the Apology Resolution—acknowledging that "the Native Hawaiian people never directly relinquished to the United States their claims to their inherent sovereignty over their national lands, either through a plebiscite or referendum." Which was exactly Robert's point the whole time. ♦

EXAGGERATED VIGOR

This one was a little bit of a thinker. When it comes to Hawaii, we immediately think of pineapple, but the pineapple industry and the complicated legacy of Sanford Dole don't seem like an appropriately respectful tribute for Wilcox. Still, there are some very Hawaiian elements in this one. Hawaii boasts some really incredible distilleries these days, and we have really enjoyed sampling Hawaiian vodkas in particular, so that's the spirit we'll highlight in this drink.

INGREDIENTS:

- ¾ ounce lemon juice
- ¾ ounce hibiscus syrup
- 1 ounce vodka
- ½ ounce ginger liqueur
- 1–2 ounces club soda, ginger ale, or ginger beer
- Slice of ginger and/or candied hibiscus, for garnish (optional)

METHOD:

Shake the lemon juice, hibiscus syrup, vodka, and
ginger liqueur with ice, strain over fresh ice,
top with club soda, ginger ale, or ginger beer, and add
garnish, if desired.

♦ MAKE IT A MOCKTAIL ♦

Leave out the vodka, and tweak the proportions
of the other ingredients as follows:

- 1 ounce ginger syrup
- 1 ounce lemon juice
- 1 ounce hibiscus syrup

Prepare as above, topping with
the soda of choice.

JOHN BROWN, THE FIRST AMERICAN TO HANG FOR TREASON

John Brown was arrested for his role in the Harpers Ferry raid in 1859, an event that set the stage for the American Civil War. The American abolitionist was subsequently convicted of murder, instigating an insurrection, and treason against the Commonwealth of Virginia, which makes him the first American executed for treason *against* the United States.

"Live your beliefs and you can turn the world around," wrote American naturalist and poet Henry David Thoreau, who was John's contemporary. John Brown grew up in a family that lived by that adage. The Browns believed enslavement was a sin against God, and John believed that he had been personally predestined to end it. Throughout his whole life—from childhood all the way up through adulthood—John had backed the antislavery movement any way he could, and he called for immediate and universal emancipation of enslaved persons in the United States. His writings on the topic were considered incendiary, and he defended violence and violent rebellion as a means for enslaved persons to claim their freedom. Many white Americans, regardless of their views on enslavement, were taken aback by his fire and brimstone, and many feared that he really would incite rebellion.

On October 16, 1859, John led twenty-one men—sixteen white men (including his three sons) and five Black men—on a raid of the Federal Arsenal at Harpers Ferry, Virginia (which is in today's West Virginia). The intention was to arm enslaved people in the area with the weapons inside, and he hoped that the raid would spark an uprising of armed enslaved persons revolting against their oppressors, particularly in pro-slavery states.

But the attack on the armory went wrong, quickly, in a few ways. Word had spread of a massive uprising of enslaved persons in the area; however, the word had *only* spread among the white community—those in the region he meant to reach, those who were enslaved, had no idea about it. Local farmers and militiamen were tipped off to stop John, but the plan went completely kaput when the US Marines (led by Colonel Robert E. Lee) arrived. The colonel immediately demanded John's surrender. John, unsurprisingly, refused and was subsequently wounded when a Marine used the hilt of a saber to beat him unconscious. Within thirty-six hours from the start of the attack, most of John's men had been captured or killed. Injured but alive, he was arrested. When asked why he'd done it, John replied, simply, "We came to free the slaves, and only that." The very fact that the raid took place *at all* not only jolted both Northerners and Southerners, it created the mythic figure of John Brown.

John was charged with three counts: one, treason against the government of Virginia; two, conspiracy to induce slaves to "rebel and make insurrection against their masters and owners"; and three, first-degree murder. He pleaded not guilty. Four other of Brown's captured men-at-arms were indicted that day, too, also on treason charges.

John's trial began with one of his court-appointed defense attorneys reading a statement claiming that several of Brown's relatives suffered from various types of mental illness, insinuating that John must, too. John, understandably, protested. This was *his* defense, after all, and he didn't want a trial held under "miserable artifice and pretext" to avoid discussing what he felt was the actual issue at hand: enslavement. The trial continued, but John did not take the stand. As a matter of fact, he showed little interest in what his defense team had to say, mainly because he was hell-bent on using the forum to discuss the injustice of slavery, not to debate treason or mental illness. The jury returned a verdict of guilty on all charges against him, but the judgment wasn't exactly a huge surprise—considering John's jury was made up of twelve pro-slavery men.

John did address the court before he was sentenced, and this was the moment he'd been waiting for. He delivered a long speech where he asserted that he "never did intend murder, or treason, or the destruction of property, or to excite or incite Slaves to rebellion, or to make insurrection, [but to] free Slaves." His full statement was published in newspapers throughout the country and convinced many Northerners who had feared his tactics that he was not the extremist they feared he was, but rather a "martyr" to the cause of freedom for everyone.

John was executed by hanging, and because of the controversial nature of the crime, admittance to view his death was severely restricted, with heavy security. John stood at the gallows, hood over his eyes, when the hangman handed him a handkerchief and told him to drop it whenever he was ready. John, ever rebellious, yelled out, "John Brown is always ready—Virginia drops the handkerchief!" The platform fell, and John dropped through. ◆

THE ZEALOT

During the American Civil War, rumors circulated among the Confederate troops that the Union soldiers got their courage from whiskey. So, in honor of abolitionist John Brown, let's make something with bourbon. This drink requires a shout out to our friend Luis, an extraordinary bartender who once served Holly a custom martini that gave her a new appreciation for bourbon. Ours is a less complex—but still tasty!—version of that inspired beverage.

INGREDIENTS:

- 1½ ounces espresso
- 1½ ounces chocolate milk
- 1½ ounces smoked bourbon
- Sprinkle of cocoa powder
- Sprinkle of cinnamon

METHOD:

Combine the espresso, chocolate milk, and bourbon in a shaker, shake with ice, and strain into a prechilled martini glass.

Sprinkle with cocoa powder and cinnamon.

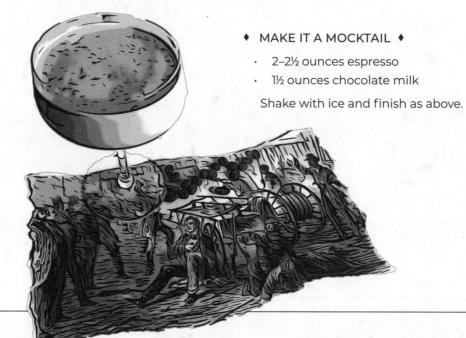

♦ **MAKE IT A MOCKTAIL** ♦

- 2–2½ ounces espresso
- 1½ ounces chocolate milk

Shake with ice and finish as above.

SIGMUND ROSENBLUM
HAD WAY TOO MANY NAMES

Mr. Constantine. A.k.a Dr. T. W. Andrew. A.k.a. George Bergmann. A.k.a. Sidney George Reilly. Whoever he really was, he did work for a time as a British intelligence officer and is, perhaps, the most accomplished spy in history.

He was born Sigmund Georgievich Rosenblum in Odessa, part of modern-day Ukraine, in 1874—*probably*. What else but a tangled web would you expect from the most accomplished spy in history, right? Much of what historians think they know about him may be false, as he was a master of deception. Over the course of his life, Sigmund invented more than a dozen identities for himself, but history probably knows him best as Sidney Reilly, his favorite of many aliases, so we're going to call him by that name. He was suave, self-confident, and charming. It's also said that he was generous with his friends, but he could be cold and pragmatic, too. Plus, he enjoyed gambling with both his money and his life.

Most—maybe all—of Sidney's actual accomplishments are murky and controversial. By nature, really. He became a businessman and con man, though his actual line of work was espionage. By the beginning of the twentieth century, he was working as an agent for British intelligence, assigned to spy on expat communities in Paris and London, with dispatches to Germany and the Russian Empire, as well as East and Southeast Asia. To talk about Sidney is to talk about his legend. Some historians see him playing a double role in several key historical events, working for the British government while also spying for Russia's Tsarist regime. It's true that he *did* establish relationships in Russia through his miracle cure business. Miracle cure business, you ask? Alongside his other professions, Sidney established himself as a chemist, and he was manufacturing and distributing so-called miracle cures to an unsuspecting public on the side, using his businesses to make and secure connections around the world. Literally, a snake oil spy.

In the aftermath of the Bolshevik Revolution, Sidney was involved in an attempt to topple Vladimir Lenin, the head of the Bolshevik Party, from power. In a twist of fate, his plan was undermined by a separate assassination attempt on Lenin, one which triggered the Red Terror that resulted in the deaths of hundreds of thousands of suspected counterrevolutionaries. He was then vilified as a key conspirator. A manhunt was ordered, but he'd vanished from St. Petersburg. It didn't take long to find him in a safe house outside Moscow, where he was arrested—allegedly for his attempts to overthrow the Bolshevik government, but there's more to it. His identity had also been discovered; he was ultimately betrayed through a five-year counterintelligence operation run by Soviet agents, called Operation Trust, which was created specifically to find the man the Soviet intelligence groups considered their most formidable enemy. A.k.a. Sidney Reilly. Ultimately, he was outed as he fled from St. Petersburg to Moscow by a man he'd considered to be an ally.

Sidney was then taken to Lubyanka prison in Moscow, where he became known only as "the man incarcerated in cell 73," since his presence was a closely guarded secret. According to the Soviet account of his interrogation, he was never physically tortured, but he was subjected to severe psychological torture that included a mock execution, an act that quite possibly terrified him enough to confess. In their account, the Soviets stated that the longer he remained alive after he had nothing left to give, the greater the chance word they had him would leak out—and that wasn't something they wanted. Thus, one evening in November 1925, thinking he was going for a walk in the woods as he was often allowed, Sidney Reilly was shot in the back and killed.

Today, many historians consider Sigmund Georgievich Rosenblum from Odessa to be the first twentieth-century super-spy, a real-life James Bond. In fact, it's rumored that Ian Fleming once admitted to a friend that his fictional British agent was based on Sidney. True? Who knows—this is a story about a spy, after all, and Fleming has coyly said the same thing about a *lot* of high-profile spies. While the character James Bond may have accomplished his assignments with gadgets provided by the creative and innovative character of Q, Sidney Reilly's accomplishments were due to his guile, his wits, and his total absolute lack of morals. ◆

REILLY'S VESPER

Sidney Reilly and his association with the character of James Bond made us think, of course, of Bond's signature martini, the Vesper. The Vesper was completely made up by Fleming instead of being based on a preexisting cocktail, so here's our twist on the recipe for the James Bond Vesper, which is as follows:

THE JAMES BOND VESPER

INGREDIENTS:

- 3 ounces gin
- 1 ounce vodka
- ½ ounce Lillet Blanc, or dry vermouth
- Lemon peel, for garnish

For our version, we're switching it up in a way James Bond would probably be horrified by, though we *are* keeping the high alcohol content (so drink responsibly).

REILLY'S VESPER

INGREDIENTS:

- 3 ounces gin
- 1 ounce vodka
- ½ ounce grapefruit liqueur
- Lemon peel, for garnish

OUR METHOD:

Combine the gin, vodka, and grapefruit liqueur in a shaking tin, shake with ice, and strain into a prechilled martini glass. Garnish with lemon peel.

♦ **MAKE IT A MOCKTAIL** ♦

Stir together 1 ounce of grapefruit syrup and 3 ounces of club soda with a dash of Angostura bitters and pour into a prechilled martini glass.

Note: If the small amount of alcohol in bitters means it's not for you, try adding a few drops of saline. You can make your own by dissolving one part salt in four parts water.

THE TREACHEROUS
RADIO BROADCASTS OF EZRA POUND

I t's said that Ezra Pound was only eleven years old when he published his first poem, a limerick. At the age of fifteen, he told his parents he was going to be a poet. And by his early twenties, with $80 in his pocket and a manuscript that had already been rejected by at least one American publisher, he left Idaho for Europe. As an American ex-pat in London, he taught, lectured, and published reviews. That same year, he self-published his first book, a collection of poems. He would go on to publish more than seventy books in his lifetime and become one of the most well known American poets in history.

There's no denying that Ezra Pound was a brilliant poet. But there's also no denying that Ezra Pound was a fascist. And an anti-Semite. And by the beginning of World War II, he blamed the practice of usury, which he believed to be propagated by a secret network of Jewish bankers, for all the evils afflicting the world. He strongly supported Benito Mussolini and between 1941 and 1943, he delivered pro-Axis and anti-Jewish broadcasts four times a week, on shortwave radio aimed at America—all to foster American sympathy for Italian fascism.

His greeting blasted over the airwaves: "Europe calling! Pound speaking! Ezra Pound speaking!" Ezra recorded more than one hundred shortwave broadcasts from Rome, each criticizing US President Franklin D. Roosevelt, Roosevelt's family, and the Jewish community. Pound also collaborated with Mussolini's fascist regime and often parroted fascist propaganda talking points on his show, and he was paid to do so.

Thanks to broadcasts that were transcribed by a US Foreign Broadcast Monitoring Service listening station, Ezra's side gig was discovered. He was indicted in absentia for treason against the United States in 1943. He answered the charge, stating, "I do not believe that the simple fact of speaking over the radio . . . can in itself constitute treason." He was apprehended in Genoa, Italy, by the US Army and temporarily held in Pisa while the FBI searched the residence where he'd been living when he was arrested. They removed articles, letters, and other documents—all classified, and all used as evidence. He was then returned to the United States and indicted for treason on November 26, 1945. His fellow writers had mixed feelings about the whole affair. Ernest Hemingway, for instance, championed for his release, while Robert Frost, on the other hand, commented that Ezra was "possibly crazy but more likely criminal." Archibald MacLeish, the librarian of Congress, said of him, "It is pretty clear that poor old Ezra is quite, quite balmy."

A board of psychiatrists appointed by the court determined that Ezra, the defendant, was "mentally unfit to advise properly with counsel or to participate intelligibly in his own defense." He was committed to St. Elizabeths Hospital, a psychiatric facility in Washington, DC, where it was ordered that he would receive treatment until it was determined that he was mentally competent enough to stand trial. For those among us who look for silver linings, there was one for Ezra; if he had been found fit to stand trial initially and was convicted, he would have almost certainly faced the death penalty.

Teasing out the artist from the fascist and anti-Semite proved difficult for some who had come to love his poetry. Fellow poets and authors rallied around him, and their pleas for his freedom kept him in the public's attention. On April 18, 1958, a US Federal District Court—coincidentally under the same judge who oversaw his 1946 treason trial—dismissed the indictment for treason that'd been lodged more than a decade prior against Ezra. Dismissed? Yes. How in the world did that happen? *Well.* Publicity, and relentless supporters, honestly. Several publications, including *The New Republic*, *Newsweek*, and *Esquire*, had begun to publish pro-release articles. Plus, Ezra had good friends and followers, who hired a top-notch lawyer named Thurman Arnold. Thurman filed a motion to dismiss the indictment, and the hospital superintendent didn't argue; au contraire, he filed a supporting affidavit stating his patient was "incurably insane," and, he continued, long-term confinement to the hospital would serve no therapeutic purpose. And just like that, Ezra was free to go, and he returned to Italy to live the rest of his life. ◆

EZRA'S WORDS

Since Ezra Pound was a man of words, the Last Word—a cocktail that predates Prohibition—is the first thing that comes to mind. This drink is usually made with the following ingredients:

INGREDIENTS:

- ¾ ounce dry gin
- ¾ ounce maraschino liqueur
- ¾ ounce green Chartreuse
- ¾ ounce fresh lime juice

For Ezra's drink, we're subbing out the Chartreuse for elderflower liqueur, to make it a bit sweeter.

INGREDIENTS:

- ¾ ounce dry gin
- ¾ ounce maraschino liqueur
- ¾ ounce elderflower liqueur
- ¾ ounce fresh lime juice

METHOD:

Put all ingredients in a shaking tin, shake with ice, and strain into a prechilled cocktail glass.

♦ **MAKE IT A MOCKTAIL** ♦

- ¾ ounce cherry syrup
- ¾ ounce elderflower syrup
- ¾ ounce fresh lime juice
- ¾ ounce ginger beer

Combine syrups and lime juice in a shaking tin, then strain into a chilled glass, add the ginger beer, and give it a gentle stir.

HOW "MEAN GIRLS" BRUTUS AND CASSIUS LITERALLY STABBED CAESAR IN THE BACK

You know that saying, keep your friends close, but keep your enemies closer? What if they're one and the same? It was on the Ides of March in 44 BCE when Julius Caesar was assassinated by those in his inner circle of senators, who stabbed him twenty-three times as he sat at the podium during a senate meeting. To the horror of everyone on the senate floor, Caesar fell at the feet of a statue of Pompey. It was a high-profile act of treason, but quite possibly the most shocking part was that the men behind the plot, Marcus Junius Brutus and Gaius Cassius Longinus, were the two men that Caesar personally considered his eyes and ears in the senate. He trusted them. These guys had known each other for a *long* time.

Caesar was an ambitious leader and powerful war hero who rose in the ranks to become the dictator of the Roman Empire. He's famously quoted as saying, "If I fail, it is only because I have too much pride and ambition." And he wasn't wrong.

Brutus, a Roman statesman, was convinced that Caesar had too much power and was growing too ambitious. Choosing what he believed to be the best interest of the Roman Republic over the life of his friend, he masterminded the plot to assassinate Caesar—and then delivered the final dagger in his back. But Brutus didn't act alone. Cassius, a Roman senator who also happened to be Brutus's brother-in-law, incited his fellow senators to kill their leader.

Expecting to be seen as liberators of the Republic, the men were instead met with accusations of treachery and betrayal. The public vilified them for treason, and in the end, they both took their own lives rather than surrender to the charges. Italian poet Dante Alighieri imagined an afterlife for them in his fourteenth-century epic poem *The Divine Comedy*, placing them in the deepest level of hell—to be chewed upon by Lucifer for all of time. ♦

ROMAN STRENGTH

In the drinking culture of ancient Rome, one of the most common beverages was posca, which was a mix of wine, water, herbs … and vinegar. Believe it or not, there are still people who make posca today, though what it tasted like in ancient Rome is really a lot of guesswork. No insult intended if that sounds delicious to you, but for us, it's a pass. However, we *do* like the idea of an herbal cocktail, one where the flavors of the herbs are really in the limelight instead of simply accenting other components.

INGREDIENTS:

- 2 sprigs fresh dill
- 2 sprigs fresh basil
- 1 sprig fresh mint
- ½ ounce lemon juice
- ¾ ounce simple syrup
- 1½ ounces vodka
- 1 ounce club soda

METHOD:

Strip the leaves from all the herbs and place them into a shaker with the lemon juice and simple syrup. Muddle gently, then add the vodka and ice and shake vigorously. Strain over fresh ice. If you like to have small bits of herbs in your drink (like we do!), use just one strainer, but if you prefer a drink without them, double strain.

Top with club soda.

♦ MAKE IT A MOCKTAIL ♦

Make as above but omit the vodka. This is also a fun mocktail to play with flavored sparkling waters as your topper instead of club soda to find the combo that makes your palate sing.

IF KŌTOKU SHŪSUI WASN'T PART OF THE KŌTOKU INCIDENT, WHY IS IT NAMED AFTER HIM?

I t began with the discovery of a cache of bomb-making materials in the small room of a lumber worker named Miyashita Takichi, who lived on the Japanese island of Honshu. And it resulted in what became known as the High Treason Incident, a socialist-anarchist bomb plot to assassinate Japanese Emperor Meiji in 1910. The fallout led to the arrest of hundreds of people, with convictions of twenty-six people on charges of high treason against the Imperial family.

Kōtoku Denjirō, better known by his pen name Kōtoku Shūsui, was a Japanese socialist who played a prominent role in introducing radical far-left ideology and radical progressivism to Japan in the early twentieth century. Authorities considered him to be the lead conspirator in the High Treason Incident—also known as "the Kōtoku Incident"—though his actual level of involvement remains in question today. Educated in both Confucian and European philosophy, Kōtoku began thinking about different political ideologies at a young age. He wrote, "I want myself to be idealist, revolutionary, progressive. I do not like lukewarm socialism, syrupy socialism, state socialism."

Kōtoku often wrote about Marxism, socialism, and, eventually, anarchism. It was when he was imprisoned for five months for press law violations—notably, it was against the law to publish about such revolutionary ideologies, as he did, regardless—when Kōtoku discovered the works of Russian anarchist-philosopher and revolutionary Pyotr Kropotkin, and anarcho-communism became an ideology he maintained until his death. Shortly after his release from jail, Kōtoku traveled to the United States, and he continued to write while abroad. He had arrived in the States as a socialist, but through his studies, experiences, and observations while overseas, Kōtoku returned to Japan an anarchist. And that made him *most definitely* a person of interest for the Japanese government, who kept a close eye on anyone who followed what they considered to be "dangerous" ideologies, including anarchism, Christian socialism, agrarianism, and Marxism.

Kōtoku and those who also held similar ideologies were part of a larger moment, where activists and intellectuals throughout the world—not just Japan—were debating imperialism and its impact. But Kōtoku took it one step further. The High Treason Incident went beyond just talking about radical topics and writing radical manifestos; it was *literally* a plan to assassinate the emperor.

After bomb-making supplies were discovered in Miyashita Takichi's room, he, among other radicals, was on the government's watchlist, and authorities began investigating his associates, including Kōtoku. In January 1911, Kōtoku was arrested, along with twenty-five others, and they were all ordered to stand trial on the grounds of high treason, known as *taigyakuzai*.

The chief prosecutor, a man named Hiranuma Kiichirō, was known to try for the death penalty in every single case that came his way, even in the cases of those who were only guilty by association or arrested on minor charges. The twenty-six cases of those implicated in the High Treason Incident were tried in closed court. In a show of benevolence by the emperor, the Imperial House personally intervened to commute the death sentences of thirteen of those defendants, but Kōtoku was not among them. He and the other remaining defendants were sentenced to death by hanging.

In a letter he sent to a friend a few days before his execution, Kōtoku wrote, "At last everything has come to an end. I feel relieved of my responsibilities. Death is like a cloud on a high mountain. When you look at it from afar, it appears in the shape of a terrible apparition, but when you draw near it is nothing. To a materialist it has no more significance than the fact that the pendulum of a clock which has been moving back and forth has come to a stop." ♦

THE EXTREMIST

This is a sad story, so we want something sweet to balance it out. Perhaps something inspired by the phrase "syrupy socialism," which conveniently overlaps with a sometimes maligned but really interesting Japanese liqueur: Midori. Sometimes Midori gets a bad reputation as a trashy, too-sweet component in cocktails. But it's super unique because it's the only honeydew liqueur, so it can be used in ways nothing else can. In this case, we're making a very simple drink that lets all the flavors come through to make a bright, fruity sip.

INGREDIENTS:

- 1 ounce apple juice
- 1 ounce Midori
- ½ ounce grapefruit vodka

METHOD:

Combine all ingredients in a shaker with plenty of ice. Shake until very cold and strain into a chilled martini glass.

♦ MAKE IT A MOCKTAIL ♦

- 1 ounce grapefruit juice
- 1 ounce apple juice
- 1 ounce honeydew syrup

Combine in a shaker with ice and prepare as above.

Note: *Still too sweet for your taste? This drink, in both its alcoholic and mocktail forms, transitions nicely to a more sippable version when you strain it over ice and then add club soda, lemon-lime soda, or ginger ale.*

PART 8

Heist Hooch

We couldn't finish a book about criminals without including some of the most expensive thefts in history. Yep, we're talking *art heists*. After all, who would—or maybe who *wouldn't*—want to display a stolen *Mona Lisa* in their home for all to see? That painting's considered to be the most recognizable piece of art of all time; it was even a major plot point (spoiler alert!) in 2022's star-studded hit *Glass Onion: A Knives Out Mystery*. Hanging that in your living room is a total power play.

As you can imagine, the list of people who crave and covet famous pieces of art goes on and on. And as for the thieves who displace these priceless pieces? Well, they may or may not know much about art, but what they *do* know is that stealing valuable artworks to trade or sell on the black market can bring them money, status, and notoriety.

Johannes Vermeer's *The Concert*—which was stolen from the Isabella Stewart Gardner Museum in Boston back in 1990—remains the most valuable piece of artwork ever stolen. When it was initially nicked, the painting was worth an estimated $250 million, and it's still missing today.

Some of the heists you'll read about next are incredibly brazen. Others are almost ridiculously simple. Is it worth it, all this burgling? Well, it turns out most art thieves never get caught (like the ones who snatched *The Concert*), so . . . we guess *you'll* have to be the judge of that. ♦

THE TIME THE SICILIAN MAFIA FED CARAVAGGIO'S *NATIVITY* TO THE PIGS

Listed in the top five among crimes that have rocked the art world is the theft of the *Nativity with St. Francis and St. Lawrence*. Experts estimate its value—if it still exists today—at a whopping $20 million. Michelangelo Merisi da Caravaggio's famous work, an oil on canvas, features the biblical scene of the newborn Christ lying in a manger. It's considered a seventeenth-century masterpiece, but it hasn't been seen since it was stolen in 1969. No one knows who stole it or why, but what might have become of it sure has sparked a lot of speculation. One prominent theory? The work was stolen by the mafia, and, quite possibly, eaten by pigs.

Caravaggio's art was well received in his day and skyrocketed him to celebrity status almost overnight—but it wasn't always his art that got people talking. His reputation for drinking, gambling, sword-carrying, and brawling preceded him, inspiring his nickname, the "bad boy of Baroque." He had a rap sheet that included everything from writing and distributing libelous poems about people he knew (often about their sexuality, that was kind of his go-to) to carrying a sword and dagger without a permit and then actually assaulting people with those weapons. Specifically, he was known to "swagger about . . . from one tennis-court to the next, ever ready to engage in a fight or an argument." Fellow painter Giovanni Baglione even once accused Caravaggio of hiring assassins to kill him; true or not, Caravaggio *was* a volatile guy, always looking for confrontation, and people were afraid of seeing what he was capable of doing. He definitely *seemed* the kind of guy who might hire assassins if you crossed him.

The part of Caravaggio's life that has really stood the test of time isn't his fondness for swords or debauchery, but rather his revolutionary artwork. He's famous for dramatic and intense uses of light and shadow, developing a technique that's known as "tenebrism." For reasons unknown, his *Nativity* attracted the attention of thieves hundreds of years after it was painted. On a stormy October night in 1969, two men in a Piaggio Ape drove along the Via Immacolatella in the historic center of Palermo, Sicily, and stopped at the Oratorio di San Lorenzo. They broke into the chapel, cut the canvas from its frame with a razor blade, rolled up *Nativity* (which had hung there for more than 350 years by that point), and simply walked out.

News of the heist was reported in Sicily's daily newspaper, *Giornale di Sicilia*, on October 20, but that's the only report that still exists to this day. The police report on the state of the oratory—a key document for investigators because it's the only known report describing the scene of the crime—somehow *also* disappeared. Hmmm . . . *curious*. Investigators formed a task force and issued a public statement that "the theft . . . may have been ordered by a gang of international, organized criminals using local operatives in Palermo." Headlines in *Giornale di Sicilia* teased a similar suspicion: that the Sicilian Mafia was behind the crime.

Francesco Marino "Mozzarella" Mannoia, a former member of the Sicilian Mafia who turned state witness, told the court in 1989, *twenty years later*, that the painting had, indeed, been stolen by the mafia—in fact, he'd been there—but claimed that they never sold it. Instead, he confessed that it was shredded and burned, though he didn't say why. As surprising as this story might seem, Mannoia is considered one of the most reliable government witnesses against the Sicilian mafia, and his account never wavered. However, he's not the only mafia man who's admitted ties to the piece. Another Sicilian mafioso, anonymous in court records, claimed that he, at one time, had custody of the painting and had intentions of selling it. When the sale fell through, he claimed that he then buried it in his backyard—but no amount of digging ever produced the *Nativity*. Yet *another* mafia hit man said that he was the one who had the *Nativity* and offered to return it in exchange for a lenient sentence, but he never did. These claims are actually all pretty tame compared to what was stated by other mafioso hit men over the years about the theft—like this one: that the piece had been stored in a dilapidated barn where it had been accidentally eaten by pigs. One more? That it had been used by Sicilian Mafia bosses as a very expensive . . . carpet.

There were also stories from journalists, though only a few, who attested that they had seen the painting, with their own eyes, after its theft. One particularly interesting claim was that the Camorra, one of the oldest criminal organizations in Italy, had obtained the painting, but it became buried under rubble in the aftermath of the Naples earthquake of November 1980. Whatever theory you believe, all roads appear to lead to the unfortunate destruction of the *Nativity*.

Of course, all of these theories are to be taken with a grain of salt, since nothing has ever been proven. In the meantime, while the investigations continue, there's a modern addition to the story: a replica of *Nativity*, made by Factum Arte for the Oratorio di San Lorenzo and unveiled in 2014, was installed in the very same place the original had hung. It's hardly the real deal, but that wasn't the point—it's better than an empty frame on a wall, right? ♦

ITALIAN STORM

This drink is inspired by two key parts of this story: the stormy conditions of the night of the heist, and the dark, foreboding colors of the painting. Plus, Italy is famous for its coffee (which is spectacular), so we're doing a coffee version of a dark and stormy.

INGREDIENTS:

- 2 ounces espresso vodka
- 3 ounces ginger beer
- Lemon juice (optional)
- Simple syrup (optional)
- Dash of bitters (optional)

METHOD:

This is one that some people will probably enjoy in its most basic, two-ingredient form. But because it involves a coffee note, we're treating it the same way we would coffee: to your taste! So, add lemon juice or syrup to taste, and if you just want to play with seasoning, get out your bitters. Have we been known to put bitters in our morning coffee? Yes.

♦ MAKE IT A MOCKTAIL ♦

This is an easy substitution—just use espresso instead of espresso vodka.

THE DAY POLISH PIRATES
PINCHED *THE LAST JUDGMENT*

T he apocalyptic prophecy involving the second coming of Christ and the rapture of souls from the Christian *Book of Revelation* in the *New Testament* has been a source of inspiration for many artists over many centuries. So many, in fact, that you'd need both hands, and maybe the hands of a friend, to count the number of famous pieces. But out of all of them, only one work has actually been both nicked and, believe it or not, also looted by pirates.

Flemish painter Hans Memling completed *The Last Judgment* triptych in 1471, which tells the story of the end of days as described in the *Revelation of Saint John*. The work had initially been commissioned by Angelo Tani, an agent of the Medici bank in Bruges, in 1465. In fact, when the triptych is closed, Tani and his wife are shown kneeling in prayer. Spanning a timeline of more than five hundred years, the work has, amazingly, never been severely damaged—despite some pretty thrilling adventures it's been on.

Those adventures began on April 25, 1473, when it was loaded, under Burgundian flag, aboard the *San Matteo*, a galley leaving from Bruges, where the piece was created. *The Last Judgment* was bound for Florence, Italy, where it would be installed. Two days later, when the *San Matteo* entered English waters, things went sideways. As a result of a conflict between England and the Hanseatic League (a commercial and defensive network of merchants looking out for each other), the *San Matteo* was stalked, attacked, and then boarded by Captain Paul Benecke, a privateer from the city of Gdańsk. *The Last Judgment* never reached Italy. All of the stolen cargo fell into the possession of Captain Benecke and his privateers—that is, government-sponsored pirates— and they offered their goods to the Gdańsk nobles first, who, in turn, gave everything over to what is now St. Mary's Basilica, in the center of the city. Perhaps unsurprisingly, Angelo objected to this plan, but since the looting was defended on the basis that the seizure had been a legitimate act of war, the case was considered closed. The triptych would remain in Gdańsk, and it was hung upon one of the pillars of the chapel of St. George, where it remained for more than three hundred years.

Fast forward to the sixteenth century: Rudolf II, Holy Roman Emperor, admired Memling's work and wanted to buy the triptych for his own personal collection. His offer, though, was turned down by Gdańsk city officials. Tsar Peter I, who also wanted the work, wasn't quite as polite as Rudolf II. He *demanded* that *The Last Judgment* be given to him as a token of gratitude for peace negotiations that had been favorable for the city. But once again, Gdańsk declined. It wasn't until 1807, when the French conquered Gdańsk, that the painting was given a new home at the Louvre in Paris, where it was erroneously considered a work of artist Jan van Eyck.

A decade later, *The Last Judgment* was returned to Gdańsk and was displayed in St. Mary's Basilica—after a side trip for a few years in Berlin. The triptych stayed in St. Mary's Basilica until the final days of World War II, when it was hidden for safety against Nazi looting; this precaution ended up being for naught, as it was eventually looted, not by Hitler but by the Red Army, and taken to the Hermitage in Leningrad.

It wasn't until post–World War II—nearly five hundred years since it had first been created—that Poland became the new owner of the piece under new international treaties, and *The Last Judgment* remains the only work of the Flemish artist in any collection in museums across Poland. In the end, Angelo Tani never got his triptych, but his triptych sure did see the world. ♦

TANI'S LAMENT

In addition to matching the colors of the artwork, we're longing to build a drink that represents *all* of the countries where Memling's *The Last Judgment* has lived—and even one where it didn't. But you have to be a little judicious in this approach, because otherwise you'll just get trash!

Since it was initially intended for the Italian city of Florence but never made it there, we're throwing the bitter aperitif Campari in this mix. For a spirit representing Poland and Russia, we're including bison grass vodka. Belgium and Germany have a *lot* of crossover crops, so this drink will also feature both apple and cherry flavors. And lastly, to commemorate the painting's brief stay in France, we'll add in some lemon juice. Citrus may not be what you think of when you think of European crops, but the south of France has become well known for its lemon groves over the years. Those are Menton lemons, named specifically for the very productive trees in that region, but in this case, regular lemon juice will do.

INGREDIENTS:

- 1 ounce Campari
- 1 ounce Żubrówka vodka
- 1 ounce lemon juice
- 1 ounce raspberry syrup
- 2 ounces cherry-infused water (see Note)
- 2–3 ounces hard cider
- Orange coin (a circular cut of orange rind), for garnish

Note: *Many grocery stores carry bottled fruit-infused waters, including cherry, but if yours doesn't, it's simple to make your own. Mash 5 cherries in an airtight container, cover with a pint of water, seal, give it a good shake, then let sit in the fridge overnight. Shake again, then strain.*

METHOD:

Add the Campari, Żubrówka, lemon juice, raspberry syrup, and cherry water in a shaking tin with ice. Shake and strain over fresh ice, then top with hard cider.

Express the orange rind over the drink, then run it around the rim of the drink.

♦ MAKE IT A MOCKTAIL ♦

This one requires a little extra tweaking, so here is the ingredients list:
- 1 ounce deeply steeped orange tea
- 1 ounce lemon juice
- ½ ounce raspberry syrup
- 2 ounces cherry water
- 2–3 ounces nonalcoholic cider

Top with cider and garnish as above.

MERRY "HEISTMAS" AT MUSEO NACIONAL DE ANTROPOLOGÍA

When thieves broke into the Museo Nacional de Antropología, or Mexico's National Museum of Anthropology, just before dawn on Christmas Day 1985, it turned out to be one of the biggest museum heists in history—and authorities had absolutely no leads.

Those merry mischief-makers made off with some of Mexico's most valuable national treasures, including priceless pre-Columbian artifacts and jewelry, as well as an Aztec obsidian monkey jar and the one-of-a-kind jade death mask of an ancient Mayan ruler. When all was said and done, a total of 140 objects went missing, and all of them were made of gold, jade, obsidian, and turquoise and crafted by the Mayas, Aztecs, Mixtecs, and Zapotecs before the Spanish conquest of Mexico. These pieces had been housed in several glass cases in three of the museum's galleries on both the first floor and in a basement exhibition area, but unfortunately, the cases had not been locked, nor were they hooked to an alarm system. Museum officials believed that the thieves had specifically targeted artifacts that were small and easy to carry—most of the confiscated works were only about an inch in size—as well as pieces that had high value on the international market, of course.

Authorities set up checkpoints at ports of exit and border crossings, figuring that the thieves would try to sell the objects abroad. But they caught no one and nothing in that net.

Why? Well, as it turned out, the items never actually left Mexico City. *Seriously.* The robbery had been the work of two suburban guys—Carlos Perches Treviño and Ramón Sardina Garcia—who may have been able to smuggle the artifacts out of a building but were far too inexperienced to know what to do with them. For three hours, they stuffed their pockets, yet they were total amateurs who didn't know how to fence the items they stole.

Authorities contacted INTERPOL and reported the theft along with detailed descriptions of the stolen artifacts to 158 countries. It took nearly four years before there was a break in the case, and it was all that was needed to arrest Carlos and Ramón, along with a few co-conspirators. At last, the stolen items were recovered from a private residence in a Mexico City suburb, where they'd been stored in a canvas bag in a bedroom closet the whole time. A pretty underwhelming end to such a legendary looting. ◆

TINY TREASURES

Because the 140 items stolen during the Christmas morning heist were all small in size, this story would be best served by a flight of mini cocktails. You could make any one of these as a shot, or scale it up for a full-sized drink by adding soda and/or multiplying the ingredients (particularly with the champagne entry).

All of these concoctions build quickly in shot glasses, so even though there are three, you won't have to spend a lot of time in prep. But DO chill those shot glasses ahead of time, and do chill your champagne. To make the green-tea infused tequila, steep 4 ounces of tequila with a bag of green tea for 30–40 minutes, shaking occasionally. Then, remove the tea bag and enjoy.

THE SPICY HOLIDAY

- ½ ounce chile liqueur
- 1 ounce champagne

OBSIDIAN MONKEY VASE

- ½ ounce dark rum
- ½ ounce banana liqueur
- 1 ounce cold coffee

JADE FUNERARY MASK

- ¾ ounce green-tea infused tequila
- ¼ ounce mint syrup
- ½ ounce aloe juice

THE SPICY HOLIDAY

- ½ ounce chile syrup
- 1 ounce ginger ale

OBSIDIAN MONEY VASE

- ½ ounce banana syrup
- 1 ounce cold coffee

JADE FUNERARY MASK

- ¾ ounce green tea
- ¼ ounce mint syrup
- ½ ounce aloe juice

WHO WAS JACOB DE GHEYN III AND WHY DO PEOPLE KEEP STEALING HIS PORTRAIT?

In 2019, a man attempted to steal two Rembrandt van Rijn paintings from an exhibit at the Dulwich Picture Gallery in London, but after being confronted by security, he fled without the art. While a gallery spokesperson declined to identify the two paintings that had been briefly displaced—they never actually left the building—they *did* clearly state that Rembrandt's portrait of Jacob de Gheyn III was definitely NOT involved. Seems to be kind of an odd thing to point out, though, right? *Well.* As it turned out, it wasn't so strange after all. Over the last century, there have been eighty-one thefts of Rembrandt paintings—eighty-one that have been publicly disclosed, that is, and that figure also does not include Rembrandts stolen by the Nazi Party during World War II. This makes the Dutch artist the second-most stolen artist in history, ranking behind Pablo Picasso, who can boast more than one thousand stolen works.

Throughout his career, Rembrandt created more than six hundred paintings, and among them is a portrait of a man named Jacob de Gheyn III, the engraver who commissioned it. In 1632, de Gheyn and his friend, Maurits Huygens, commissioned similar, companion portraits, in which they wore similar clothing—black doublets and ruffs style—and face in an opposite direction. Kind of the ultimate bestie portrait set of the seventeenth century. There is, though, one big difference in these portraits: one of them has been stolen. *A lot.*

The *Portrait of Jacob de Gheyn III* has picked up the nickname "The Takeaway Rembrandt" over the years because it's been stolen four times in less than twenty years: first in 1966, then in 1973, again in 1981, and, yet again in 1983. Each time, it's been nabbed in a different fashion, but in every instance, it's been stolen from the Dulwich Picture Gallery. Thankfully, the painting has been recovered each time it's gone missing, though it's been recovered in, let's say, a *variety* of unexpected places.

The first time that the portrait was stolen, it was included in a bigger heist involving the theft of eight Old Masters from the Dulwich Picture Gallery on December 30, 1966. It took a team of twenty-one detectives to recover the stolen works, but they did so within a couple of days of the theft. (You have to admit—that's pretty amazing.) Following an anonymous tip, the paintings were found wrapped in brown paper underneath a bush in The Rookery, a formal garden in Streatham Common in London. However, after that theft, the museum, for reasons unfathomable to us, failed to improve the security around that and other paintings.

The second heist of the *Portrait of Jacob de Gheyn III* happened in 1973, when a visitor to the Dulwich just simply took the painting off the wall, stuffed it into a plastic bag, and rode off on his bicycle. (Who's wishing for heightened security measures now, eh?) Eight years later, in August 1981, thieves nicked the portrait a third time, in a daytime heist at the Dulwich, with a snatch-and-grab technique. The thieves had initially planned to blackmail the gallery for the return of the painting but were apprehended in a taxi after the theft, with the portrait wrapped rather unceremoniously in a pillowcase. It was returned to the Dulwich once more.

And then, in May 1983, security informed the gallery director, "We have some bad news, sir. The Rembrandt is gone again." Despite a newly upgraded security system, "The Takeaway Rembrandt" was stolen yet *again*, in a daring heist that took the thieves through the gallery's skylight, *Mission Impossible*–style. This time, it took three years for authorities to recover the work, where, on an anonymous tip, it was found in a box on a luggage rack in a British train station and army base in Münster, Germany. Since then, the portrait has stayed in place at the Dulwich—hopefully well-secured and for good, but what are the odds? ♦

THE BFF

The idea that de Gheyn and his BFF wanted to have matching (or at least similar) portraits is objectively the most adorable thing we've ever heard. It reminds us of the way kids will climb into a photo booth together and take pictures. So, let's make a cozy drink that best friends could share. This beverage is served hot, makes enough for two, and mimics the color of the stiff white collars sitting atop the darker garments that both men wore in their portraits.

INGREDIENTS:

- 10–12 ounces hot black tea
- 1 ounce black spiced rum
- 1 ounce Chambord
- Splash of demerara syrup
- 2–3 ounces heavy whipping cream, whipped
- Sprinkle of brown sugar
- Sprinkle of coconut sugar

METHOD:

Stir together the tea, rum, Chambord, and syrup in a cocktail glass, then split into two mugs, ideally glass.

Spoon the whipped cream on top of your tea, then sprinkle with brown sugar and coconut sugar.

We like to leave the layers for serving, but we find the flavor is more enjoyable when the cream is stirred in.

◆ MAKE IT A MOCKTAIL ◆

- 10–12 ounces black tea with nutmeg or cinnamon added
- 1 ounce raspberry syrup
- Splash of demerara syrup
- 2–3 ounces heavy whipping cream, whipped

Build as above.

THERE ARE FOUR VERSIONS OF *THE SCREAM* AND THEY KEEP GETTING CARRIED AWAY

Norwegian artist Edvard Munch created four versions of his famous painting, *Der Schrei der Natur*, known to English-speaking audiences as *The Scream*. Two paintings were made with tempera, and two drawings were also made with pastel and crayon. Three of the works in this collection are housed in the Munch Museum and the National Gallery of Art in Oslo. The fourth, which is considered by many to be the most valuable because its frame features a poem handwritten by Munch himself, is privately owned.

Of the four, two versions of *The Scream* have been stolen; the first painted version, in 1994, from the National Gallery in Oslo, and a pastel version in 2004 from the Munch Museum.

In 1994, Norwegian professional footballer Pål Enger used a ladder to climb up the walls of the gallery, smashed a window, and then he simply took *The Scream* off the wall. The painting wasn't alarmed or secured behind protective glass—it was open for the taking. Curiously, he went on to claim that it was his theft of *The Scream* that made the painting famous in the first place. (An interesting theory, but, sorry, Pål, it wasn't you.) Pål and his accomplices were apprehended after trying to fence the piece to an undercover Scotland Yard officer claiming to be an art dealer at the Getty Museum. Pål received a six-year prison sentence, and *The Scream* was returned to the National Gallery.

A decade later, in 2004, *The Scream* was stolen by two armed men carrying .357 Magnum pistols and wearing ski masks. They left with a pastel version of *The Scream* as well as another work and what's more, they pulled off their heist in broad daylight. Two years later, Norwegian police reported that they had recovered the pastel piece, undamaged, and had arrested three men for their participation in the heist: Bjoern Hoen, the mastermind, as well as Petter Tharaldsen and Petter Rosenvinge. ♦

BLOOD AND TONGUES OF FIRE

Perhaps the most touching part of *The Scream*, in all its incarnations, is the poem that Munch inscribed into one of the frame edges, describing the moment of inspiration that led to the creation of the art:

> *I was walking along the road with two Friends*
> *the Sun was setting—the Sky turned a bloody red*
> *And I felt a whiff of Melancholy—I stood*
> *Still, deathly tired—over the blue-black*
> *Fjord and City hung Blood and Tongues of Fire*
> *My Friends walked on—I remained behind*
> *shivering with Anxiety—I felt the great Scream in Nature.*

That is a slightly edited version of the poem, copied from one he wrote in his diary. The "blood and tongues of fire" phrase is especially evocative, so we'll create something deep red in color with a hot, spicy note.

INGREDIENTS:

- 4 ounces cranberry juice infused with jalapeño (soak 3–4 slices of jalapeño in the juice overnight, then strain before use)
- ¾ ounce habanero syrup
- ¾ ounce lemon juice
- 1½ ounces rye whiskey

METHOD:

Combine all ingredients in a shaking tin, shake with ice, and strain over fresh ice.

♦ MAKE IT A MOCKTAIL ♦

Make as above, but substitute strong black tea for the rye or omit it completely for a spicy, fruity drink.

THE SKYLIGHT CAPER A.K.A. CANADA'S BIGGEST UNSOLVED ART HEIST

The Musée des beaux-arts de Montréal, or the Montreal Museum of Fine Arts, lost more than a dozen works of art in what the journal *Canadian Art* called the largest art theft in the country's history and nicknamed the Sky-light Caper. This takes us back to a night in 1972, when a man wearing climbing spikes scaled a tree to gain access the museum's roof. He lowered a construction crew's ladder down to two additional men waiting below. Together, they entered the building through a skylight that was under repair; its alarm had been deliberately disarmed during construction on the building, a fact the men knew. They then rappelled down through the skylight with fixed nylon ropes into the galleries on the second floor. Catherine Schofield Sezgin, contributor to the Association for Research into Crimes Against Art, later summed up the stranger-than-fiction endeavor, saying: "It was a very cinematic theft."

Disguised in ski masks, the burglars spent roughly thirty minutes gathering up paintings and objects. They had planned to exit the museum through the same skylight they'd used to enter, and they had MacGyvered quite an elaborate pulley system to hoist the works back up to the roof so they could haul them away. At the very last minute, though, they changed their plan—they collected their loot at the loading dock instead, planning to escape with the museum's small cargo van. (Though the pulley system is undoubtedly cool, the van sure does sound faster.) When one of the men accidentally triggered the alarm, however, the trio was forced to flee on foot with only what they could carry: eighteen paintings and thirty-nine smaller pieces, mainly jewelry—which, to be fair, was still quite a bit of booty. Police later concluded that the missing paintings were all small enough to be easily stacked together, for a quick getaway. The same could not be said for the pile of art they left behind.

Tragically, the thieves had completely ransacked the galleries; there were shattered display cases, torn backings, and hundreds-year-old frames cracked to pieces. Investigators didn't have a lot of information to work with initially, but they had a few details to help them get started: there were three male suspects, two of whom were approximately 5-foot-6 and had long hair, and two of whom spoke French (the third spoke English).

As their investigation continued, authorities grew increasingly suspicious about the fact that these thieves had somehow known that there was one skylight with a deactivated alarm, and investigators considered the possibility that the theft was an inside job. However, after interviewing museum staff, they dismissed this theory—after all, no one from the inside would have tripped an alarm. Museum employees also reported something interesting: in the weeks preceding the theft, some had seen at least one man sitting on a folding chair on the rooftop of an adjacent building, smoking cigarettes—and, apparently, as the thieves knew about the disarmed alarm on the skylight, monitoring the museum's renovations. Now *that's* what we call a clue!

What followed the heist was a series of seemingly arbitrary yet absolutely related events (stay with us here). Someone claiming responsibility for the theft directed museum officials to go to a payphone outside McGill University's Roddick Gates, where they could expect to find a discarded cigarette package on the ground. Once there, officials found a pendant in the package, which was one of the stolen items. Next, museum officials received a brown envelope labeled "Port of Montréal." The contents were all photos of the missing paintings, with a requested ransom attached. The museum didn't pay, but, instead, asked for a show of good faith. The thieves sort of complied. They returned *Landscape with Vehicles and Cattle*, but what they returned was a forgery. (To be clear, they hadn't created or commissioned it; this painting had initially been attributed to Jan Brueghel the Elder but upon its return, it was determined to actually be the work of his students. It was unclear whether or not the thieves knew that—but probably not.)

The thieves continued to bargain, and the museum countered by asking for another show of good faith. Meetups were bungled, and in the end, nothing was recovered from the heist—but no one was arrested, either. A last apparent effort to exchange the artwork for cash came when an anonymous caller contacted the museum, offering information that could lead to the missing paintings. Undaunted, investigators followed the lead, and an insurance adjuster contracted on behalf of the museum went on what became a fourteen-hour wild goose chase across Montréal, from payphone to payphone, following "clues." The whole thing turned out to be a literal run-around, and nothing came of it but a wasted day.

Fifty years later, no one has been asked to visit another payphone. Nothing has been inadvertently brought to auction. Nothing's been intercepted or discovered during a police raid at the home of some criminal kingpin. And the mystery just keeps getting more and more mysterious. ♦

SKYLIGHT

OK, throw us a bone here and don't be pedantic about the time of day that this heist took place. What we *really* want to do here is create a drink that invokes the idea of the daylight sky, while also mimicking the bright sky in the painting *Landscape with Wagon* by Brueghel the Elder, one of the paintings stolen in this heist. This drink involves floating one spirit on top of another for visual effect. But in this case, we've thinned out the blue curaçao we're using with a little bit of vodka to invoke the sky (because liqueurs are heavy enough that they can and will sink to the bottom of a drink if they're not thinned out).

INGREDIENTS:

- ¾ ounce limoncello
- 4–5 ounces ginger ale
- ½ ounce blue curaçao plus
- ¾ ounce vodka mixed together

METHOD:

Into a glass with ice, pour the limoncello and the ginger ale.

In a separate glass, pour the blue curaçao and vodka and mix.

Pour the blue mixture down a bar spoon with a flat disc end to float it on top of the drink.

Note that this is a presentation drink—it looks beautiful in the layered form, but you should mix it before drinking!

♦ MAKE IT A MOCKTAIL ♦

- ½ ounce lemon juice
- ½ ounce simple syrup
- 4–5 ounces ginger ale

Build as above.

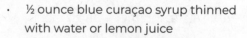

- ½ ounce blue curaçao syrup thinned with water or lemon juice

THE GENTLEMAN THIEF
OF VENICE

Vincenzo "Encio" Pipino was an Italian thief whose efforts to look like an eccentric, polite gent—and *definitely not a thief*—earned him a very specific nickname, the Gentleman Thief. He became an unlikely hero of sorts among Venetians, since his heists were successful and the art he stole always seemed to turn up again; plus, he was nonviolent and, most considerately, he never left a mess behind.

His story itself could take up an entire book, but let's hit the highlights. Encio began stealing—primarily pastries—when he was just a kid, before moving on to pickpocketry, which seems like a legitimate leveling up in terms of the criminal hierarchy. He carried out roughly three thousand art thefts at museums, galleries, jewelers, and private residences across Venice—*just* Venice, and all close to St. Mark's Square. Interestingly, he had a particular weakness for nabbing any fine clothing he found along the way.

But one of Encio's biggest criminal feats was that he was the first thief to successfully rob the Doge's Palace, in October 1991—and he did it all by himself. His target was the *Madonna col Bambino*, a Bartolomeo Vivarini work displayed in the Sala di Censori, and he successfully pinched it for the Mala del Brenta, a criminal organization based in Veneto, Italy. The painting, you may be surprised to hear, was returned within a month. Most interviews with Encio throughout his life suggest that he never really intended for the art he stole to ever leave Venice. Instead, he would ransom or resell stolen goods and was known for giving tainted money to those less fortunate (lest you think he sounds saintly, it must also be said that he paid himself, too, for his efforts). Unusual for an art thief, it's also well-reported that he was friendly with the police. Allegedly, he would return the art he stole, undamaged, in exchange for favors; one notable anecdote we found was a request for a berth at a covered dock in return for lost treasure. ♦

LIFE OF CRIME

Because Vincenzo, also known as Encio, started stealing at the age of eight, it only makes sense to whip up a beverage that is Italian in its roots and would also be appealing to kids (only in its mocktail iteration, of course). In Italy, *acqua frizzante*—sparkling water—is particularly popular with all ages. So, in this case, we're combining that with juice and a bit of sweetener to make something as refreshing as a Mediterranean breeze. If you really want to lean into the sweetness, use a fruit soda instead of juice.

INGREDIENTS:

- · 1 ounce raspberry syrup
- · 2 ounces pineapple juice
- · 1 ounce gin
- · 4 ounces sparkling water

METHOD:

Fill your glass with ice. Pour in the raspberry syrup, then the pineapple juice, then the gin, then the sparkling water. Give a gentle stir.

◆ MAKE IT A MOCKTAIL ◆

Simply leave out the gin and add a little extra juice and sparkling water.

THE DAY THE REMBRANDT WENT MISSING AT THE ISABELLA STEWART GARDNER MUSEUM

Rembrandt van Rijn's *Christ in the Storm on the Sea of Galilee* is widely considered to be one of the most striking works from the Dutch Golden Age, and the biblical scene is an example of his early style, which centered around bright colors and bold brushwork. Created in 1633, it's also Rembrandt's only painted seascape. The piece is a visual representation of a passage in the Christian Bible's *New Testament* (Matthew, 8: 23–26):

> *And when he was entered into a ship, his disciples followed him.*
> *And, behold, there arose a great tempest in the sea, insomuch that*
> *   the ship was covered with the waves: but he was asleep.*
> *And his disciples came to him, and awoke him, saying, Lord, save*
> *   us: we perish.*
> *And he saith unto them, Why are ye fearful, O ye of little faith?*
> *   Then he arose, and rebuked the winds and the sea; and there*
> *   was a great calm.*

The work was acquired by the Isabella Stewart Gardner Museum in 1898, where it was on display in the Dutch Room as part of the museum's permanent collection—that is, until 1990, when it was stolen in a famously bold heist. Disguised as police officers, two thieves entered the museum under the guise of following up on an emergency call they'd allegedly received. Once inside, the duo stole thirteen paintings in total, including *Christ in the Storm on the Sea of Galilee*.

Though *Christ in the Storm on the Sea of Galilee* has yet to be recovered—in fact, more than thirty years later, none of thirteen missing pieces from that heist has been—its empty frame still hangs in its place at the museum, frozen in time. ♦

GLOOMY SEAS

Rembrandt's *Christ in the Storm on the Sea of Galilee* is truly a visual feast, and the fact that it remains missing is especially sad because it was Rembrandt's sole seascape. Perhaps because of our gloomy reactions to this tale, we keep thinking about the dark storm clouds that hover over the boat in the painting, and we want to somehow re-create that deep grayish blue hue in liquid form. It won't calm the seas like Christ did in the biblical story, but this drink might help soothe our blues about the painting's missing status.

INGREDIENTS:

- 1½ ounces white rum infused with butterfly pea flower tea (see Method)
- ¾ ounce lemon juice
- ½ ounce blue curaçao
- ¾ ounce simple syrup
- Club soda, to taste (1–2 ounces)

METHOD:

To infuse the rum, steep 4 ounces of white rum with 1 tea bag of butterfly pea flower tea in an airtight container. Let steep for 30–40 minutes, shaking occasionally, then strain into a clean vessel. You'll have extra to play with later on!

Place all ingredients in a shaking tin with ice. Shake, then strain over fresh ice and top with club soda.

♦ MAKE IT A MOCKTAIL ♦

Make as above by making tea with the tea bag and water instead of rum, and using blue curaçao syrup instead of liqueur.

THE DAY THE DALÍ
ESCAPED FROM PRISON

This is one of those stories where truth really is stranger than fiction. To begin . . . maybe the only thing that could seem more unreal than an original Salvador Dalí painting being stolen from the walls of the New York City Department of Corrections is that an original Salvador Dalí painting ever hung in a Rikers Island jail mess hall to begin with. Who would have ever guessed?! Dalí's artistic creations span not only painting and illustration but photography and film, and for many people, he's best known for his Surrealist pieces. He was also, without a doubt, a professional provocateur. As *Smithsonian* magazine once wrote, "Dalí without the antics is not Dalí." *Truth*. Keep in mind that this was also a man known to announce his arrival with a booming, "Dalí is here!" What charisma, to be Dalí!

In February 1965, Salvador Dalí was invited to visit a Rikers Island inmate art program under the cheeky marketing banner, "Salvador Dalí Goes to Prison." Dalí was open to endorsing pretty much any product you put in front of him—including himself—and the potential and inevitable press coverage that would accompany the invite was hard to turn down. He planned to go, and as amazing a story as that could have been, it turned out that it just wasn't meant to be; the day of his scheduled visit, Dalí woke up with a fever. To make up for his cancellation and as means of an apology, he sent the prisoners a custom Dalí: a Surrealist crucifixion scene, made with pencil and India ink on paper. He signed and dated it in the lower corner and included this note (that sure could have benefited from spellcheck): "For the dinning [*sic*] room of the Prisoners Rikers Ysland [*sic*]. Dalí." The piece adorned the mess hall of the building then known as the Correctional Institution for Men for sixteen years until an inmate threw a coffee cup at it. Neither the inmates, nor the beverages, posed any real danger, though. But we can't say the same about the prison guards and officials.

After the coffee mug incident of 1981, the Dalí piece was removed from the mess hall. It was appraised and authenticated and placed into storage, where it was . . . promptly forgotten about. The work didn't resurface again until sometime in the 1990s, when, reportedly, the drawing was recovered from the trash by a corrections officer. It eventually found its way to a lobby wall in the Eric M. Taylor Center of the prison. In all likelihood, most employees of the Department of Corrections and visitors probably didn't even notice it, nor the framed note from the warden explaining that the image was indeed a genuine Dalí. And there it hung in its original gold frame in a glass case, next to a soda vending machine, until March 1, 2003, when the piece went missing. And it hasn't been seen since.

So, what happened? Well, the heist began with a fire drill staged by four prison officials. The theft itself was fairly basic. One person manned the fire alarm. Two people worked as lookouts. And a fourth person was responsible for switching the real Dalí with a forgery. But the plan itself wasn't executed quite as neatly as it had been imagined. During the next guard shift change, a corrections officer coming to work reported that there was something *odd* about the Dalí and said that it appeared to be a fake—which it very obviously was. Investigators would later find out that one of the thieves drew a replica; a really, really *bad* replica. The only people who had access to the artwork weren't inmates, but guards, since the inmates didn't have access to that lobby. By June 2003, two assistant deputy wardens and two corrections officers were arrested and charged with second-degree grand larceny; three of them served time and the fourth was acquitted.

And what about the missing art? Well, according to court records, the thieves claimed that they'd destroyed the piece in a panic, shortly after it was stolen. As heartbreaking as it may sound to us, those who knew Dalí seemed to overwhelmingly agree—with a hearty laugh—that he would've considered the whole incident rather hilarious. *He would have loved it.* ◆

DALÍ'S ANTICS

We just can't get the image of Dalí walking into any circumstance by announcing "Dalí is here!" out of our heads. This cocktail references Dalí's Spanish roots, and one of the ingredients is a vanilla liqueur made in Spain that is truly exceptional thanks to its flavor and the depth of its spice notes. Additionally, this drink resembles the original art, including the various ink splotches and the splatters of food leftovers it received while posted over a trash can in the Rikers Island mess hall.

INGREDIENTS:

- 1½ ounces vodka
- ¾ ounce Licor 43
- ¾ ounce heavy cream or half-and-half
- 3 drops Angostura bitters
- Sprinkle of black salt

METHOD:

Combine the vodka, Licor 43, and heavy cream in a shaking tin. If you have a frother, this is a great time to use it! But otherwise, you can just shake the tin vigorously without ice. Add ice and give it another shake.

Strain into a chilled glass with a couple of pieces of ice in it.

To the top, add the bitters (they will spread) and black salt.

♦ MAKE IT A MOCKTAIL ♦

Brew a vanilla tea and an orange tea together in 1 cup of oat milk or almond milk by simmering on low heat for 10 minutes, then letting it steep as it cools.

Once cool, add 3 ounces to a shaking tin; shake it, and pour into a chilled glass with ice as above.

Add a drop or two of vanilla extract and black salt on top.

THE MAN WHO THREW A PICASSO IN THE TRASH

Spanish painter and sculptor Pablo Picasso is a world-renowned artist who created more than twenty thousand works of art over the course of his lifetime. He's perhaps known best for his role in pioneering Cubism with Georges Braque, as well as for his famous "Blue Period" pieces. It's worth noting that despite all of his artistic acclaim, Picasso was also a problematic figure due to his chauvinistic and abusive behavior. So for this tale, we'll be focusing on the theft, and *only* the theft, of his 1911 Cubist oil on canvas painting, titled *Le Pigeon Aux Petit Pois*, or *Pigeon with Green Peas*.

Le Pigeon Aux Petit Pois was stolen from the Musée d'Art Moderne de la Ville de Paris on May 20, 2010, in a heist that included five paintings in all, and totaled more than $100 million. Just before 4 a.m. on the day the painting was stolen, the museum's alarm system was malfunctioning—apparently, sometimes fate smiles on those planning an art heist? A masked thief then clipped a padlock, broke a window, climbed inside, and promptly stole the Picasso. Other stolen works included *La Pastorale* by Henri Matisse, *La femme a l'eventail* by Amedeo Modigliani, *L'olivier pres de l'Estaque* by Georges Braque, and *Nature morte aux chandeliers* by Fernand Leger. Each painting was cut from its frame, and most shockingly of all, the whole incident took no more than fifteen minutes. Each painting was worth millions, but the Picasso alone had an estimated value of about $25–$28 million at the time—it was perhaps the most valuable.

Unlike many art thefts that often lack clues and go cold, it wasn't long before officials working the case picked up a lead: the thief behind the heist was a man named Vjeran Tomic, nicknamed the Spider-Man of Paris. He was convicted of stealing "cultural goods belonging to humankind's artistic heritage" and served an eight-year sentence. Vjeran and his accomplices claimed that, panicked, the works were burned and trashed after they were stolen. Many don't believe that story, but who's to say? ♦

TIPSY PIGEON

Since we're focusing exclusively on the painting in this story, we're gonna have that theme travel over to the cocktail, as well. If you look at the right-hand side of the painting, you'll notice what looks like a cocktail glass. Because of the Cubist style of the piece, we're left to wonder if that rounded shape is a garnish or if the orange-tone angled shape is, or if perhaps they both are. For this drink, we're splitting the difference, and garnishing with a lemon coin.

INGREDIENTS:

- ½ ounce lemon juice
- 1 ounce Chartreuse
- 2 ounces cognac
- 1 lemon coin (a circular cut of lemon rind), for garnish

METHOD:

Shake all ingredients in a tin with ice until very cold, then strain into a chilled glass, and garnish with a lemon coin.

♦ MAKE IT A MOCKTAIL ♦

This will combine the cognac and chartreuse segments into one component with a combination of teas, and it brews enough to make several servings!

Simmer 2 cups of water with 1 black tea bag, 1 rooibos tea bag, and a sprig of dill for 10 minutes. Turn off the heat and let steep as it cools. Once cool, strain into a clean vessel.

INGREDIENTS:

- 3 ounces combination tea
- ½ ounce lemon juice

- ½ ounce simple syrup
- 1 lemon coin, for garnish

Shake in a tin with ice, strain into a chilled glass, and garnish with
    a lemon coin.

A FINAL TOAST!

Though we've always been fans of a good story and a good drink to go with it, the real inspiration for *Killer Cocktails* started from our podcast: *Criminalia*.

When we first started brainstorming the show, we were ready to dig in and take a closer look at some of history's crimes and criminals to see if we could find commonalities between the past and the present. Would these crimes from the archives of history look different with a little distance on the timeline? And with a little bit of modern perspective added, would any of these perpetrators emerge as sympathetic characters? As it turns out, yes, some of them did—but for the most part, not really!

Our first season of *Criminalia* focused on female poisoners, which got us thinking about the foods and beverages that people have consumed day in and day out over the course of history. Of course, not all people have personally prepared the food and drinks they consume, meaning that many times, it's made for them by other people. There's a *lot* of inherent trust in that exchange—it leaves a lot of room for both creativity *and* catastrophe. Leaning into the former (rather than the latter), we decided to start featuring beverage recipes—a pick-your-poison sitch—with each story. And we had so much fun with it, that we haven't stopped since.

And here we are! We hope you've enjoyed this raunchy ride into the dark corners of days gone by, and whether you tried one of the recipes we included or branched out to create your own, we raise our glasses to you, the reader, in a final toast.

CHEERS!

SOURCES

We've infused a lot our modern perspective into the storytelling of Killer Cocktails since it's important for us to consider the differences between how these criminals would've been regarded at the time of their crimes vs. how they'd be received in this day and age. Historical context, while enjoying a criminally good drink—if you will. Was this woman really a witch, or did she have some knowledge or skills that made her threatening to the general establishment? Did this man really commit treason, or was it just pro-nationalist propaganda? We've put everyone from poisoners and pirates to (con)artists and art thieves in the hot seat here, so if you'd like more information about the criminals and crimes featured in this book, please check out our list of resources.